# Late Call

## Book One of the Call series

Emma Hart

*I don't understand how a woman can leave the house without fixing herself up a little, if only out of politeness.*

*And then, you never know, maybe that's the day she has a date with destiny.*

*And it's best to be as pretty as possible for destiny.*

Coco Chanel

# Chapter One

This is taking forever.

It doesn't matter how selective you are, how tight you squeeze, or how fast you go. There's always one that'll take longer to come than everyone else you know. It doesn't happen often and they definitely don't go on my regular client list. I get paid for this but I sure as shit don't have the patience to bounce on some guy until he decides he wants to shoot his load.

He grunts and groans beneath me, his lazy thrusts no match for my desperate ones. *Jesus fucking Christ, will you come already?*

I steal a look at the clock on the hotel nightstand. Five minutes left. Time to end this. I cringe and creep my hand around his thigh to his backside. God, I hate this part. I squeeze his cock at the same time I slip my finger in his asshole—

"Oh god!"

And there it is.

I give him a saucy wink and get off of him. Finally. I've been on top of him so long my legs have forgotten how to work, but he paid for an hour so an hour is all he's gonna get.

There are four golden rules in this business. Every escort I know abides by them. At all times. They're non-negotiable. Ironclad. Set in friggin' stone.

Get the money first.

Don't go over the time.

Don't fall for your client.

And no freaking sob stories.

Unfortunately for me, that last rule is one no one bothered to tell this guy. I'd barely tucked the envelope full of his money into my purse before he started telling me about his pregnant wife who isn't up for sex.

Hey—don't judge me. This is my job, and if a guy chooses to cheat on his wife with me, then that's his deal. There's a reason I don't ask personal questions, and that's it. Getting names and shit is what I pay my agent twenty percent for.

I button my coat and leave the hotel room as quickly as I entered it. There's only one hotel I'll work in in this city and that's because I know the concierge. Connor is a darling, and despite my constant refusal to sleep with him, he always covers my back.

"Busy?" I sidle up to his counter and prop my chin up on my elbow.

His glittering blue eyes look down at me. "Busy keeping you off my boss's radar."

I grin and slip a fifty-dollar bill into his hand. "You're a doll, Con."

"You know you don't have to do that every time."

"Just keeping you sweet."

"There are plenty of ways you can do that, Mia."

"Oh, sweetie, you know where I stand there. I don't do personal relationships. They just don't work when you have my job." I straighten and touch his arm. "When I stop to settle down with a white picket fence, a chocolate Lab, and two-point-five snotty kids, you'll be the first person I call."

"Better be. Until then, I'll just stand here behind my little desk waiting for you to come to your senses and fall madly in love with my boyish charm."

I laugh and peck his cheek. "I'm sure you will."

He grins, that exact boyish charm glinting in his eyes. "Marc has your cab outside."

"Thanks, hon. I'll see you soon," I say. I throw a casual wave over my shoulder as I step outside. Evening is falling across Seattle, the lights from the buildings illuminating the darkening sky and drowning out the stars.

"Ms. Lopez." Marc tips his hat and opens the cab door for me.

"Marc." I shoot a dazzling smile his way and get into the car, smoothly passing him a ten-dollar bill as I do so. He returns my smile as the cab pulls away, and I relax back in the chair, breathing deeply.

The ride home is when Mia Lopez becomes Dayton Black, when the call girl becomes the real girl.

Until my cell buzzes in my hand and my agent's name flashes on the screen. I swallow my sigh.

"Monique."

"You're late, Dayton."

Fuck.

"I had to wait for the cab," I lie, mouthing, "Sorry," when the driver glances at me in his mirror. "I'm on my way now."

"Five minutes." The line goes dead.

I let out that sigh and lean forward. "Hey, can we go to 2440 Cascade Way in Bellevue instead?"

"Sure thing, lady."

"Thanks."

I stare out the window and stay in my state of limbo between the two versions of me. How could I forget to go to Monique's after Mr. Can't Come? It's a Friday, and she takes her share of our earnings every Friday. Her share. Shit. Do I even have that?

I rifle through my purse, barely breathing, until I feel the envelope hidden in the lining. At least I was thinking this morning... Discreetly, I count out her share from today's earnings and tuck it into the envelope as we pull up outside. Thirty of my hard-earned dollars fall on the driver's lap with a, "Keep the change," and I run— as well as someone can run in four-inch heels—up the path to Monique's idyllic suburban dream house.

You know, the kind usually reserved for families with two-point-five bubbly, screaming kids and a bouncing puppy. Not a woman with a hot tub and an escort agency who mothers a teen with a penchant for crashing his car.

I knock twice and let myself in. I've been in this house more times than I can count in the last five years. It's comfortable here— from the white walls with an accent wall in each room to the endless photographs wherever you walk. The pictures are all of Monique with her girls in various cities around the country, from Vegas to Miami to New York.

"You're late," Monique repeats her earlier words, and I sit in the only empty seat around the table. "If you tell me you went over the time, shit's gonna hit the fucking fan, Dayton."

"I haven't gone over the time since you took me on, Mon, and I'm not starting now. The cab was late. I'm here now. Can we get on with this?"

My agent cocks her head to the side, her lips quirked. "Hot date tonight?"

"If you can call my slippers, ice cream, and Liv a hot date, then yeah. Smokin'."

"Funny. All right, girls. Show me what you got." She makes a 'gimme' motion with her hands, and one by one, brown envelopes rustle out of purses and onto the table.

"One and a half."

"Seven hundred."

"Seven fucking hundred? You on your period?" Monique snaps

at Lori. "Get a damn implant. I don't have the time for you to have a week off. Robyn, you better have better than that shit."

"Three." Robyn smiles, dropping the envelope on the table.

Monique nods.

"Two."

"Eighteen hundred."

"Twenty-six hundred."

"Another three."

Monique nods after each amount, finally turning to me. "Dayton?"

I place my fat envelope on the table and look her in the eye. "Six thousand, four hundred fifty." I slide it along the table to her.

"Four hundred *fifty?* Where the fuck did the fifty come from?"

"You shack me up in a hotel with a guy who takes longer to come than a porn star on Viagra, you pay the concierge to keep it quiet."

"It's a good fucking thing I like you, Dayton. If you were anyone else, you'd be on your own with the shit you pull." Monique opens the envelope and leafs through the amount. "As it is, you just got my kid a new car."

"Good. Tell him not to crash it this time. I'm not buying him a fourth." I stand.

"Where do you think you're going?"

"Home. I have a hot date, remember?"

"Ooooooh," my best friend, Liv, coos. "Six gees?"

"Don't forget the four fifty."

"Fifty? Oh, concierge."

It really says something when my best friend gets it and my

agent doesn't.

"What do you do with all the money? If that's twenty percent, then you took home like thirty thousand fucking dollars this week."

"Twenty-five. I pay off this place, expand my shoe collection, buy out Agent Provocateur and occasionally La Perla, and save the rest for a rainy day. Oh, and taxes. They kill me." I stab my spoon into my tub of Phish Food. "And if you remember, I take cheapskates like you on vacation now and then. But this doesn't happen every week." I lick the spoon clean. "A couple extra clients dropped in, so voilà"

Liv grins. "Sometimes I wonder if I'm in the wrong industry. Shit, I show my tits all the time and I don't make half as much as you."

"That's 'cause your tits are for the camera. Mine are for touching."

"Point made and taken."

"Anyway, you know we're selective on my clients. Not selective enough sometimes, but they're all big payers. What I earn in a month takes most of the other girls a year."

"You get all the big jobs? Don't the others get pissed?"

"Probably, but it's some money or no money. It's not like I haven't worked for them. I'm the best in the fucking city at my job and they all know it."

And it's the truth. I have the most clients, and they just happen to be the ones who pay the most. Fuck well, get paid well. That's how my life works.

"Yeah? Fuck anyone lately who can get the girls a good job?" Liv pats her natural double D's. "Because *my* agent is shooting more blanks job-wise than he is dick-wise."

"No, but I have a client in two days who might be willing to have a free hour of my time for a double page spread of you. And cover."

"And cover?"

"Liv, my hourly rate is more than most people's daily wage. Yes, the fucking cover too. And to sweeten…" I jump up and tug Liv upstairs and into my lingerie room. What else am I gonna do with a three-bedroom house? I'm a call girl. I live and breathe lingerie.

I grab the dark pink bodice with black lace detail that I ordered last week and show it to her.

"Oh!" She takes the hanger and gives it a once-over. "Yep. This is cover-winning lingerie, Day. Every time."

"I know." I smirk. "He has a thing for these, and a nice new one will do the trick."

"Mm… Is he coming here?"

"Yep."

She shivers as we head back down. "I don't know how you can do that in your house."

"It's no different than someone who works from home on their computer or something. I just have a bedroom instead of an office. It's not like it happens in *my* room. I built the extension for a reason."

I built it two years ago after buying this place when my client load got too big for constant hotel jumping. It's an extra two rooms—one's a normal bedroom while the other carries the kinkier stuff. I'm prepared for every situation.

"Okay. You know, we've been friends for eight years and I still don't think I get why you do what you do."

I smile wistfully. "Yeah, I never imagined I'd drop out of college for the thing I did to get me *through* it in the first place."

"Hello?"

"I have a job for you."

I let my groan out and lift my legs out of the water. "It's my day off."

"I don't give a fucking shit if it's your day off." *Tell me how you really feel, Monique.* "This is an easy one. Rate and a half."

"Tell me more."

"He's taking over his father's company and he has a function tonight. His father is expecting him to show with a date. This is where you come in. He's paying extra for short notice."

"Okay." I wrap a towel around me and walk into my room. "So who is it?"

"He's requested to stay anonymous until you arrive and he'll introduce himself then. His profile is too high to deal with the stigma of hiring an escort." The bitterness filters through her tone, and I feel it. Judgmental douche. "So you have to agree to keep that private."

"Right." I draw the word out. "Because talking about my clients is something I do every day. What do I wear?"

"Something classy. It's a multimillion-dollar company, so something fucking expensive. Something that makes everyone look at both of you. Tonight is about him and stroking his ego."

"Got it." I pull out a brown-grey knee-length dress with a pencil cut and lay it out on my bed. "And sex?"

"Not required. Date only."

"Huh. That doesn't happen often."

"I'll text you the details. Don't fuck up."

"Never do."

I toss my phone on the bed and peruse my collection of lingerie, looking for the perfect set to wear under my dress. Sex may not be on the cards, but that doesn't mean I can't wear nice underwear.

Give a girl a matching bra and panties and just the knowledge of its existence on her body will add a level of confidence she didn't know she had.

Fortunately for me, I have more than enough confidence. At least Mia Lopez does.

Southfall Hotel. 7pm to meet, function at 7:30. Money on arrival. Receptionist Rachel is expecting you.

I nod once and throw my cell back on my bed to get ready. I know the Southfall well. I've been there several times before as a paid date. The functions are held in the largest room, and you have to be somebody to get in there. It's one of the most exclusive hotels in the city.

I fix my dark hair to the side, letting curls fall over my shoulder, and slip my feet into some brown heels. Diamond earrings glitter in my lobes, and after a coat of lipstick, I tuck it into my purse.

I climb into the waiting cab and stretch out my legs. A lick of nervousness flares inside me. Not knowing the client's name before a date is always unnerving—especially when they're a last-minute hire. Usually I have time to research them, even if it's only basic details. Tonight, I have thirty minutes to know everything about my client and the company he's taking over.

That alone is worth my rate and a half.

I pay the driver and step into the Seattle evening. The Southfall is right on Elliot Bay, and the gentle breeze from the water wraps around me, bathing me in comfort. I pause in my steps to glance at the boats lined up, remembering a time when my father's bobbed along there.

I shake my head. There's no time to be Dayton tonight. If I'm being paid, I'm Mia. Dayton has no place in this high-class world of deception and pleasure. She's too pajamas-and-ice-cream for this shit.

The doorman opens the door for me. My heels click on the marble floor as I approach the reception desk.

"Can I help you?" The receptionist looks up, and I glance at her nametag. *Rachel.* Perfect.

"Yes. I'm here for the function this evening."

"It's on the second floor, ma'am. The South ballroom."

I place my hands on the counter, twenty dollars poking out from beneath my pinky finger. Her eyes find it.

"I'm here for the function."

"Ah, yes. Of course. Excuse me, Ms. Lopez." She picks up the phone. "Ms. Lopez has arrived. Please take her to the reserved private booth in the bar."

Two seconds later, a boy no older than nineteen steps next to me. "If you'd follow me, Ms. Lopez."

"Thank you, Rachel." I shake her hand, mine coming away empty, and follow the young boy.

Money gets you everywhere in this world, and for me, it's almost like my calling card. I show you green, you know who I am and why I'm here. I show you green, you shut the fuck up and be discreet.

"Ms. Lopez." He pulls a curtain to the side slightly.

"Thank you." I pass him a ten as he leaves and turn into the booth.

I pull the curtains shut behind me, and just like that, Mia gives way to Dayton, because I look into a pair of eyes I haven't seen for seven years. Disbelief and shock ricochet through my body.

It can't be. It's not possible.

But my gaze follows the shapely, stubbled jaw and pink lips of the man I fell in love with one beautiful summer in Paris seven years ago. Before everything went wrong.

"Aaron?"

# Chapter Two

My body jolts as if it's been struck by lightning when his eyes rise from his hands resting on the table and connect with mine. I can barely breathe, and through the skipping of my heart, I'm consumed with a longing I haven't felt in years.

His blue eyes slowly trace every part of my face, his own disbelief as evident as mine must be. Finally, they come to rest on mine, and he stands slowly.

"Dayton?"

"What…" I put a hand to my chest. "*You're* my client?"

Aaron motions for me to sit, lowering himself down when I do so. "You're my date? I hired a Mia Lopez?"

"Mia is my working name," I say quietly. "Being an escort is a double life."

"I can't believe this." He pushes a button and a waiter appears. "A bottle of Pinot Gris. Two glasses," he orders, the guy disappearing quickly. Neither of us speaks again until he returns and places the tray on the table.

My heart pounds as Aaron pours two glasses. In the five years I've done this, since escorting became my life, I've never had a client I know. I've never had to worry about anything other than getting the job done. Now, sitting in front of Aaron Stone, I know this job is anything but simple.

I drain my glass as a brown envelope appears on the table. Taking it silently and slipping it into my purse is the single most awkward moment of my life. Aaron pours me another glass.

"Thank you."

"This was unexpected."

"Ya think?" I raise an eyebrow. "I can't say I'm in the habit of having a previous personal relationship with my clients."

And what a relationship we had. Six weeks filled with fun, kisses, and endless passion in the city of love.

"I'd imagine not." He pauses, dropping his eyes to the table before bringing them back to mine. "Can I ask why?"

"Why what?"

"Why you do this?"

"That's a bit personal."

"Dayton, I've seen every inch of your body. Don't fuck around and tell me it's too personal."

"You're my client," I remind him, sitting up straight. "Our past is irrelevant here. You're paying me to do a job, and I'm going to do it. No personal details. Tell me what I need to know so I don't look like a complete idiot when I'm out there tonight."

He clenches his jaw and reaches up to adjust his tie. "Dad has decided to step back from the company, and this is one of many events designed to introduce me to the people I'll be working with when I take over in just under two months."

"The modeling agency?"

"We branched into advertising and rebranded the summer after Paris. It went global three years ago, and now there are offices in Australia and Europe as well as here."

"Impressive. And you needed a date because?"

"Because if I turned up alone, the vultures would get me."

My lips twist. "The vultures?"

"The daughters of my mother's friends. They're single."

"And you're the perfect target. Nice to know I'm hired to be a buffer."

"I'm sure Mia Lopez is used to it."

"Oh, she is. But we both know there's not a chance in hell I'll get away with being Mia tonight."

He studies me intensely. His tongue traces a path across his bottom lip, and my eyes flick there before I can stop them. He smirks.

"Mr. Stone?" a voice asks from behind the curtain.

"Yes?"

"Your father is asking for you, sir."

"Tell him we'll be there momentarily."

"Of course."

Aaron looks at me again and reaches a hand across the table. His fingers curl around mine, sending jolts up my arm. "Day, you don't have to do this. You have a working name for a reason. I won't ask you to jeopardize that for me."

I slide my hand from his and stand, smoothing out my dress. "You hired me to do this job, and I'm going to do it. Besides, I can't have you being eaten alive by the vultures, can I?"

His eyes light up when his smirk turns dangerously sexy. "Very true."

He stands, and for the first time since I walked in the booth, I take note of how he looks. His black-and-white suit is perfectly tailored to the body that's bulked out since I last saw it, the jacket stretching across broad shoulders and tucking in at his waist. Dark hair curls against the collar of his white shirt and frames his face perfectly.

Aaron Stone cuts a damn fine figure in that suit.

His hand rests on my lower back as he leads me toward the elevator, and boy am I glad I passed right on over the backless dress in my closet. I'm not sure I could deal with such intimate skin-on-skin contact with this man without being swamped by the past. God knows I can barely breathe through this as it is.

My back straightens a little more each minute his hand is resting there. I take a deep breath and remind myself to act as Mia would. I have to be Mia. I have to be unaffected yet believable.

The elevator doors open and Aaron closes them again. I look up at him, frowning.

"What are you doing?"

"Dayton." He pushes some hair back from my face, looking at me almost tenderly.

I swipe his hand away. "Standing in an elevator isn't going to change the fact I have a job to do, Aaron. Can we get on with this?"

He sighs, following it with a small smile. "Fine. But what do I tell my parents when they inevitably recognize the girl who stole me for the duration of our vacation seven years ago?"

Shit. I didn't think of that. "You let me think of that."

The doors open again and we walk toward the ballroom.

"Last chance," he murmurs.

"Shut up and open the damn door for me."

I hear his quiet laugh before he opens the door. Men in suits and women dressed in expensive dresses fill the buzzing room. A bar takes up one corner and tables line the walls, leaving the main floor free.

As I am standing here in the doorway, surrounded by Seattle's elite, it's so very easy to see why this is the top hotel in Seattle. This room reeks of money and class.

Aaron leads me inside, and almost immediately his parents appear in front of us. His mom looks the same as she did back then—perfect brown hair without a grey in sight and flawless skin any woman would be jealous of. Her blue eyes, the same as Aaron's, survey me before widening slightly.

"Well I never. Dayton Black?" She places a hand on her chest.

I smile. "It's lovely to see you again, Mr. and Mrs. Stone."

"I don't believe this is the little teenager who had our son performing disappearing acts for weeks on end." Mr. Stone beams at me.

"I plead the Fifth. He acted of his own accord." I return his smile and he laughs. He leans forward to kiss me on the cheek, Aaron's mom doing the same.

"And none of this Mr. and Mrs. stuff. Brandon and Carly," he insists. "Can we get you a drink?"

"A bottle of wine would be great, Dad," Aaron answers.

"Aaron, darling, why didn't you tell us you were bringing Dayton?" Carly questions him as we walk toward the bar.

"Yeah, about that," he replies uncertainly. I try not to roll my eyes.

"We ran into each other a few weeks ago," I cut in. "Completely by chance. I think both of us were really shocked, right, Aaron?"

He struggles to keep a straight face. "Right."

"We've been out for drinks a couple of times. Catching up, you know? Then this afternoon he calls me out of the blue and tells me he needs a date for tonight. And well, how could I say no to this face?" I raise my eyebrows and brush my thumb across his jaw, giving him a fond smile.

"You didn't say you'd seen her!" Carly taps his bicep.

"I wasn't aware I was supposed to, Mom."

"Well it would have been nice to know she was still in Seattle and you were back in contact."

"We've only seen each other a few times."

"Stop grilling him, Carly. He's a grown man now. Let him have his secrets." Brandon places a bottle of wine and four glasses in front of us then pours. "Well, it sure is a lovely surprise, Dayton. How are your parents?"

Be Mia. Be Mia. Be Mia.

"They, uh… They actually passed away five years ago." I look down, feeling the same sting that always accompanies the mention of them. Aaron's hand creeps across my back to my waist. He steps slightly closer to me and I take comfort in the gesture.

"I'm so sorry." His dad takes my hand briefly. "That must have been terrible so young."

I nod and take a deep breath. "Yes, but my aunt Leigh was there for me. I got through it eventually."

Aaron squeezes me gently. "Mom, Dad, I think Mr. Warner is trying to get your attention."

Carly turns. "Of course. Brandon."

He steps up, she links her hand through his elbow, and they head in the direction of the guy who was waving at us.

I sigh deeply and sip my wine, using all the restraint I have. I doubt chugging would be acceptable.

"Thank you," I say softly to Aaron.

"You're welcome." He stands in front of me, gazing down at me with his piercing eyes. "I didn't know your parents passed."

I smile wryly. "Yeah, well. It's not exactly a conversation starter, is it?"

"I suppose not. How did they die?"

"Plane crash," I say flatly. "They were flying back from New York. The plane had some technical difficulties and went down. No one survived."

"I'm sorry."

"Why? You aren't the reason they crashed." My fingers flex around the stem of my glass.

Aaron wraps his other hand around my neck and brings his lips to my forehead. Warmth and tingles travel through me at the contact. It's been so long since I had a touch like this—tender, gentle, almost loving—that I almost forget one of the rules of my life.

No personal feelings for clients or any of their actions.

"What are you doing?"

"After politely dismissing herself from Mr. Warner, my mother traveled across the room to Mrs. Royce. Once there, she will have proceeded to tell her the story of how we found each other again after seven long years of being apart, and isn't it great how we're reconnecting? And don't we look so good together? And Mrs. Royce will have agreed and voiced how beautiful our babies would be," he replies in a hushed tone with a hint of amusement. "And this will happen with every one of my mother's friends throughout the night. I'm merely keeping her happy, Dayton."

"Aaron?" An older lady approaches us, and Aaron winks at me before dropping his hands.

"Mrs. Warner. May I say how lovely you look this evening?"

"You may, but it won't get you anywhere. Well, maybe a little." She looks at me and winks. I smile politely.

"Mrs. Warner, this is Dayton Black, my date for this evening. Dayton, this is Mrs. Warner, my mother's closest friend. Her husband is an investor in our company."

"It's a pleasure to meet you, ma'am." I shake her hand.

"And you, my dear. Carly has told me how the two of you met. How wonderful you found each other again after all this time!"

Here we go.

"Is that everyone yet?" I whisper in Aaron's ear. "I'm not sure how many more times I can listen to "How delightful you ran into each other!" and any and all variations of that sentence."

Aaron laughs quietly into my hair. "Most, but not all."

I groan. "How about an escape outside for five minutes?"

"I think we can manage that." He wraps an arm around my waist and, keeping his head down, pulls me through the room to the doors. We slip out, surprisingly unnoticed, and run into the waiting elevator. Neither of us says a word until we reach the sidewalk.

I step from his hold and cross the street. The wall overlooking Elliot Bay is cold and rough when I rest my arms on it and lean forward. The cool night breeze teases through my hair, and I close my eyes into it, taking deep breaths. On nights like tonight, when so many things are expected of me, it's hard to stay composed.

I'll take the fucking over the escorting part of this job every time. It's simple and I know exactly what is expected of me. It's planned and it's *controlled*. It's in my comfort zone, but this...

Escorting is improvisation. Every word, every look, every movement. It's all spur-of-the-moment actions and decisions. None of which I can dictate.

"Why do you do this?"

"I thought I put that in the personal box."

"You did." Aaron smirks in that dangerously sexy way that does stupid things to my stomach and leans against the wall next to me. "But I'm asking again."

"I do it for the same reason other people work. I need to pay the bills."

"Really?"

"Is it that hard to believe? Really?" I turn my face toward him. "When my parents died, I lost everything. I was at college and suddenly lost my home and all my financial support. By the time my fees were paid, there was next to no money left. I couldn't get a job, so I went to my aunt's old agent."

"Monique?"

"She took me on and gave me a job. Aunt Leigh let me move in with her during breaks from school, and by the time I was twenty-one, I had enough money saved to put down the deposit on my own house."

"Impressive. So you do it for the money?"

"Well I certainly don't do it for the lack of fucking orgasms."

"That bad, huh?" His smirk changes to a grin.

"Aaron, there's no reason in the world anyone would do this job except for the money. Besides, I'm not paid to orgasm. I'm paid to make them. And occasionally, I'm paid to be a date for pretty little rich boys." I smile back.

"Pretty little rich boys who pay more than necessary in desperation to please their parents with a beautiful girl?"

"Exactly."

"Then it's a good thing you're worth every cent, isn't it?"

I stand up straight, my eyes on his. "That's what they tell me."

Aaron's eyes flash with an emotion that disappears too quickly for me to register it. He holds my gaze for a long moment, seemingly looking right through me and my façade. He takes a step closer to me and holds out his arm.

"Shall we go back inside?"

"Are they likely to send out a search party?"

"I wouldn't put it past my mother."

I loop my arm through his, focusing both my mind and my body on the job. Not the past. Ours or otherwise.

"For the record," he says as we walk through the lobby, "she probably thinks we sneaked off to make out like teenagers."

"I think your mom is too excited about this totally coincidental meeting."

"You and me both, Day. That was an impressive story you told earlier, by the way."

"Thanks." I reach up and fluff my hair slightly.

"What are you doing?"

"Making it look like we snuck off to make out like a couple of teenagers." I wink and give myself a final once-over in the elevator mirror. We creep back into the ballroom and I wipe under my lip, removing a bit of imaginary smudged lipstick.

A tantalizing smile teases his lips, his eyes flicking to my mouth. He pauses for a moment and raises his thumb to my mouth, rubbing it over the same spot I just touched.

"Missed a bit," he breathes, running it across my bottom lip. I hold my breath at the intimate touch and his eyes find mine again. "Got it."

"Good," I mutter.

He leads us into an empty corner, his hand firmly placed on the small of my back.

I ignore the pounding of my heart and subsequent heating of my body as he pulls me into him, pressing our sides together. "Do you think anyone noticed we disappeared?"

"Not sure." He looks around. "But they definitely noticed we came back."

I follow the direction of his gaze to his parents. Carly is whispering in Aaron's dad's ear. Brandon has a smile on his face, a mixture of amusement and pleasure that makes me bite the inside of my cheek in a reaction that is all too genuine.

The teenage dreamer lingering inside me kind of wishes we had snuck out for a make-out session. She remembers all too well the consuming feeling of Aaron's lips on mine.

I do too. It's hard to forget something that made you feel so alive.

"Do you think anyone else will bother us?"

Aaron turns his face back to me. "Of course they will."

Nope. I'm done being bothered tonight. A tiny, crazy part of me wants to savor these moments we have together, because I know reality will intrude once more tomorrow.

I curve my body into his. I slide my hands up his chest, feeling the solid muscle beneath, and curl my fingers around the lapels of his suit. He presses me into him even farther until I'm flush against him and lowers his mouth to my ear.

"What are you doing?" His lips brush over my earlobe as he speaks. The strangely intimate touch ignites a spark of lust in the pit of my belly. It feels foreign and unwelcome, the desire bubbling in my lower stomach stronger than I've felt in a long time.

I tilt my face into his, feeling the slight scratch of the stubble coating his jaw against my cheek. "My job title might be escort, but I spend half my life as an actress. If the women in this room want to believe we're reconnecting romantically, then they can for tonight."

"I see." He slides his hand down my back and runs it over the curve of my ass. It settles on my hip as the other snakes upward and into my hair. "Don't you think this is a little rude?"

"Says the man running his hands over my body and whispering in my ear."

I feel his smile against the side of my head. "Touché, Miss Black. Touché."

"Anyway, this is exactly what you're paying me for. Keeping the vultures away."

"I'm an idiot for not paying for you all night, the vultures be damned."

I raise my eyebrows. "If you'd known it was me, would you have?"

His face turns to mine, the tip of his nose brushing across my cheek. "If I'd have known it was you, I would have paid triple for all night."

A knot forms in my throat and I swallow it down. Where the fuck is Mia when I need her? Oh yeah—the bitch up and left the second she looked into Aaron Stone's blue eyes.

Even in my job, sometimes pretending is just too much of a stretch.

# Chapter Three

"Aaron Stone? The guy you met in Paris?"

"Know any other Aarons, Aunt Leigh?"

"Of course I do, Dayton. I know several of every man." She snorts and sits opposite me. "What you gonna do, girl?"

"Same thing I do every day. My job."

She snorts again.

"Seriously. I mean it. Running into him was a shock, but it was a one-night job."

I'm still reeling from that shock. I barely slept last night after leaving the hotel. My mind was full of Paris seven years ago as I remembered the hopes of a naïve seventeen-year-old girl. As I remembered the feeling of falling in love for the first time.

And the memories were full of his piercing blue eyes, looking at me with amusement, tenderness, and heat. They were full of his fingers trailing across my body, touching deep enough that they seeped into my bones despite barely skimming my skin. They were full of promises and believing… And an inevitable goodbye.

"Dayton!" Aunt Leigh snaps.

I drag my gaze from the window back to her. "What?"

"One-night job my ass. You've been staring out of my window for the last five minutes chewing on your lip. My rose garden is pretty, but it isn't that fucking pretty!"

I click my tongue. "I'm... I don't know. I'm shocked, all right? Jesus, I haven't seen him for seven years. Then he's my goddamn client? He doesn't even live on the West Coast, so what the hell is that about?"

"It's about life throwing you a curveball. You gotta swing with it, sugar, or it's gonna hit you in the gut."

"Because my *client* being the only guy I've ever loved isn't enough of a hit in the gut?"

She shrugs and lights a cigarette. "Dayton, it doesn't matter if you loved the guy. Shit, honey, it doesn't matter if you've fucked him six ways to Sunday. What matters is he knows your real name. What matters is he knows where to find you."

"You think I don't know that?"

"Oh, you know that. I just don't think you have a clue what to do about it."

Goddamn, I hate it when she's right. But that's the problem with having an aunt who used to do this exact job. You can't get anything past her.

I grab my purse and stand. "You know what? I'm going to see Liv."

"Do what you want, sweetie, but do me a favor."

"What?" I pause at the front door.

"Just remember—call girls don't fall in love."

I stare into the glass in my hand and twist it by the stem. The remaining wine swirls in circles, rising up the sides of the glass and dropping back down with a tiny splash with each full circle. Sitting here in the wine bar Liv works in, I can almost pretend Aaron Stone didn't explode back into my life, that I'm waiting for my best friend to finish work like any other twenty-four-year-old.

But I'm not any other twenty-four-year-old. I never have been. I never will be. And I'm okay with that.

Becoming a call girl was my choice, and when the time came, I chose to make it a career. I've always known the rules, and hell, I watched Aunt Leigh's marriage break down because of her unwillingness to give it up. She chose escorting over love, and I understand it. I get why.

Being an escort gives you control. Sure, the client plans it from the location to what happens. They pick how they want you to look—girl-next-door, dominatrix, or just plain sexy—and they choose how everything unfolds, but the second the money leaves their hand, the control switches. It's up to me to give them everything they want. The look, the feel, the whole experience. It's like porn without a camera.

I relish the control. There's nothing in this world like having someone at your every command and sometimes at your mercy. It's invigorating, a rush like nothing else. It's compelling and addictive. And it's a constant. It'll never change—and that's why I love it.

As long as men need sex, I have a job.

But with love... With love, you surrender control. Love is promising to give someone everything and not expect anything in return.

This is the very reason call girls don't love. We don't love, we don't lust, and we don't spend our days thinking, *What if?* Being a call girl is taking and giving without really giving any of yourself at all.

I don't give my name, my age, my likes or dislikes. I don't give anything except what the client pays for, and there's only one part of me they're paying for. They don't pay for the story of my parents' deaths, of how I took this life because it was a quick and easy fix for me financially, or of how I dropped out of college and a chance at my dream career because this was so much higher paid.

And isn't everything about money?

You pay me it to fuck you, and I take it. That money gives me pretty things—a house full of beautiful clothes and shoes—and that money gives you the time of your fucking life. The same money keeps our tryst hidden from prying eyes and silent from oversensitive ears.

It also guarantees that you'll be back again and again.

Usually that's a good thing. Usually clients know nothing about you. They don't know your bra size or how you gasp when lips brush a certain spot on your neck, and they definitely don't know what it feels like to be truly inside of you, connected in every way.

Usually clients aren't Aaron Stone.

"Thanks," I mumble as Liv fills my glass.

"Looks like you've had a shitty day." She sits opposite me with her own drink, her eyes soft and nonjudgmental. Thank fucking god I have a best friend who gets me.

"Apart from my aunt pointing out my latest client knows exactly where to find me followed by reminding me we don't fall in love, it's hunky-fucking-dory."

"Back up. I missed something."

"I had a late call last night—a function for some guy taking over Daddy's company. Just a date."

"And? The big deal is?"

I bury my face in my arms on the table. "The guy was Aaron."

My best friend says nothing, and I know I've truly shocked her. Liv always has ten words where two will do. "As in?"

"Paris Aaron. Summer-fling Aaron. Love-of-my-motherfucking-*life* Aaron!"

"Well, shit."

"Shit? Shit? That's all you have? Because I have some words that are several letters stronger than damn shit!"

Her shoe comes into contact with my shin.

"Ouch!" I sit up and glare at her.

"Pull it together, Dayton," she orders. "You don't lose your shit over a guy. Ever."

"This... This shocked the ever-loving life out of me, Liv. I had no idea it was him. He was an anon and he thought he'd hired Mia Lopez. The girl he got was little old me."

"I can't see how it's such a bad thing."

Jesus Christ. Every brunette might need a blond best friend, but next time I'll have a switched-on one, please.

"Do I need to spell it out for you?"

She nods.

"One"—I hold up a finger—"personal relationships are off-limits with clients. Pretending to be a girlfriend is different, but you never, ever fall in love with them. Two, Mia Lopez is that for a reason. She separates the pretend from the real, the working from the playing. And three, Aaron Stone knows my name. He knows who I am. There are a handful of people in this city who really know who Mia Lopez is, and he's now one of them."

"Okay, but it's not your fault you have a personal relationship with him. If you'd known it was him when Monique called, you wouldn't have done it, right?"

"Obviously not. You don't mix business with pleasure in my life."

"So you don't even..." She raises her eyebrows.

"Liv."

"Sorry. Sorry. I'm just sayin'..."

"No. I don't. Can we get back to the problem now?"

She shrugs one shoulder and leans back, tilting her glass side to side. "I get everything you said, babe, but I just don't see the problem. He needed a date for one night and you did it. It's not like you're going to see each other again, is it?"

"See you again soon, Mr. Michaels." I shut the door to the extension and lean against it. God. He's always a tiring one. There are only so many ways you can have sex with a fifty-year-old man before you're afraid you'll break his back—a memo he didn't get, because he thinks taking Viagra before he gets here will make it nice for us both.

Thank God my fake orgasm would show up a porn star's.

I leave Monique's twenty percent in the envelope, and tuck my share into my purse, ready to deposit it in the bank tomorrow. The only thing on my mind right now is a hot shower to scrub old man off me and then sinking into a bubble bath until I turn into a prune.

The water practically burns my skin as I stand beneath the spray, but I definitely feel cleaner when I get out. If I lived anywhere other than Seattle, the water bill would kill me, even with my higher-than-average earnings. As it is, it costs me more to heat the water than it does to use it, and my water tank barely holds enough to wash a freaking bunny rabbit.

This job requires shower after shower after shower to scrub old man and sneaky husband off my body—something that would be slightly more bearable if there was the chance of an orgasm once in a while. But no. No orgasm. Not even a tremble of one.

That's why I have Mr. Jack Rabbit under my bed.

Yep, that's me. Dayton Black, high-class escort and responsible for my own orgasm since 2006.

I'm about to dip my toe into my corner tub when my cell shrills. Fuck that. Monique won't call when she knows I've just finished with a client, and anyone else can just wait. I let it go to voicemail, and I'm about to sit down when her voice rings through my house.

"Dayton, get your ass to my house now. We need to talk."

Aw, shit.

What was that about her not calling?

I throw on some sweatpants, a tank, and Ugg boots and shove my still-wet hair into a ponytail. She wants me now? She takes me as I am now.

The drive across Seattle to her suburban dream is surprisingly stress free, and when I pull up, she's standing with her hands on her hips in her doorway. Her lips are pursed and her brows furrowed in a look I know too well. It's a look that says only one thing—my agent is pissed. Incredibly so.

"Inside," she barks.

I look to the sky and follow her in. Monique in a bad mood is never fun. For anyone.

She sits me at the kitchen table and leans against the side. "Why the fuck didn't you tell me you knew him?"

Of course.

"He was an anon. I didn't even know myself until I got there."

"An ex-boyfriend? Fuck, Dayton. Why didn't you get the hell out of there?

"Rule one hundred seventy thousand and ten of being a call girl: you don't run out on a client once you're introduced. Ever." I fold my arms across my chest. "I had a job to do, Mon. He paid, I delivered."

"No personal relationships!"

"*After* hire!" I argue. "I haven't seen Aaron Stone for seven years and I never thought I would again."

Monique's eyes flit across my face, examining every feature, and she finally relaxes. "Do you still have feelings for him?"

"No."

"Good. Because he's your client again."

I'm sorry. What?

"He called this morning. He's traveling to his father's other offices—Vegas, Sydney, Milan, London, and Paris. He needs someone to accompany him for the next six weeks, and you're the lucky fucking girl."

What?

"And you're telling me this why?"

"Because you're going."

"But you just said—"

"Oh, believe me, Dayton. This has been fucking killing me all day, but Ross said I should just let you do the job. You have a past, but he thinks you're too smart to go fall in love again, right?"

"Right."

"And Mr. Stone is paying triple your damn rate to get you on his arm looking pretty. But you listen to me. You go out? He buys you dinner. You need a new dress? He buys that fucker too. You need your hair done? A bikini wax? Your eyebrows shaped? He pays for every fucking thing you need. Even if it's a candy bar."

"I don't depend on a guy to buy me stuff, Mon. I'm pretty damn sure I can afford to get my eyebrows shaped."

She leans forward and slams her hands on the table, her light blue eyes piercing mine. "You need something, he buys it. Capiche?"

My jaw tightens. "Capiche."

"Good. Now go home and pack. You're leaving at seven a.m. for Las Vegas."

"Seven a.m.?!"

"Seven a.m., and your share of the first week's money will be in your account by the time you land."

"Fine. What am I doing?"

She smirks. "You're his girlfriend."

Fantastic.

# Chapter Four

If one week ago you'd told me I'd be staring at three large suitcases wondering what the hell I was doing getting ready to travel around the world with Aaron Stone, I wouldn't have believed you. Hell, if you'd told me I'd see him again, I wouldn't have believed you.

From the moment my seventeen-year old self touched back down in Seattle from Paris, he became little more than a memory. Every thump of my aching, broken heart reminded me of our promise to each other—one summer. Eventually, the pain receded, and six months later, my heart was beating to its own rhythm once more.

Now I'm making sure I have everything I need for six weeks away, and I'm wondering how I've come to belong to Aaron Stone once again.

I slide my feet into grey suede knee-high boots and tuck my cell into my pocket. My stomach is rolling with apprehension, and my heels click against the wooden floor of my living room. I keep alternating my glace from the window to the clock, even though there's still five minutes until he arrives.

And I don't even know what I'm more worried about—seeing him or spending six weeks with him and keeping to the rules of my world.

Three soft knocks at the door echo through my house, and I take a deep breath. I'd rather be doing anything but this. Anything at all. I'd even take Mr. Can't Come right now. I flex my fingers around the door handle and pull it open before I have second thoughts about something I can't change.

My eyes comb over his jeans and well-fitting blazer that's open at his waist. A white shirt collar peeks above the V-neck of his sweater, and my gaze finally finds his face. There's a five-o'clock shadow lining his strong jaw, and soft pink lips are teased into a tiny smile, one that's reflected in the blue eyes staring down at me.

"Aaron," I say as softly as he knocked.

"Dayton. Are you ready to go?"

I nod once and step to the side so he can pass me.

He takes my suitcases to the car while I grab my purse. I lock my front door, and when I turn, I notice that he's holding the car door open for me.

"Enough suitcases?" he asks, a glint of amusement in his electric blue eyes.

"Oh, didn't you know?" I pause before lowering myself into the car, looking at him pointedly. "Girlfriends of the rich don't travel light."

I tear my eyes from his as I sit. As he slides in beside me, he sighs, and I look out of the window. It wasn't until I saw him standing in front of me that I realized how pissed I am about this. One coincidental night doesn't equal a fucking worldwide rendezvous.

Buying Mia Lopez for one night doesn't equal buying Dayton Black for six weeks.

Silence stretches between us, the tension building until it's tight enough it'd snap if one of us sighed too hard.

"Day—"

"Don't Day me. Just tell me why."

He reaches forward and shuts the glass partition. "Dad asked me if you were coming—"

"Don't try and put this on your dad."

"—and I said no." He gives me a look that makes me close my mouth. "The more I thought about it, the more I wanted you to come with me. After seeing you the other night, I wanted to catch up and get to know you again. This was the only way."

"By fucking *buying* me?"

"Would you have come otherwise?"

I bite my tongue. We both know the answer is no.

"Exactly. I just wanted to spend some time with you again. Is that so bad?"

It is when you're the one person who could shatter everything I've strived for seven years to build.

I don't answer him, instead turning back to the window. His eyes are searing into the back of my head the whole way to the airport, tempting me to turn. When we reach the airport, I open my door and get out of the car before he can do it for me.

Wordlessly, I follow him to the small private jet owned by the company. His arm snakes around my waist and I glare at him.

"See that girl standing by the stairs? That's my father's second assistant. Try not to look too pissed off at me."

"I'll be as sweet as sugar," I snap quietly. A smile replaces my frown when we approach the tall, blond girl with a catwalk figure.

"Mr. Stone." She flicks her hair and beams at him. Jesus, her eyes are undressing him right here. "And this must be Miss Black?"

"That's me." My smile turns tight, and she notices, quickly diverting her eyes to the clipboard in her hand.

She clears her throat. "Well, Mr. Stone, your father wanted me to tell you that everything you need is on the plane, and you're booked to stay at the Dorgate."

"Presidential suite?" Aaron questions.

"Yes, sir. You have use of the company card." She hands him a slick, black American Express card. "Anything bought while you're away is to go on the bill, and it'll be sent to your father when you check out of each hotel."

"Thank you, Sarra. Is that everything?"

"Yes, sir. Have a good trip." She flashes me a quick smile and gets in the car we just left.

I feel Aaron's eyes on me and turn my face toward him. "What?"

"I think you scared her." His lips twitch.

My own lips curl in response and my eyebrows rise. "Hey, she was trying to hit on you. It's my job to scare people off. That's why you hired me in the first place, remember?"

I climb the stairs to the plane, but before I can get inside, Aaron wraps an arm around my stomach and brings his mouth close to my ear.

"Correct. I hired you in the *first* place to scare the vultures off. This time I hired you to be yourself, because believe it or not, all you have to do is be in the same room as other girls to scare them off."

"Flattering," I retort dryly.

"Beauty is intimidating, Dayton, and you're the very definition of the word."

"Smooth. Do you use that often?" I push his arm from me and take myself to the plush, cream seats.

"No." He sits opposite me. "I'm not in the habit of lying to people who matter to me."

I raise an eyebrow as an attendant comes out and he orders two coffees for after takeoff.

"What if I want tea?"

That smirk appears again. "You hate tea."

"I used to."

"Would you like tea?"

"No." I sit back and cross my legs. "I hate tea."

Aaron shakes off his jacket and leans forward. "Are you going to be this difficult the whole time?"

"Oh you better believe it, baby. Difficult is my middle name."

The pilot's voice comes over the speaker and instructs us that we're about to take off. I clip the seatbelt around my waist and turn my attention to the window and the rising sun filtering through the faint Seattle skyline.

Nerves bubble up inside as the plane moves, and I tilt my head into the chair, my hair falling and covering my face. I screw my eyes shut, fear slithering through every part of my body, freezing me, and holding me hostage. I don't move until we level off and are surrounded by fluffy white clouds.

The coffees are placed in front of us, and I take a long sip and try to calm my breathing.

"You haven't flown since, have you?"

My eyes snap up to Aaron's. "What does it matter?"

"Dayton."

"No. I haven't. This is the first time I've been anywhere near a plane in five years, to be honest. I've never had to."

"We could have driven to Vegas."

"And you're driving to Sydney? Milan? Paris?" I raise my eyebrows. "I'm sure I can manage two hours on a plane."

He nods but says nothing back to my bravado. Because we both know that's what this is. Bravado. I'm more scared than a claustrophobic person trapped in an elevator.

I drop my eyes to my mug and watch the dark liquid swirl inside it. "So," I say after a long moment of silence.

"So," Aaron returns.

"I need to make sure I'm on the same page as you with this 'relationship' thing."

"What do you need to know?"

For some reason, asking him the questions I'd ask any other client makes me want to blush.

And I don't blush.

Ever.

"This arrangement… What's expected in public?"

"For you to act as a normal girlfriend would. The way you did the other night. We're in the honeymoon stage."

"Fabulous. And in private?"

"We'll be sleeping in the same bed, if that's what you're asking. Don't forget my father booked our hotel rooms."

I meet his gaze. "Of course. And sex?"

His eyes cloud over with heat at the word, making my stomach muscles tighten. "Optional."

Let's rephrase that.

Sex: optional but inevitable.

I press my fingertips to the ceiling-high glass windows that stretch the length of the main area of the suite. From this position, on the highest floor of the hotel, I can see the whole strip stretching out before me, lit up so brightly it barely seems like night is falling.

Vegas—it's a whole other world filled with temptation and greed. It doesn't matter how much you have when you're here because you always want more. More risk, more money, more everything. It's a city I've always avoided despite my job. I always told myself I'd never give in to the lure of Sin City, yet here I am.

At least *I* didn't bring me here.

"You're missing half your robe," Aaron's voice travels across the room.

"In that case, you should call the concierge. God forbid I should be wearing half a robe." I drop my hand and walk toward him, ready to get dressed for the night.

He stretches his arm out across the door, stopping me. "Why would I do that?"

"You tell me." I turn my face toward him.

"There isn't a thing that would convince me to tell the concierge." He drops his eyes to the opening at my chest and brings them back up. "Especially when you forget to put underwear on beneath it."

"Ah, yes. I forgot. You get to look at your girlfriend that way."

"Just exercising my right to look at my *girlfriend*."

I push his arm down and grab the door. "Yeah? Now I'm exercising my right to lock this damn door behind me." I slam it, the noise echoing around the bedroom, and turn the latch.

So I'm bitter. Who gives a fuck? I think I'm allowed to be.

I open my suitcase and pull out a tan chiffon dress with a black lace layer over it. This is one of my favorite dresses despite only having worn it once. And it looks perfect with the black purse and tan heels I conveniently packed. So it's not as garish and glittery as Vegas demands, but it's classy and sexy.

My middle names. If you discount Ms. Lingerie.

I throw on some makeup and step into some black lingerie. And pause.

The lock clicks on the door, and before I can grab the robe again, Aaron strolls into the room.

"What the hell, Aaron?"

Those electric eyes comb over my body, his gaze touching every inch of my body, sweeping over my exposed curves smoothly. I put my hands on my hips as if the simple movement can distract me from the feelings running through my body.

I'm looked at every day in every way, but I can't remember the last time someone looked at me the way Aaron is right now. His darkened gaze, full of hunger and want, isn't for the body. It's for me.

He finally brings his eyes to mine and grabs a bow tie from the bed. "I'm still getting ready."

"So you picked the lock? You didn't think to ask if I was dressed?" I snatch my dress and slink into it.

"Underwear is dressed." He smirks. "Do you want me to zip you up?"

I try and fail to get the zipper on my back up. "I suppose."

He stands behind me as I turn. I can see us in the floor-length mirror in front of me, but it can't distract from the buzz that moves over my skin when his fingers brush my back.

"You're angry with me," he murmurs.

"Did you expect me to be sunshine and rainbows?"

"No." He slides my hair over my shoulder and brings the zipper the rest of the way up. His eyes meet mine in the mirror. "But I didn't expect you to be this pissed either."

"You show up in my life after seven years—as my *client*—then buy me for six weeks."

"It wouldn't bother you normally."

I sigh. "Being bought is my job."

He drops his eyes to my back and strokes the back of my neck with his thumb. "So why does it matter if I have? After all, it's your job."

*You bastard.* "Don't fuck with me, Aaron. You know exactly why it's different."

"Because you loved me once."

I swallow and step forward where he can't touch me anymore. Twelve hours and this conversation is already pushing boundaries. Pushing my rules. "Yes."

He nods and wordlessly puts on his bow tie. I grab my brush from the dresser and run it through my dark hair, keeping my eyes on a part of the mirror where I can't see him.

I should have said no. I should have turned this job down.

"You should wear your hair like this." Aaron once again comes behind me and pushes my hair over my shoulder. He's fully dressed now, the sleeves of his white shirt creeping below his black jacket. "It suits you."

I snap the band on my wrist. "I'm wearing it up."

He takes my wrist and slides off the band, tucking it into his pocket. "Wear your hair this way."

"Are you asking me as my client?" I ask through a tight jaw.

"I don't ask people things, Dayton. I tell them. You included."

There's an undertone of something in his voice—of power. Of the power he'll hold in a few short weeks, but more than that, the power he already holds. Because he's right. He doesn't ask people. He's never asked me anything.

Even when we met, he didn't ask me for a date. He *told* me I was going out with him. Just like he told me when our dates became something more. When he told me he'd booked a second hotel room across the city for us. Just us.

I never said no. It never crossed my mind to.

"Your wish is my command," I mutter under my breath, grabbing hair pins instead. He quirks an eyebrow but doesn't say anything, finally leaving me in peace. Once my hair is pinned to the side—per my *client's* request—I slip on my tan heels and grab my purse.

Aaron's waiting for me in the main room, looking out over the strip like I was not so long ago. I pause here at the door and let my eyes run over him shamelessly. He's gorgeous—truly gorgeous. He wears his suits in a way that's effortlessly sexy, and I haven't seen him in an outfit yet that hasn't been tailored perfectly to fit his body.

Granted, I've only seen three outfits, but I'd imagine the others are the same.

"Are you done?" His eyes find mine, and the sparkle in them

tells me he caught me ogling him.

"Yep." I move toward the door.

"Wait." His long stride swallows the room as he walks to me. "Give me your hand."

I hold my hand out and he pulls a glittering tennis bracelet from a box I didn't know he was holding. I open my mouth when he attaches it around my wrist, but he speaks before any shocked words can leave me.

"Don't." He meets my gaze. "I can't say I'm giving this out of the goodness of my heart."

"So why are you?"

He rubs his thumb along the underside of my wrist, alongside the bracelet. "It makes a statement. It tells everyone you belong to me."

"I'm pretty sure the money deposited in my account at noon does that."

"And you and I are the only people who know of that. The guys downstairs don't, but they know this." He taps it and drops my hand. "Which means you're safe from any unwanted advances."

"I wouldn't say I'm safe, exactly."

"Trust me, Day." He brushes the backs of his fingers along my jaw, his eyes tracing their path, and drops his voice. "When I come on to you, it'll be because you want it. Very much."

He opens the door and leads me to the elevator. Once inside, he punches the button and wraps an arm around my waist. Heat radiates from him into my side, and I clutch my purse tighter to distract myself from the way his fingers are flexing at my waist.

"Try not to sass me too much tonight."

"I'm not promising anything."

# Chapter Five

Aaron eyes me over the top of his cards, and I bring my glass to my lips. We've been at this table for an hour, but this is the first game I've played. If my daddy taught me anything, it's that you don't play poker 'til you know a guy's tells.

And I know Mr. Stone is bluffing.

He studies me for a long moment before resting his elbows on the table and placing his cards facedown on it. "You're bluffing."

"Try me." I lick my lips. "Unless you're scared."

The guys around the table watch us with amusement, and my fighting talk gets an 'oooh' out of someone.

"Scared? Not of you, Bambi."

I ignore the old pet name and tilt my head. "Show your hand."

Slowly, he flips the cards and spreads them across the table in front of us. "Full house."

"Ooooh," comes from the guys who all folded.

I shrug a shoulder and sigh. "Dammit."

Aaron smirks.

"You should have listened." I lay my cards out. "Four of a kind. Read 'em and weep, handsome."

The smirk drops from his face when his eyes crawl over my cards. "Fuck."

"Hard luck, buddy." One of the guys—I've never been good with names—pats his shoulder as they file out of the room.

I grin at Aaron across the table.

"I can't believe you just beat me at poker."

I pick up my glass again and empty it, keeping my eyes on his. "I can't believe you're surprised."

"I suppose I shouldn't be." He stands and walks around the table to me. He spins my chair so I'm facing him, and I tilt my head back to look at him. "What other tricks do you have stashed up your sleeves, hmm?"

"If I tell you, they won't be tricks any longer." I run a finger down the lapel of his jacket, the white tip of my manicure a stark contrast against the black material. "And they won't be half as fun."

He raises a dark eyebrow. "I guess not. Just don't beat me at blackjack. I'm not sure my ego can take the battering."

"Oh, I might just beat you at everything for calling me Bambi."

"It slipped out."

Now I raise an eyebrow. "The last time you called me Bambi you'd followed me to the Charles de Gaulle airport because you were worried you wouldn't get to say goodbye. Now you're saying it over poker?"

He smiles and leans forward. "Like I said, it slipped out."

"And I'm calling bullshit. You knew what you were saying."

"Maybe. Maybe not."

His eyes dare me to keep arguing with him, but the lingering memory of the past begs me not to. I need to remember I'm not here to relive the most amazing summer of my life, no matter how hard it is to avoid.

Who the fuck am I kidding?

"Come on. Since you won, you can buy me a drink." Aaron takes my hands and eases me up from the chair.

"You're going to let a woman buy you a drink? Damn."

"Good point." He pulls me closer to him. "I'll buy you a drink, and we'll make this an 'I owe you.'"

"We will?"

"Yes, and I'm about to cash it in."

"You are?"

"The head of the Vegas office will be meeting us at the main bar in twenty minutes with his wife." Goose bumps erupt on my skin where he trails his fingers up my arm. "He'll be calling my father as soon as he gets to work tomorrow, who, per my mother's request, will ask about us. I think he should have something good to report back, don't you?"

I purse my lips. "That's what you're paying me for."

He dips his head forward. "So take the favor and make it twice as good." His breath crawls over my mouth with his words, the warmth making me part my lips. It carries a lingering scent of the whisky he's been sipping all night, a woody smell reminiscent of oak.

"You have no idea what you're asking me to do," I warn him.

"That's the fun part."

I flatten my hands against his chest and push him back. "I'm serious, Aaron. This is my *job*. Giving people something to talk about is what I do when I escort."

His eyes hit me, deadly serious. "Give it your best."

I pick my purse up from the table and pause in the doorway, glancing over my shoulder. "As you wish."

I slip my hand around his arm and add some extra sway to my hips as we walk through the casino. Eyes follow me wherever I go, and I'll bet anything that the swish of my dress is exactly what they're looking at. I raise my right hand and smooth my hair back, letting everyone get a glance at the bracelet glittering on my wrist.

Their quiet groans form an ironically loud chorus of music that makes my lips twitch. This is where I'm comfortable, where I'm home. Men watching me, wanting me, wishing they were the guy whose arm I'm clinging to. That's my life. That's where I excel. Making them watch me. Making them want me.

And their wives? Their girlfriends? I excel at making them wish they *were* me.

We walk through into the quiet restaurant and I take a seat at the bar. Aaron orders a glass of wine for me and a bourbon for himself, turning to me when the guy goes to get our drinks.

"Don't think I didn't notice what you did back there," he says in a low voice.

"I have no idea what you're talking about." I give him my best innocent eyes.

His lips quirk into that smirk, and he steps forward when the barman disappears again. He rests his hand on my waist, his fingers flexing against the lace of my dress, and drops his eyes to mine.

"No, you have no idea of the effect you have on men simply by walking past them."

"Not at all." I run my fingers up his stomach, ignoring the feeling of solid muscle there, and tweak his bow tie. "It's not my job to know the effect I have on them, rather, merely to affect them."

"Well let me say you do it"—he bends his head toward mine— "spectacularly."

"Thank you." I pull on the tie harder and it unravels, hanging loosely around his neck. Then I undo the top button of his shirt.

"What are you doing?"

I lean up and rest my mouth by his ear. "Giving people something to talk about. Isn't that what I'm supposed to be doing?" My thigh brushes against his as I cross my legs.

"It's absolutely what you should be doing." Aaron says his words into my hair, and I turn my face into his.

"Then you should stop questioning me and allow me to do it."

His hand flattens against my back, drawing us closer. "You play a dangerous game, Dayton."

"It's only dangerous if you don't trust the person standing in front of you—if you don't know their breaking point."

"What makes you think you know mine?"

I smile against his cheek. "Have you forgotten? I know your breaking point *and* your tipping point, and I know exactly how to get you there."

"It's been seven years, as you keep reminding me. What if it's changed?"

"I'm very good at adapting." I pull back so a whisper of air hovers between our lips. "But it hasn't changed a bit."

"She thinks she's so smart."

Another smile tugs at my lips, and I whisper, "She knows if she drops her hand and brushes it against your groin, you'll be hard and ready to take her in the first possible place."

"Is that right?"

"Mhmm. A wall is the likely choice…" I rest my fingers against his belt, and he tenses. "Looks like she's as smart as she thinks she is if you're tense at my fingers sitting here…nowhere near the erection you're failing to hide."

He chuckles low, a raspy tone to it. "Your game is very, very dangerous, Miss Black."

"And you get to play it for a whole six weeks. Aren't you lucky?"

He curls his fingers around mine at his belt. "The only luck here will be if we leave Vegas without me fucking you against every wall of our suite."

The promise in his voice makes my breath catch. I have no doubt he would do that, if only I'd let him.

Heat floods my body and pools in my lower stomach at the thought, moving down slowly until the heat becomes a slight throb in my clit. *Sweet Jesus, a sentence has never sounded so sexy.*

"And the tables turn," he murmurs, moving my hand away. "Tell me, Dayton. Are you as easy to turn on as you used to be?"

"I dare you find out," I breathe.

He turns his face into my cheek and I feel his lips curve against my skin. "I think I already did."

"Excuse me, Mr. Stone?" the guy behind the bar says.

"Yes?" Aaron stands and looks at him as if he hasn't just made me clench my—thankfully already closed—thighs together.

"Mr. Duvall has asked me to pass on his apologies, but he and his wife won't be able to make it tonight due to her ill health."

Aaron nods. "Thank you. Pass on our regards, and I hope Mrs. Duvall is feeling better soon." He turns to me. "She's pregnant—four months, I think."

"And you were going to drag her into a casino restaurant?" I raise my eyebrows.

"She's lived in Vegas for five years. She breathes casinos."

I roll my eyes. "Well, if they're not coming, then I'm going to turn in." I throw back the last of the wine—something I wouldn't do if this restaurant wasn't empty—and stand. "Excuse me." I tap Aaron's solid chest.

His lips turn up. "What for?"

I sigh. "Don't be difficult, Aaron. You're in the way."

"I'm waiting for the erection you caused to disappear."

"Yeah? Considering the way it's pressing against my hip, I don't think that's happening anytime soon, and I consider myself an expert on the male anatomy." I step the side. "Are you coming?"

Poor choice of words, Dayton.

Aaron caught it too, if the spark in his eyes is anything to go by. He slides his empty glass across the bar and wraps his arm around my stomach as we walk.

"Is that an invitation?"

"As much as you'd like it to be, I'm afraid not. I need my beauty sleep."

"I could call it in."

We step into the elevator and I eye him. "You could."

The doors close. He slides his hand up my back to my neck, his thumb brushing my skin. "So why aren't I?"

"You tell me." My eyes meet his with a questioning turn of my head.

"I don't know. But I know I'm dying to kiss you right now."

"Until we're in the room, I'm your girlfriend."

The doors open. He follows me to the suite door and stops me from opening it. "And once we're inside the room? What happens then?"

His breath fans over my neck, and I tilt my face into him. "You're the client. That's for you to decide."

He laughs quietly. "When you stop seeing me as a client, I'll be sure you tell you my decision."

This isn't working.

I turn the treadmill up to the next level and pick up my pace. An all-morning session in the gym followed by a swim is my plan to shake Aaron off me—that is, from under my skin. 'Cause dammit, the bastard has snaked his way under it already.

This is what I get for not listening to my gut feeling. This is what I get for not listening to my agent's gut feelings. *Stupid, stupid, stupid!*

I need to separate the two Aarons in my mind, take away the young man I fell in love with. I need to tear that version of him up into a thousand little pieces and let them crumble all over the floor. Then step on them. I need to separate the man and the client.

In my heart, I honestly believed I'd put those weeks behind me. I'd accepted them as a once-in-a-lifetime opportunity to experience the kind of world-tilting love everyone should feel at some point. Hell, I knew that was all it could be. One summer.

We agreed that from the start, when we realized what we felt was stronger than friendship. We agreed we'd spend the summer together and then, when we got back to the US, we'd each go about our lives on the opposite sides of the country. Seattle and New York. Two different worlds. Both of us knew it wouldn't have worked. He was at college, I still in high school…

We agreed to six weeks and sealed it with a kiss, the kind of kiss that made me wonder immediately if we'd made a stupid choice. But it didn't matter, because it was done. We were young and crazy, and neither of us really thought about what would happen after.

Neither of us really thought about what would happen when we fell in love then ripped our own hearts out.

Neither of us realized just how painful that would be, but it had to be done. So I boxed away the pain and I moved on to what needed to be done. And when my parents died, everything changed in a way that made me glad we'd said goodbye. My life took on a whole new twist.

I accepted escorting as the reality of my life. I saw it for what it is—the money and the lingerie and the men who can't get themselves off.

I never, ever imagined I'd see Aaron again.

I still don't believe I have.

I can't believe he's fucking with my twenty-four-year-old mind as easily as he stole my seventeen-year-old heart.

And that, in essence, is everything this trip is. A mindfuck. I don't believe he wants to get to know me at all. Hello, this is the twenty-first century—you use coffee for that shit. *Not a six-week worldwide trip.* No, the second the shock faded from his eyes, an age-old hunger took over.

All Aaron Stone wants is what's inside my very pretty pink lace thong.

Well, mostly inside.

He's playing the game well. He could get it any time he wants. It's what he's paying for, essentially. Hell, the guy could tell me to get on my knees and wrap my lips around his cock and I'd be completely powerless to deny him it.

In this game where the rules dictate we both hold equal parts power, he has the edge. I can't use mine until he uses his. I can't seduce him until he gives me permission.

Because the bottom line remains—he is my client.

Not my ex-boyfriend.

Not the love of my fucking life.

My client.

And call girls don't fall in love. But then falling isn't the problem. That comes when you've already fallen once, because you know the quickest way down.

I run faster, stamping him out of my mind with every beat of my feet against the treadmill. I'm sweating him out, panting him out, pushing him out with sheer determination, and reminding myself of what I do.

I get paid. I fuck. That is the essence of my job. The essence of *me.* I change my name for it, for my anonymity, but Mia and Dayton are the same person. I don't have different personalities—not really. Mia has the same quirks as Dayton, they like the same things, and they act pretty much the same way.

Mia just gets a lot more sex. However unsatisfying it may be.

Yes, there's no difference. They're the same person, but I'm more Mia than Dayton. Much more—and that makes being two people much easier.

Mia is…stronger. She has more sass and confidence and sexiness, and she lacks the broken past Dayton has. She lacks all the memories and heartbreak that go with it. She doesn't get nostalgic when she hears certain songs or visits certain places. There's no ache when she looks in the mirror and sees her mom's eyes in place of her own or the curl at the ends of her hair, reminiscent of her father's.

She sees strength. Confidence. Determination. Beauty.

Mia is the girl I always wished I could be.

Perhaps the two sides of me are a lot more different than I thought.

I step off the treadmill and leave the gym. Strength. That's what I need to be now. I need to be Mia, all day every day, if I have any chance of leaving this job the way I came into it.

And if I get desperate, then, well… I'll just stick Post-it notes on the bathroom mirror to remind me to sort my shit out.

The indoor pool is quiet, so I quickly change into my swimsuit and dip under the water. It's warm against my skin, soothing and relaxing me. I immerse myself beneath the water and swim from one end of the pool to the other.

I swim the length repeatedly, back and forth, only pausing to take a breath of air. When I swim, my mind is completely clear. All the thoughts melt into the water around me, forgotten in an instant.

Some people use alcohol or drugs to deal with the past, others use sex or gambling, but I use exercise. It became an addiction at one point, something I couldn't live without, but sharp-tongued

Monique kicked my ass and whipped me into shape. Aside from Liv, she became my best friend.

"So this is how you keep those gorgeous curves in check."

I jolt around, and the first thing I notice is a shiny pair of black shoes. As my eyes travel up the body of the person they belong to, my surprise turns to annoyance.

"Aaron."

"You could sound pleased to see me once in a while, you know." He loosens his tie and shrugs off his jacket.

"You could wear something other than a suit. It's a Saturday, you know."

"I don't know if anyone in the business would be impressed if their future CEO walked into the office wearing jeans and a polo shirt."

"You own a polo shirt? Wow." I lift myself out of the pool.

"Several." Aaron follows me with his eyes as I walk to my towel and wrap it around my body.

"How did you know I was here?"

He pulls a ten-dollar bill from his pocket and holds it up between his fingers. *Ah.* Of course. Money talks.

"Only ten dollars? I'd be offended if I cared."

"It actually cost me a hundred." He opens the door and lets me pass. "For some reason, the concierge was reluctant to tell me where you were."

"Imagine that." I step into the elevator.

"And he asked me to hand you back your fifty dollars." Aaron takes my hand and tucks the bill into my palm. "Nice try, Dayton."

*Bastard.* "I'll have to remember to offer him a special rate next time."

Aaron slams the suite door behind him, and I glance over my shoulder. His eyes are hard, the bright sparkle replaced with a gaze of granite. I'm about to drop my towel when he pulls me back against his chest and cups my jaw with his hand.

His lips, close to my ear, brush against my skin when he speaks, his words steady and controlled. "Are you telling me you'd fuck the concierge?"

"Take what you want from it." I clench my teeth together.

"Are you telling me you'd fuck the concierge?" he repeats, a hard edge to the words. "To avoid me?"

My lips twitch. "That's exactly what I'm telling you."

I slide my hand behind me to push him away, but he's quicker, and he grabs both of my wrists in his large hand. He releases his grip on my jaw and tugs the towel down.

"You're on my time, Dayton. Every second of your time belongs to me, or have you forgotten that? Your actions, your clothes—they belong to me too." His hand runs down my side, his thumb brushing the side of my breast, his fingers grazing along my bikini line. "And your body? That belongs to me as well."

I turn my face away. "Only because you pay for it."

"I don't care how you belong to me." He pulls my face into his. "Just that you do. And as long as you do, no one gets to fuck you. Not the concierge, not a waiter, not a guy from the casino." His breath coats my lips in a swath of heat and desire. "The only person who gets to see you, touch you, and make you come is me. Do you understand that?"

I bring my eyes to his in a silent defiance.

He grips my jaw a little tighter. "*Do you understand that?*"

"Yes. I understand it." I snatch my hands from his grip and knock his fingers from my jaw. "I belong like you, like a pretty little possession."

"You belong to me, but nothing like my possession. As much as I'd love to possess you and your naked body, you're your own person and I respect that. Until you push me. Push me and you'll find out just how fucking possessive I can be."

"I think I have a pretty good idea."

He spins me into him, slides his fingers into my hair, and pulls my head back. "You have *no idea* just how thoroughly I could possess you, Bambi."

"Don't call me Bambi."

Our lips are a whisper apart as he dips his head to mine. "You've always been Bambi to me, and I'm not changing it now just because you've decided to ignore our past. I refuse to ignore it, so get fucking used to it." He brushes his lips across my cheek. "Get ready. We're going to dinner at seven."

# Chapter Six

I haven't said a word to Aaron Stone for two hours and seventeen minutes. Not that I'm counting, of course, and not for his lack of trying to make conversation. As it is, I've made it through a whole dinner and a drink with only speaking to the waiter.

Because he's royally pissed me off.

What's even worse is that the possessive shit he pulled, the grabbing and the whispering and the sexy-ass threats, turned me on. Panty-changing, leg-clenching, pussy-throbbing kind of turned on. I loved it and hated it at the same time.

Love it because the only thing that's turned me on in at least two years is battery-operated. Hate it because it's *him*. Enough said.

"You have to talk to me sooner or later."

No, I don't.

He raises an eyebrow. "How long are you going to keep this up?"

*I'm not falling for that.* I smile tightly at him.

"Fucking hell, Day." He rubs his hand down his face and sighs. "You're being incredibly immature, do you know that?"

As if to validate his statement, the urge to poke out my tongue overcomes me. I beat it down. Just.

I take my purse and stand, turning away. His chair scrapes

against the floor as he gets up after me, and I hear his shoes squeak against the tiled floor of the restaurant behind me. We leave the busy restaurant, together yet apart, and I head toward the casino. If the next six weeks follow the pattern of the last two days, I'll be in a perpetual state of annoyance.

Aaron's hand finds mine and pulls me back into the wall of an empty hallway. He stands in front of me, his eyes searching for my gaze, his free hand holding my jaw much the way he was earlier. He tilts my head back so my eyes crash into his.

"We can't go in there if you're not talking to me. Too many people I know."

I raise my chin defiantly.

"You're not going to say a word?"

I stare at a spot on the wall over his shoulder.

"Fine. That's fine"—he bends his head forward—"because there are other uses for your mouth."

My eyes close at the firm touch of his lips on mine. They're warm and soft with a lingering taste of the oaky whiskey he drinks. Caressing and gradually more probing, they're everything I remember and more.

I drop my purse, and his fingers curl around the back of my neck as mine grip the lapels of his jacket. Our bodies push together, and when his arm snakes around my back, holding us together, a small gasp leaves me at our full-bodied contact.

His kiss is as engulfing and suffocating and intimate as it was before. Only now it's laced with a power and determination he didn't know then, with the possessive, domineering streak he showed earlier.

"You're a bastard, Aaron Stone."

"I know, but it worked." The lips that were just covering mine are now curled in a smug amusement.

"A woman ignoring you is *not* an excuse to kiss her."

He runs his thumb across my mouth. "I didn't see you using these for anything else."

"Really? They were about to tell you where to go."

"Behave." He kisses me again, once, deeply, and tugs on my bottom lip. "I'd hate to say something that would make you ignore me again."

"I bet you would." I uncurl my fingers from the material of his jacket and flatten them against his chest. "You're lucky you're paying for that. Anyone else would have felt the damage of my heels."

Aaron laughs, his hand still firmly on my neck. "Oh, Bambi. I didn't pay for that kiss. I stole it."

"Then, perhaps"—I step into him and slide my hands over his shoulders—"you should give it back."

He barely has time for his eyebrow quirk before I tug his face to mine. My lips mold against his forcefully, and he wastes no time pulling me into him again. I nip at his bottom lip and run my tongue across it after, soothing the tiny sting and then smiling against him at the flexing of his fingers on my back. Gently, I coax his lips apart and flick the tip of my tongue against his. My fingers tangle in his hair and he groans quietly into my mouth at the tiny pull it causes.

His tongue explores my mouth the way mine does his, and briefly, it occurs to me that we're making out in a hotel hallway like a couple of teenagers, exactly how we used to. The kisses were simply more desperate and wanting instead of the point-making charade it is now.

I can feel him growing hard inside his pants, and his erection digs into my stomach. I trail my fingers down his chest and cup his cock, rubbing my thumb along the side of it, and he tightens his grip on my neck.

I break the kiss and rest my cheek against his. "You might have stolen the first one, but you definitely just paid for it."

"You're pushing me, Dayton. Very close to the edge." He takes my hand from him and holds it behind my back. "Keep it up and you'll find it's a long fucking way down."

A breathy laugh leaves me. "I dare you to take me there."

"Do you have any idea how easily I could tease your body into coming for me?"

"And there is our difference. You seduce women for fun, Aaron, and I seduce men for a living. I seduce without *being* seduced, and that's a skill in itself. I don't get seduced. Ever."

"Really? Because..." He slides a hand down my body and between my legs quicker than I can realize his intentions. He slips a finger along my underwear, feeling the dampness there. "You feel seduced to me."

I pull back and look him dead in the eye. "Don't ever confuse a natural response to kissing with my being seduced. The last client that did that found himself without a regular fuck for six months."

"You're so difficult," he murmurs. "I don't remember you ever being this headstrong."

"I wasn't." I step from his hold. "But a lot of things can change in seven years. You ought to remember that."

It's nine a.m. on a Monday fucking morning, and I'm not in bed. There are *so* many things wrong with this, least of all the fact I'm in the building that houses Stone Advertising's offices, ready to sit by idly as my 'boyfriend' picks two new models.

Yep. Casting call number one and I have no coffee. Even if I did have coffee, I'd need something stronger in it because acting like a coolly jealous girlfriend is going to drive me insane by lunchtime.

A young intern hands me a mug of the much-wanted coffee

with a mumble. I watch her as she turns to Aaron and hands him one too, this time with a bright smile and wide eyes. *What the fuck is it with females going all doe-eyed and charmed around him?*

He smiles as he thanks her, and she practically pants and runs away. That'll be it. The panty-dropping smile that hasn't yet worked on me. Clearly I'm immune to that one, huh? I roll my eyes.

"Jealous already?" he murmurs into my ear.

"Green as can be." I bring the mug to my lips, inhaling the strong scent of coffee. "Don't you know how threatening teenage girls are?"

He laughs lowly and places a hand on my back. "Then it's a good thing I prefer a real woman, isn't it?"

The door opens and the first model strolls in. She's all…well, bones, to put it bluntly. There's nothing to her apart from skin. No curves. Nothing.

"This is the kind of girls you work with?" I turn my face and raise an eyebrow.

Aaron taps my nose. "Try to behave yourself."

"Always do," I mutter into my mug as he takes a seat.

Four other models join her, all of varying body types. One is curvier, another clearly packs a bit of muscle, one is slim but less curvy, and the last is basically the second girl with curves. They're all completely different.

And each of them knows how to work it, how to manipulate the small panel in front of them. Despite this, it's plain to see where all their eyes are—on the man in the middle. The one relaxed back in his chair with his foot resting on the opposite thigh, his fingers adjusting his tie, and his eyes on no one in particular. As they each introduce themselves, Aaron nods, but his expression never changes.

The curvy girl seems put out by it the most, and she flicks her light hair over her shoulder with a sense of entitlement. Oh, god. I hate these snobby bitches. Someone should tell them that you're not entitled to anything just because you were blessed with good looks and a great rack. Get off your high horse and work hard just like the rest of us.

She places her portfolio on the table with a beaming smile and an unnecessary wiggle of her body. I cough from my perch on a desk in the corner, and both she and Aaron look at me. She with annoyance, he with amusement.

I hold up my empty mug. "Sorry. Went down wrong." My lips curve in a polite smile, and I cross one of my legs over the other. My dress rides up slightly, exposing my thigh, and the darkening in Aaron's eyes tells me he saw more than just my thigh.

The door closes behind her as she leaves the room, and I lean back on my hands as the other girls all come forward and leave their portfolios on the table. Aaron's gaze flicks to me every other minute, and I feign complete ignorance, even though I can feel it burning into me.

"What do you think?" Eric Duvall, the British guy, asks Aaron when the room is empty.

"What did they want?"

Eric holds up a sheet of paper. "Blond, curvy but not heavy, slim but not skinny."

"And the only blonde there was on the skinnier side of slim."

"The curvy girl, uh…" Another guy shuffles paper. "Connie. She's so light she'd pass for blond."

I bet that's not all she passes for in your mind, buddy.

"No." Aaron shakes his head. "She's too dark for blond. Dayton? What do you think?"

"Hmm?"

His lips quirk up. "Connie—the first girl that left. Could she pass for blond?"

"Sorry, but no. Light brown and blond are different. She'd have to get highlights, and since this is only one shoot, it's a big ask."

"One shoot with the potential to front the campaign," the guy who wants her puts in.

"But why ask her to take the risk? There are probably a hundred blond girls out there who would be suitable. Of course, this is only my opinion—and I know nothing about modeling." I shrug a shoulder.

Eric Duvall smiles gratefully at me and turns to Aaron. "Shall we put out another call?"

"Yes—and be specific. Don't miss a detail—hair, eyes, weight. Everything. This is a large contract we can't afford to lose."

"Will you be here next time?" the other guy asks.

"No, we leave for Sydney on Thursday." Aaron stands, and the other guys follow suit. "Obviously I expect a full report including portfolios via email before the end of the day, and it goes without saying that no one will be chosen without my approval."

"Of course." They shake hands.

"Thank you for coming today, Adam. I know you're busy with the L'amour contract."

"It was a pleasure." He nods and leaves the room.

"Eric, how's your wife?"

"She's well, thank you. Bloody awful sickness is taking its toll on her now, poor love." He shakes his head.

"My ag—" I catch myself. "My friend swore by popsicles when she was expecting her son. She said they kept her hydrated as well as settled her stomach."

"Really? I'll get some on the way back home tonight. Thank you, Dayton."

"You're welcome." I smile.

He checks his watch. "Excuse me. I have a meeting for another contract in ten minutes, so I really must be going now. Dayton, it was a pleasure to meet you." He takes my hand and presses a kiss to my knuckles. "And, Aaron, I'll be sure to touch base with you and your father tonight to let you know the outcome."

"Thank you, Eric. Good luck with the meeting." Aaron shakes his hand and closes the door behind him. He pauses in front of it, raising his eyes to mine. "Subtlety isn't a strong point of yours, is it, Dayton?"

"I have no idea what you're talking about."

"Of course not." He loosens his tie, letting it hang around his neck, and the now open top button of his shirt reveals a hint of muscle on his chest. "I have to say, I found it very convenient how you just had to cough when Connie was very obviously bending in front of me."

"She was? I didn't notice."

Aaron places his hands on the desk either side of me, and one of his thumbs brushes my thigh as he does so. "And I definitely have to say, it was a nice move with the leg cross. If there were anyone else in here who had seen that, there'd be some happy wives tonight."

I don't fight the twitch of my lips. "Again, I have no idea what you're talking about."

He laughs once and leans in, ghosting his lips along my jaw, barely touching my skin. "That pink thong you're wearing—as fucking gorgeous as it is—doesn't cover nearly as much of your pussy as you think it does."

My breath catches when he wraps his fingers around my thigh, dangerously close to that thong. The phone rings and he presses a button on it without moving from me.

"Yes?"

"Your food is here, sir."

"Send it in."

I raise an eyebrow at him. "Food?"

"It's almost lunchtime."

I look at the clock on the far wall. "Ten thirty isn't lunchtime."

He smirks and answers the door. He locks it without saying a word and sets the paper bags on the desk next to me. "Maybe I wanted you here alone."

"Really, Aaron, you don't need to lock me in an office to fuck me. That's why we have a hotel room."

His eyes darken a shade. "As much as I'd love to lay you back and fuck you until you scream my name on this desk—and I will, one day—that's not the reason I've locked you in here with me. You're here because you're going to talk to me."

"And if I don't want to?"

"Then tough shit, because you can't run from me in this building."

"You left the key in the door." I glance over his shoulder. "I could easily leave."

"You wouldn't get past security on the door. They have instructions that you aren't allowed to leave unless you're accompanied by me."

"Are you kidding me? You have me on some sort of bullshit office-arrest so we can *talk?*"

Am I hearing him right? Is he being fucking serious? I shove him away from me and stand. Anger floods my body, making my hands tremble from their resting place on my hips, and I bite the inside of my lip. There isn't a single part of me that can believe this.

"Dayton." He says my name slowly, and a hint of annoyance threads through it.

"No, Aaron. Don't stand there and fucking '*Dayton*' me. I don't want to talk to you about anything other than the reason we're here."

"I want to know you again. Shit, I need to know you again."

"You don't get to do that. My clients don't know anything about me."

"I'm not your normal client."

"Normal or not, you're still my client and I'm still a call girl. My clients don't know my real name, for God's sake, and you have that. I don't get personal on a job. The only thing that matters is the lingerie I'm wearing and how hard I have to fuck until the guy comes. Not my past. Not what I've been doing since you saw me last."

Aaron chucks his jacket on the chair and eyes me as he rolls up his shirtsleeves. His gaze roams over my face until I feel like every inch of it has been scrubbed raw by the swirling mass of emotion in his eyes.

"Is that what matters? How hard you'd have to fuck me until I'd come for you?"

"I never said that."

"Yes you did. We've already established you're wearing very revealing, bright pink underwear, so let's get part two over with." His voice turns husky. "I'm easy, Day. You could fuck me hard and fast or you could fuck me slow, and I'd come for you. Inside you, over you… As long as you fuck me the same way I'll fuck you, like you'll never get enough of me being inside you, I'll come for you." He steps a little closer, his eyes never leaving mine. "Are we clear?"

*Fuck yes, that was clear.* I swallow hard and fight the urge to squeeze my thighs together. Crap. I'm so turned on I think he just fucked me with his words.

"That doesn't mean I'll tell you anything. That just means I know how you like sex."

His lips quirk and he sits behind the desk, the Vegas skyline stretching out behind him. He looks totally at home sitting there, a figure of power and pure sexuality who can word-fuck me like nobody's business.

"I hope you like this office, because we're not leaving until you talk, and I don't care what self-erected walls you have to tear down so you do." Calmly, like he can't sense my annoyance, he grabs a bag and pulls out a Subway sandwich.

Ladies and gentlemen, meet the future CEO of Stone Advertising. And he's eating fucking Subway.

He nudges the bag toward me, and I shake my head.

"I'm not hungry."

"Eat it."

"I said I'm not hungry."

"And I said fucking eat it, Dayton."

I clamp my jaw and grab the bag. Domineering asshole. This is why I do men in short doses. I can't deal with the "do this, do that" crap. I'm too headstrong for it, and I like winning my battles too much to put myself in a situation where I might have to pick them.

I bite into the sandwich and the taste of club sandwich assaults my senses, the different meats mingling together in my mouth. And there's extra cheese. *Toasted.* My eyes narrow and flit across to Aaron.

Never trust a guy who knows your favorite sandwich without asking you.

"Whenever we went for lunch at that little English café in Paris and it was on the menu, you'd ask for a club sandwich with extra cheese," he explains before I can say a thing. "And you sent back three of them because they weren't toasted, even though you'd asked for it to be. Since Subway doesn't do those, I improvised."

I lower the sandwich and perch on the corner of his desk. "How do you even remember that?"

"The things we remember the clearest aren't necessarily the big, heart-stopping moments everyone expects. They're the little things that add up. The little things most people look over but that mean the most."

Silence hovers between us for a moment, growing steadily more tense and awkward.

"If I believed in romance, I'd be a puddle right now." I take the last bite of my lunch and wad up the wrapping.

"You believed in romance once."

"Once." I cross the room and drop the wrapper in the trash can.

"That was before I realized love hurts. I gave love up the day I signed the contract with my agent. Love hurts, but pleasure doesn't and neither does power. I had to choose, and I chose pleasure and power."

"There isn't a part of you that believes in love? Really?"

I glance over my shoulder. "Do I believe it's possible? That it's real? Tangible? Yes. I believe everything you can tell me about love, but that doesn't mean I have to believe *in* it. It doesn't mean I have to believe—or want—it in any part of my life."

I feel his thumb stroke the back of my neck before I realize he's behind me. He drops his wrapper in the trash can in front of me and runs that hand down my bare arm.

"You loved me once. You loved me like I was the air you needed to breathe, like you needed my touch to keep you alive. You loved me the very same way I loved you. Obsessively. Insanely. Relentlessly. Don't tell me you don't believe in love when for six short weeks, all those years ago, you couldn't possibly live without it."

"And don't tell me I do believe in love when for months after, all those years ago, I *had* to live without it." I shrug him off me and walk to the door. "We've talked enough. I'd like to go now."

# Chapter Seven

I pinch my nose and take a deep breath as I drop beneath the water. The bathtub in this suite is a huge corner tub, and it's currently so full with bubbles I can barely see the wall behind it.

Water. It's my soother. My cleanser. Swimming, a bath, a shower—it doesn't matter. Swimming is for frustration, a shower for a quick fix, and a bath when things are so fucked up.

The water ripples when I come back up for air. I lean my head back against the tiles and let out a long sigh.

I miss Seattle. I miss the certainty and structure of my days. The regular clients, the nights with Liv, the frequent calls and texts from Monique. In reality I'm only a few miles away, but it feels like a whole world. It's been six days yet, it feels like a lifetime. I miss my lingerie room, my bedroom-come-closet, my client extension. I miss brusque texts and excited phone calls, and hell, I even miss Liv's whining after work because the hot guy she works with *still* hasn't noticed her, no matter how low she unbuttons her shirt.

I glance at the clock I brought in and sigh again. Business nights for Aaron mean business nights for me, and although we're only going for a casual dinner and a couple of hours in the casino, I have to remember that I'm working. That's it. *Working*.

The cold air of the bathroom hits my skin the second I ease

myself from the bath. I shiver and wrap the towel around me, savoring the fluffiness of it. What is it about hotel towels? God.

Empty. That's the only way to describe the suite. Silent. Lifeless. Empty.

I grab my cell from the side and text Aaron's number. What do I wear?

The response is immediate. Something Vegas. But classy and sexy. Something that is so very you.

Another message comes before I've had time to finish unzipping my suitcase.

Something that makes every guy in the casino want to fuck you.

Now that I can do.

I whip a bright pink, white-spotted lingerie set out, remembering how he liked the set I wore yesterday. Fuck. Why does that even matter?

The dusky pink lace dress I pull out after makes all those thoughts disappear, and I slide it over my wet hair until it hugs my body to perfection. Bobby pins slide into my hair perfectly, holding it to one side the way I know Aaron likes.

The dress. *Classy,* he said. The hair. *Sexy,* he said.

White-heeled pumps fit my feet perfectly, and I grab a matching white purse. I slip my credit card, cell, and lipstick inside it.

*You,* he said. White depicts innocence, but it's also deceptive. That's me all over. Deceptive.

Where do I meet you? I brush some mascara across my lashes, making them curl at the ends, the perfect accent to my smoky eyes.

"Right here." Aaron appears in the doorway, perfect and poised. His suit is crisp and tailored, and it hugs every part of his body from his shoulders to his ankles. His pants hug his fucking ankles, for the love of God.

I sweep my eyes across his face, his jaw that's holding a hint of a perfectly trimmed five-o'clock shadow, and over his hair that's swept to the side.

"That didn't take you long."

"I knew you were waiting." His fingers brush mine as he hands me my purse.

I curl my fingers around the satin. "I'm ready now."

The elevator suffocates me as he moves closer through our journey down. The air gets gradually heavier, more pressing, until I'm so focused on breathing, on the rhythmic in-and-out and the rise and fall of my chest. So much so I can barely feel Aaron's hand curving around my waist and pulling me into his side.

"You have to kiss me tonight," he says into my ear in a low voice.

"I know." I tilt my body into him, a rare streak of vulnerability going through me. I take a deep breath. "Tell me what you want me to be."

The door opens and he pulls me to the side. The bright lights and loud shouts of the casino melt into nothing at the hot sensation of his hand sliding from my side across my stomach. They fade into silence at the buzzing across my skin, at the absolute hum through my veins.

His fingers caress my cheek gently as they glide up it and around the back of my head. "Be you. The sexy, carefree, gorgeous you."

I take a deep breath in. "Mia or Dayton?"

My skin tingles at the way his other hand trails down my side. "Be *you*, Bambi. Be Dayton. I don't care a single bit for your alter ego. Be the gorgeous, amazing, and enticing woman I know is in there hiding."

I don't know if I remember how to be myself, even as the blaring noise of the casino surrounds us and envelopes us. The last time I was truly myself was the day I walked away from him, so what he's asking is absolutely a challenge.

"Be the person you fight against every day." His lips brush across my jaw. "For me."

"That's a dangerous thing you're asking. For *both* of us."

"What's dangerous is this dress." Appreciation fills his tone. I try to ignore the spark of pleasure that sneaks through me.

"I mean it." I bring my eyes to his. "You're playing with fire, Aaron. People who do that get burned."

"I don't play with fire, Dayton. I stoke it and make it burn hotter and faster until it consumes everything in its path. I'll never take a spark where I can have a roaring flame." Heat flares across my lips as his mouth hovers above mine. "Playing would imply I'm not being serious. I'm always serious when I want something. And right now, I want you. I want you, and I want you to go out there and act like you fucking want me."

"Are you asking me or telling me to do that?"

"I'm telling you you're going to go out there and act like you want me until you actually do. Until you want nothing but me and my body. Over you, under you, inside you… Go out there with me and don't leave until there isn't a part of your body that isn't crying out for mine."

He draws back and pulls me with him. His steps are stronger than mine, more assured, more determined. Try as I might, I can't match them. My head is spinning too much. Not because of the request, but because I already want him. Because it's impossible not to want him when he turns heated, darkened blue eyes on me. Because it's impossible not to in the face of pure, unadulterated lust.

Even now with his hand at my side, I can feel sparks emanating from his fingertips and spreading through my stomach. They all head downward. God, they head downward until I'm afraid a mere glance from him will have me aching in desperation.

We approach the casino bar and Aaron steers us toward two

other couples. Two sharply suited men and two beautifully done-up women. They reek of class and money. Of everything I pretend to be each and every day. Of what I'm pretending to be now.

Aaron introduces us, and the whole time pleasantries are being exchanged, his eyes flit to me. I avoid his gaze, instead flicking my eyes over his shoulder, to his forehead, at his lips. I ignore the tightening of his grip at my waist and sink into him a little farther, a faked yet convincing smile on my face. I pretend and pretend and pretend until my cheeks hurt and my stomach aches from laughing.

When Antony Barnes says that they're leaving, I almost breathe a sigh of relief. Until Aaron lays a hand on my cheek and turns my face into his. Until his takes my lips with his, soft and gentle and full of too much realness for it all to be a show.

And I realize the 'leaving' refers to the guys. Now I have to sit here at a table near the restaurant bar with two women whose names I barely remember.

"So, Dayton." The blonde turns a genuine smile on me. "What do you do?"

"Me? Oh." I wrap my fingers around the stem of my wine glass. *Fuckfuckfuck.* "I'm all dot com. Design—websites, graphics, book covers, and the like."

"Oooh, really?" The darker blonde—is it Abigail?—asks. "Anything we'd know?"

"Oh, no. Nothing big. Mostly for self-published authors. There's a big market there right now."

"Oh, that's lovely. I don't have much time to read these days."

Thank you, Mom, for always making me believe in books. "That's a shame."

"Yes. I wish I did, but Antony is forever off on business and dragging me to functions like this."

The light blonde rolls her eyes. "Yes, it's a hard life."

"Just because you enjoy traveling, Brea, doesn't mean we all do." She stands. "Excuse me for a moment."

"Of course." I give my politest smile and lift my glass.

How long do I have to do this shit? How many *times* do I have to do this? Small talk and pretending to give a crap about rich bitches wasn't mentioned when I agreed to this.

I seriously need to get Monique to draw up contracts for jobs like this.

"Ugh." Brea tops up her wine and holds the bottle over my glass. I nod in reply, and we sit in silence while she fills it. The empty bottle hits the table with a dull clunk, and a sigh leaves her dark red lips.

"I love this, you know? This lifestyle. The traveling, the dinners, the parties, the nights out... It's not something I ever expected I'd have. I've been with Patrick since we were seventeen and I helped him build his business—from selling soap samples out of the trunk of my car. Some of us"—she nods in the direction Abigail left—"were born into a life of privilege."

Oh, sweet Jesus. Is this my welcome into the Rich Bitch Wives Club? I want my invitation revoked.

"I know how hard our husbands work to give us this."

Or they just buy you because they're presumptuous bastards.

"And it riles me that she takes it for granted, you know? Not to mention she doesn't work. At all."

"Do you?" *Crap.* That came out bitchier than intended.

Brea laughs. "You sound surprised. I do, yes. I work in Rick's company. We own it jointly. We started it together."

Well, shit me. "That's great!"

"It sure is. I do all the designing and fragrance testing, and I leave all the business stuff to him. I could never do what he does."

"I don't think I could do what Aaron does either. The amount of offices he'll take charge of in a few weeks is, quite honestly, scary."

"Absolutely." She nods. "Have you been together long?"

I nearly choke on my wine but swallow it instead. Somehow. Why am I not prepared for this?

That's right. I'm Dayton, not Mia. Stupid damn client orders.

"Um, not really. We knew each other a long time ago." My lips curl into a small smile.

"A second-chance romance? Oh, how romantic!"

"Something like that."

A second-chance romance with a tidy six-figure sum behind it. *Sweep me off my feet, baby.*

"Are you in Vegas for much longer?"

"Only tonight. We're flying to Sydney tomorrow afternoon."

"What a coincidence! We have some new samples, so we're taking a working vacation over there, starting Saturday. It would be great to catch up—you know, get away from the men for a few hours."

Congratulations, Dayton Black. You're the newest member of the Rich Bitch Wives Club.

Abigail never came back—not that it bothered Brea any. She filled the very awkward conversation with her life story.

She's twenty-four, Patrick is twenty-six, and her severe allergies lead to the start-up of their business. When he unknowingly bought her a soap basket that sent to her the hospital, he set about trying to find a soap without the ingredient she's allergic to. Failing that, he made one.

I think I just heard the greatest love story of the twenty-first century. I also think I need to vomit.

"You look tense." Aaron steps behind me and rests his hands on my shoulders, his thumbs digging in at the bottom of my neck.

I bend into his touch, unable to help the sigh that escapes me. "So would you if you'd had the night I have."

"Same again." He nods at the bartender and sits me on a stool. "Let me guess. You got the soap allergy story too?"

I turn. A small smile plays on my lips. "For real? He told you too?"

"Oh yes. He wants us to do his marketing."

"No wonder his wife was so far up my ass she could see my brain," I mutter.

Aaron laughs, a rich sound that curls my toes. "Dayton," he admonishes. There's nothing to it. He's merely masking his amusement. "Behave."

"Not often I get told that. In fact, it's almost always the opposite."

His thumbs stop moving, and my hair flutters away from my ear when he leans forward. "How much wine have you had?"

I prop my chin on my hand and reach for my glass with the other. "If there were such a thing as too much wine, I'd go with that."

"I'd say, in this case, there might be."

"Pfft. Wine is the greatest invention. Next to the vibrator, of course. They're equally fabulous."

"And you'd know this…?"

"Because I own several. All right with that, Mr. Stone?"

I hear his breath catch before I feel his fingers grip my waist.

"Say that again," he demands, his voice low against my ear.

"Say what? About the vibrators?"

"After that."

"Mr. Stone?"

"Yes. That."

His growing erection presses against my back, and I smile sexily.

"Aha. Some things *do* change, don't they?" I clasp my hands in my lap just in time. The feel of him pressing against me makes me want to reach my hand back and cup him, wrap my fingers over his hard length, but that would be awkward in the middle of a crowded Vegas casino.

Oh, fuck awkward.

My hand comes between us and I trail my fingers down his erection. His grip on me tightens, and I can feel his restraint. Feel him fighting the urge to jerk his hips and push his cock right into my hand.

"It didn't change until roughly five seconds ago," he responds in a gruff voice. "The only places I get called Mr. Stone are in the office or a boardroom. How the hell do you make it sound so fucking sexy?"

I spin on the seat and curl my fingers around his silky red tie. I tug him down to me until our breaths mingle in the space between our mouths.

"I'm a master of manipulation, Mr. Stone. I could take the most menial object or phrase and turn into the object of your greatest desire if that's what I wanted."

He sinks his fingers into my hair. "And you wanted my name to sound sexy."

"If I'd wanted to do that, you'd be dragging me out here while fighting the urge to pull my dress up and expose my very expensive, very pink thong that doesn't cover a lot at all. If I'd wanted to do that, we'd be back in that suite right now with you begging me to allow you inside me." My smile grows. "No, I didn't want your name to sound sexy. I wanted it to sound enticing."

"Color me enticed," he murmurs. "More about your thong than the way you said my name."

"It's bright pink and has white spots."

He pauses then pulls back, his eyes a swirling mass of amusement and heat. "You are the only woman I know who would talk about her underwear so publicly. Not to mention sex."

I finish the last of my wine and stand, smoothing my dress over my thighs. "Why wouldn't I? Underwear isn't anything to be ashamed of, and sex most definitely isn't. I'm not exactly the type to sit in the corner and blush at the mention of the word 'pussy' or 'cock.'"

The elevator doors close and cold glass hits me as I'm spun into the wall.

"There aren't many women who can say those words and not make them sound crude."

"They're crude words. They're not supposed to sound sexy. At least alone. Accompanied by someone who can talk as well as he can fuck? They're the sexiest words in the English language."

His heavy exhale covers my mouth. "What are you doing to me, Dayton?"

I move my hips forward and smirk. "Do you need me to answer that?"

He takes my bottom lip between his teeth and tugs lightly, sending a lightning spark right down to my clit. I don't need or want him to answer it.

I don't want words. I want skin-on-skin contact. Mouths against mouths. Tongues tracing necks and trailing across stomachs. Hands grasping and toes curling and lips parting and breath catching.

I want every single fucking thing I know I'll regret tomorrow.

The air in our suite is heavy as we enter it. I can feel Aaron's eyes tracing my body as I drop my purse on the sofa and move to the windows. Vegas shines up at me the very same way his want shines over my body. It illuminates the room the same way he illuminates me.

Aaron and Las Vegas have a lot in common. Vegas is Sin City for a reason, and Aaron is the walking embodiment of that. They're both tempting yet obvious, filled with sexual domination that's attracting and compelling. They make you need them, even if you know they're the very worst thing for you.

Temptation and sin have no bounds.

Vegas has no bounds.

Neither does Aaron.

And the two combined makes me want to destroy my own.

"You're drunk," he whispers in a low tone from just behind me. "You should go to bed."

"I'm not seventeen anymore. I can handle my wine, thank you."

"It's not that I'm worried about. It's about having you standing in front of me after acting like the woman I know."

I turn and press my back against the glass. "You're too caught up in the past."

He runs his thumb down my jaw to my bottom lip. "In the past? No. It's not the past I'm caught up in."

My eyes fall to our shoes. "It's barely been a week. You can't possibly be caught up in anything else other than the need to be inside me."

"You have no idea." He steps closer, pressing his body against mine. Hot. Hard. "Right after I spoke to you at the Tower, you nearly tripped but caught yourself at the last moment. I knocked your coffee all over you, and I've never seen anyone more shocked in their life. Like you expected no one to be there although I'd spoken to you. Your eyes met mine." He tilts my face up, and I open my eyes to his. "And I knew. I knew then, seven years ago, that no one would compare to the girl standing right in front of me. The second our eyes collided, I knew you were something so much more than I'd ever imagined, and I had to have you. Even if it was just for a moment, I had to make you mine.

"If I knew then, standing in front of you for the first time, that I was captured, caught, royally fucked, then don't tell me now that I'm not. Don't stand there with a guard around your heart and your memories and tell me that I'm not still caught up in the person who stole my heart and ran fucking marathons with it."

"Fuck you and your memories."

"And fuck you and your defiance, Dayton. Just for five goddamn minutes, surrender control. Let me in."

I draw in a deep breath. No, no. My job is the epitome of control. Every detail of my life—controlled. My orgasms—controlled Every. Fucking. Thing.

"No." I push back into the glass harder.

Aaron's hand slides to my side and undoes my zipper. He tugs the dress down roughly until it's pooled at my feet and my bare skin is against the cold glass.

"You can surrender by choice or I can make you," he whispers in my ear. "Either way, you're coming tonight."

"People could see me. Probably can," I breathe unnecessarily. We're so fucking high up that the only thing that would have a chance at seeing me is the International Space Station.

"Yet the only person who will see your face as you come is me." Aaron kisses down my jaw, and I tilt my head back. Fucking wine. Fucking job. Fucking—

His lips take mine in a deliciously rough way. I grab his collar and hold him against me, kissing him with the same fervor he's kissing me with. Fuck. I'm kissing him so desperately that I'm practically begging for him to make me come right now.

His fingers trail down my body, curving over my breasts and sliding down my stomach to the top of my underwear. He runs his finger beneath the material and around to my ass. He cups it tightly, pulling me forward so I can feel how turned on he is. So I can feel the hard length of him against me.

My clit throbs and my pussy aches at the feel of him against me, and his fingers trailing around the top of my thigh sure as shit aren't helping.

Sense says that I need to push him off of me and lock myself in the bedroom, but my body has taken over. It's telling me that I need him and the release he can give me.

"Fucking hell. Dayton." My name is a harsh hiss when his fingers creep beneath the material of my panties. I gasp at the touch of him against me and push my hips into him. Gently, slowly, he pushes two fingers inside me and small cry leaves me.

I've forgotten what it's like to be touched by someone who cares about more than their own pleasure. What it's like to have lips against your neck, a hand flat against your back, fingers stroking and slipping into your aching pussy. What it's like to have someone touch you for you.

Aaron pushes his lips against mine as he curls his fingers inside me. His thumb flicks across my clit with each movement of his wrist, sending pleasure ricocheting through me.

"You're so wet," he murmurs against my lips. "And it's for me. Isn't it?"

I gasp and claw at his back as a wave flows through me.

"Dayton." He nips my neck. "Answer the question?"

"The...what? Oh god."

He pushes his thumb down hard on my clit. "This. How wet you are. It's all for me, isn't it?"

I want to grit my teeth even as I moan loudly. "Yes."

"Say it."

"Can't." Oh fuck. Wave after wave floods my body, pushing me to the edge, and he stops. Takes his hand. Fucking bastard. I'm teetering on the edge of a runaway oblivion.

"Say it." He rubs my clit to make his point.

I thread my fingers into his hair. "Yes. It's for you. I'm wet for you, *Mr. Stone.*"

"Fuck." He plunges his fingers back into me and I ride his hand until I'm over the edge, blinded by heat and pleasure. Thrashing against him and crying out into his shoulder. Holding him to me and squeezing his fingers inside me with everything I have.

And he never lets go. He stands there, his fingers curved inside, his thumb pressing my clit, and waits until I calm.

I open my eyes to his. He takes his come-covered fingers and slides his hand over my hip to my ass.

"I forgot how devastatingly beautiful you look when you're coming apart in my arms."

I hold his gaze, mine never wavering, never flitting away, never doing anything but returning the intensity coming from the brilliant blue of his eyes. "That was your reminder."

"Oh no, Dayton. That wasn't a reminder. That was only the beginning."

# Chapter Eight

I flinch at the sharp tear across my skin and mutter a few choice words. *Fuckshitcrapouch!* The young esthetician looks at me apprehensively, and I cover my eyes with my hand.

"I'm a wimp. Ignore me."

That earns a small smile. She spreads some more wax onto my skin, and I grit my teeth because I know this one is gonna hurt. The sides always do. Tear. Wax. Tear. Each strip gets another hiss of breath, a curse, a punch to the bed.

"Do this quickly. I mean it. Whip it off," I beg as she applies the wax to the very back of my core, right by my ass.

"Absolutely, Miss Black." She's as good as her word. The wax barely dries before she rips it off with the vigor of a mother pulling a Band-Aid from a screaming child.

"Sonofa…" I bite my tongue and kick my heels against the bed.

Brazilians. Fucking hate them.

"Thank you." I smile at the girl, albeit a tight one, and wrap a fluffy robe around me. Sweet god. My legs bend into a half-squat position and I do an odd half twerk. The tender, itchy feeling I always experience after… I let out a long breath. I really need to invest in laser hair removal.

I walk through the spa barefoot to the private elevator that will take me to the presidential suite. The Cheshire Hotel is easily the most exclusive and expensive I've ever stayed in. It's obvious in everything. The décor, the furniture, the way the staff treats their well-dressed, well-mannered, good-looking clients.

Aaron and I certainly got star treatment.

Australia is hotter than I imagined it would be in March, and although I'm not short of clothes to wear, nothing seems light enough. And what is light enough is courtesy of Agent Provocateur. Not suitable for public viewing.

I shrug off the robe and step into my underwear. Nothing in my suitcase is even remotely appealing to wear in this unexpected heat wave. The temperatures are hovering around one hundred thanks to a late-summer heat wave, and if I make it through this without melting, I'll be amazed.

The suite door closes. "Dayton?"

"In the bedroom." My cheeks flush. This is the first time we've spoken since we left Vegas—since he pinned me against a glass wall and fucked me with his fingers until I came spectacularly. We both slept during the flight and he left early this morning while I was still in bed.

My skin hums with awareness when he walks into the room, and a low, appreciative chuckle leaves him.

"Not what I was expecting to see, but welcome all the same."

I flip him the bird over my shoulder. "I have nothing to wear."

"You're standing in front of three suitcases. How can you have nothing to wear?"

"I didn't pack for a trip to the surface of the sun."

Aaron unzips his own suitcase on the other side of the room, and I hear the swish of material as he changes. "It's not that hot."

"Are you kidding me?" I spin. And stop dead at the sight of him.

He's wearing a white polo shirt that stretches across his

shoulders and hugs his torso like a second skin, and his shorts hang just below his knees. There's even a pair of sunglasses resting on top of his head, and I can't help the way my eyes travel over his body. From his head to his toes, I appraise him. Heat floods my body when I catch sight of his fingers on his hips, remembering them inside me last night.

"Don't look at me like that," he warns, his eyes hot and heavy and lidded. They hold me captive, turning the heat spreading through my body up a notch.

I straighten. "Like what?"

"Like there's nothing you'd rather do right now than rip these clothes off me and fuck me."

"Maybe that's what I'm thinking."

He smirks and moves to me. "No you're not. You're remembering the feel of my fingers inside you last night." Those same fingers tease the hem of my panties. "You're remembering how easily I made you come all over them."

I exhale loudly and knock his hand away. "Stop playing with me, Aaron. I'm not a toy."

"Actually…" He trails his hand up my body and cups my chin. "You're whatever I want you to be, remember? I just have more respect than to treat you like a toy. I told you last night. I don't play. Whether that be with fire or games. I'm not the one hiding my desire behind a thick wall of defiance."

"Hiding my desire? I think you found it last night, don't you?"

He tilts my face back, his lips curving deliciously. "For a second, until you locked it away again."

I step back and turn to my suitcase. "If you're going to fuck me, just do it. It's part of what you pay for."

"If you're going to let me fuck you, just do it. And again—I don't give a shit what I pay for. When I fuck you, it'll be because you need it so badly you won't be able to breathe. When I fuck you, it'll be because you'll feel like you'll die if you don't have me inside you. I won't be taking you to bed just because I pay for it."

I grab a dress and ignore him. My core is aching too much to respond, because if I do, it'll be to beg for that fuck.

"Get dressed. We're going out."

"Where?"

"To buy you something suitable for a week on the surface of the sun, Bambi." He walks through the door, and I throw my hairbrush after him.

"Stop calling me that!"

Aaron reaches across the table and threads his fingers through mine. I look at our hands. Large and small, two different shades of tan, linked together and held there by his tight grip. His tan is likely more natural than mine. I can't imagine Aaron Stone lying on a tanning bed for ten minutes twice a week.

He rubs his thumb across the back of my hand. "So. Dot com work, huh? How's that working for you?"

I bite the inside of my cheek and gaze at the harbor through the café's window. "Shut up."

"I've heard it can be a lucrative business."

"Aaron."

"Particularly with the e-book boom lately. How have you managed to take time off?"

I look at him, unable to hide the stupid grin on my face. "Shut up."

"That's what I was going for." He returns my smile. "Seriously, dot com? That was the best you had?"

"I was put on the spot! It was the first thing I thought of."

"You realize they'll try to look you up, don't you?"

"Then they'll find themselves incredibly surprised if they happen to come across Monique's website."

He quirks an eyebrow. "There's a website?"

"Why? Wishing you'd thought to try before you bought?"

"No. I'm thinking I'm not a fan of your picture on there for the world to see."

"It's pixelated. You can't tell it's me."

"I'd know your face anywhere."

"It's good you didn't go on the website then, isn't it?" I tap the back of his hand with my fingers. "How did you get her number?"

"A friend of mine has used her...services...before."

"This could get awkward very quickly," I mutter.

"Not you. He said he saw Shelly or someone." He pauses, and I nod. "I had no idea who I was booking when she gave me your name."

I smile wryly. "That's the reason we have two. Working with people you know is off-limits and not something that's ever happened to me. But it did to another girl. She was due to meet him for an evening function but he was the brother of a high school friend. Monique had to send another girl out pronto."

"You all grew up in Seattle? Isn't that risky if you don't want to be found out?"

"The risk is...well, irrelevant. It doesn't matter where you do it, there will always be the chance you'll run into someone you know. It's why there's always one or two of us off. We're always ready to jump in for another girl."

"Or for calls like mine."

"Or for late calls, yes. I happened to be the lucky one that night." I roll my eyes.

"Hey." He tugs on my hand and I lean across the table. His thumb teases across my bottom lip and he keeps his eyes firmly there. "No luckier than I was when it was you who walked into the booth."

"There's nothing lucky about me walking into your booth. I've wrecked more guys than I've made."

"And you did both to me, once upon a time." He leans in and brushes his lips across mine. "But it was lucky because every time I've been in Seattle, I've always thought about you. Wondered where you were living, what you were doing, if you'd met anyone or had kids. And now I know."

I pull back slightly, this revelation making my head spin. "Why didn't you ever look for me?" Is that hurt in my voice? Fuck. No. *Get back in your box, teenage Dayton.*

His blue eyes find mine. "I don't know. I didn't know where to start, and I was a little scared. We promised each other we'd be just a summer romance, a fleeting fling in a European city. I should have forgotten you the second we got back to the US, but I never did. I was afraid if I found you, you'd tell me my worst fear. That it was just a fling and wasn't anything real. I loved you too much to hear those words."

My throat constricts and my chest tightens. I struggle to swallow the emotion in my throat. This… This is what I wanted to avoid. What I never wanted to know.

"I wanted to leave that summer as it was," he continues, his thumb once again rubbing the back of my hand. "Six beautiful weeks of you and me wrapped in our bubble of passion and love and bliss. I didn't want anything to ruin that."

"Maybe… Maybe that was the best idea," I manage in a voice calmer than I feel inside. Inside, I'm a raging mess of longing and remembering and need.

"Would it have made a difference? If I'd looked for you and found you?" He pushes some hair back from my face in a move that seems too soft. Too tender. Too loving. "Would you have let me love you the way I did in Paris?"

I draw in a deep breath. "At first. But not...after. Not after. Excuse me." I pull my hand from his and force myself to walk into the ladies' restroom. I want to run. I want to run and hide and make sense of this shit.

"Remember, call girls don't fall in love."

Aunt Leigh's voice fills my mind, ringing out in my ears and reverberating through my body. The words wrap around me, reminding me, taunting me, striking me, and bringing a pain I didn't know existed.

I lock myself in a stall and put the toilet seat down. It's hard as I sit and bury my face in my hands. Call girls don't fall in love. They don't feel anything other than physical things for their clients. They don't feel tingles at the touch of their lips, a hum when they enter the room, a buzz when their eyes darken. They don't get shivers at a hand on the bases of their backs and their bodies don't go into overdrive when lust-filled eyes appraise them.

"Remember, call girls don't fall in love."

I lean my head against the cubicle wall, staring at a spot on the door, and whisper, "Unless there was always a small part of them that never let that love go."

The new dress Aaron bought earlier is lightweight and flirty while still giving the impression of class. I stare at the water of the pool swirling around my feet and grab my cocktail glass. He's having a conference call with his dad in the US, which means I have the next while to myself. To think.

Or I would if the concierge didn't approach me.

"Miss Black? There's a call from America for you."

I accept the phone he offers. "Thank you." I wait until he leaves, and when I'm alone once again, I hold it to my ear. "Hello?"

"Dayton!"

"Liv? Why are you calling me, you crazy bitch?"

"Because I'm half-asleep, and fuck it all, I miss my best friend!"

"And drunk."

"I'm sorry. Did you not hear that? I fucking miss you!"

Definitely drunk.

"I know. I miss you too, Liv. You'd love it here."

"Wait. Where are you?"

"Sydney." I kick the water. "By the pool with a Blow Job in my hand."

"Babe, that better be the cocktail or I wanna know why you're talking and not sucking."

I laugh. "It's the cocktail. I've never seen a bartender blush so much."

"You did it deliberately. Okay. Enough bullshit. How's McDreamy?"

"You mean Aaron."

"Pssh. I want details."

"Of what? How he's my client and I'm working?"

"Fuck you, Dayton Lauren Black. If you think for one second that I, your best friend, believe you can sleep in the same bed as that gorgeous man and be at his side most of the day and not want him, you need a slap upside the head."

I look down and sigh. "I don't want to talk tonight. Are you free tomorrow? Uh, my tomorrow."

"Tonight?"

"Yeah."

"Skype date?"

"As long as you bring Pop Tarts."

"On it, babe. Just... You're okay, right?"

I smile sadly at my feet. "Yeah, I'm okay. No losing my shit over a guy, remember?"

"Good. I don't look forward to getting on a plane to kick your ass. I'm going to bed now because this chat has probably cost me a hundred bucks already because my stupid plan doesn't include stupid international minutes. Goodnight, I love you, and absolutely do not be good." She kisses down the phone and hangs up. I shake my head and grab my flip-flops.

I leave my cocktail on the table and walk to the main lobby. My eyes find the concierge desk. They must have switched shifts while I was talking because now a young guy is sitting behind it. He looks uncertain, his eyes flitting about nervously. And goddamn, I'm a bitch, but I'm using this to my advantage.

I saunter up to him with my best smile. "Hi there." I look at this name badge. "Steven."

"Uh, hello there, madam."

"Dayton Black. I'm finished with my call. Here's your phone." I shoot him a dazzling smile and he accepts the phone with a shaky hand.

"Thank you, Miss Black."

"Steven, I was wondering…" I lean on the counter. "Could you do me a little favor? I need to send a message to someone back in Seattle, but my international thing hasn't been set up yet."

"Um. Of course I can. If you just, uh…" He grabs a pen and paper and gives it to me. "Write the details down here. I'll do it right away."

I smile widely and scribble a note.

*To Monique Park, from Dayton Black.*

*Pay Liv two hundred for international calls. I owe you—take extra from the next.*

*And get my cell sorted so it works. I don't wanna be*

*paying her crap again. Thanks xo*

I hand him the message with her contact details and touch his arm. "You're a doll, Steven. Thank you so much."

"You're... You're welcome, Miss Black. Oh, Mr. Stone. Can I help you?"

The hair on the back of my neck prickles, and I turn to Aaron. He's amused and pissed off simultaneously. I rest my hand against his chest.

"Hey, baby. Did your call go well?"

"It did." He wraps an arm around my back.

"How's your dad?"

"He's fine. Are you harassing the concierge?"

I raise my eyebrows and glance at Steven. "Of course not. He's just sending a message for me, and he's been so helpful. He's a real doll."

"I'm sure he is," he says. "If you'll excuse us, Steven, I believe I need to have a chat with my woman."

*With my woman?*

He guides me into the penthouse elevator without a word. We make the journey in complete silence, his hand curved at my hip and his eyes forward. His body is tense, and annoyance radiates from him.

What did I do now?

The concierge—oh. I threatened to sleep with one just a few days ago. Double oh.

Aaron moves me out of the elevator and into our suite. Still keeping his silence, he pulls off his tie and rolls up the sleeves of his shirt. I stand by the doors and sink my teeth into my lower lip in feigned ignorance.

After a small slice of forever, he turns. Dark blue, angry eyes hit me. "You seem to have a thing for concierges."

"I needed to send a message to Monique."

"And you needed the concierge for that?"

I wave my phone before throwing it on the sofa. "No international calls yet. I'm like a hermit."

"And you needed to get the message to her right fucking now?"

"Yes."

"Why?" He flattens his hands against the door.

I tilt my head back to look at him. "Because my best friend is an idiot who thinks calling Australia from Seattle is a smart idea when her only steady income just about pays her bills." I jab him in the chest. "My message to Monique was to pay her the cost and then some in case she calls me again and to sort out my international shit. Don't worry. I wasn't trying to fuck the concierge. Not that I wouldn't, given the chance. He's kind of—"

Aaron takes my lips with his and cuts me off. He wastes no time sweeping his tongue through my mouth, dominating the kiss and every one of my thoughts. He tugs my bottom lip between his teeth. My stomach coils, and each time I feel his teeth against my lip, the same old ache starts up. It deepens, spreading from the tip of my clit to right inside me, and I squeeze my legs together. Holy...

"The next time I see you talking to a concierge, any concierge, I'm doing that right in front of him."

"Oh, please. You say it like it's such a hardship. You'd love to do that in public."

"And let every guy in the immediate area know you're off-limits? Damn straight, *baby.*"

"I'll keep that in mind."

He rubs my swollen lips. "You were being very unfair to him, you know."

I straighten. "I was not!"

"You were. I watched you the whole time. You had the guy completely spellbound, Dayton. You don't realize how incredibly beautiful you are, and you emit a raw sexuality that makes every guy you pass look at you. It's palpable. I know exactly when you walk into a room because of it. It hits me full force. I know how far away from me you are because I feel it."

*I* have a raw sexuality? This coming from the guy who makes my skin hum so badly I turn into a walking vibrator.

"Do you feel it now?"

"Feel what?"

"My 'raw sexuality.'"

"I can't not feel it. It calls out to me, and that's exactly why I can't touch you again right now. If I touch you, being mad at you and wanting you this badly will end up in you coming again. Likely on my tongue."

He pushes away and strolls into the kitchen area. My heart is pounding in my chest as I imagine me pressed against this door and him on his knees. As I imagine my legs hooked over his shoulders and his hands cupping my ass and holding me up and his tongue gliding along my pussy and across my clit…

I glance up and meet his eyes. "Fuck you," I mutter, turning to the bedroom. "Fuck you one hundred times over."

"You will. Soon enough."

# Chapter Nine

Aaron's arms slide around me and grab the mug of coffee I just made.

"Hey! That's mine." I spin right into his grinning face.

"It was yours. I have to run." He downs it. "I won't be back all day—probably just in time to get ready for the party tonight."

"Okay." I tilt my head back. "What do I wear?"

A smile curves his gorgeous lips, and he brushes his thumb across my cheek. "Not that it matters what you wear, but it's formal. So something long but sexy."

"Long but sexy?"

"Excuse me if I want everyone to know the most beautiful woman in the room belongs to me." His smile widens as he leans in and touches his lips to mine. "Behave today. I left you my card on the nightstand. Go and buy that something long but sexy."

"What if I have something?"

"I don't care if you have something. I'm telling you to go and buy a dress, Dayton, so do it. I want you there tonight in something *I* bought you."

I narrow my eyes. "I can buy my own dress."

"But you're not going to. You're going to take my goddamn card and buy yourself something."

"*Your* card?"

"Yes, my fucking card. Jesus Christ, Day. I have the company card. You have mine. I am buying you a dress, not my father. Spend whatever."

The hardness in his eyes tells me that he isn't budging, and I give in. Reluctantly. Because I despise things being bought for me.

"Fine. I'll take your card and buy a dress. But I'm warning you, Aaron." I skip from his hold and point my finger at him, walking backward to the bedroom. "I'm buying the whole shebang. Dress, shoes, purse, jewelry. *All* of it."

He opens the elevator doors and smirks. "Get your nails and hair done while you're at it. You have a few split ends."

"Fuck you!" I shout as he disappears behind the closing doors.

Do I?

I grab a section of hair between my fingers and pull it in front of my face. My eyes flit over it, examining it, and I drop it with a curse.

"Bastard," I mutter to the buzzing of my phone.

Kidding, he texts. Your hair is perfect.

I'm making you pay for that, asshole.

Good.

I toss my phone on the bed and look at the time. Shit. Skype date with Liv!

I run into the front room area and pull my laptop from its case. The Wi-Fi connects in seconds, and two minutes later, I'm staring at the blond bombshell that is my best friend.

"Spill. Everything," she demands.

"Hello to you too. I'm having an okay time but I miss you like crazy. Hope everything is good in Seattle." I stick my middle finger up.

Liv laughs. "Everything is fine in Seattle, I miss you ten times more, and you should be having an amazing time. Not an okay one. I mean, hello! Have you seen Mr. Aaron Stone? He's a walking fucking orgasm."

"Considering I see him every day and sleep next to him each night, I'd say yes, I have seen him. I'm very well acquainted with him and his looks."

"Sarcastic bitch." She sighs. "Seriously, babe, what's up? You look like you need a girls' night."

"Oh, Liv. I do. So badly." I rest my head on my hand and stare at my screen. "This job is impossible."

"Nah, it's not, baby girl. You can get through it. Only four and a half weeks to go, right?"

"Right." I sigh. "Liv?"

"Yeah?"

I chew on the inside on my lip as I mull over what to say. "Have you ever wanted someone so badly it hurt to look at them? Like, your world would fall apart if you didn't have at least one touch from them each day? Like nothing else matters except the all-encompassing feeling of their lips against yours?"

"Yeah, I feel that way about you every day." She laughs. "Kidding. Kind of. Um, not really."

I sigh again, more heavily this time. "It sucks. It sucks Big Foot balls, for real."

Her eyes soften. "If you want him that badly, why don't you have him?"

"Because. It's dangerous. I already have to kiss him a hundred times a day, touch his cheek, stare into his eyes like I'm helplessly in love with him… If I had to have sex with him too, I think I'd die."

"You haven't had sex with him yet?"

"That's what you took from that?"

"Seriously? You sleep next to that each night and you don't fuck his gorgeous brains out?"

"Liv!"

"Who the fuck are you and what have you done with my blunt-talking best friend?" She taps the webcam to make her point. "Sex is your fucking job, Dayton. It's what you do for a living."

"He hasn't called it in. He said on the flight to Vegas it was optional, and he's since said he won't until I want him for him. Until I don't treat him like he's my client."

"But he is your client."

"Exactly."

"I don't get it."

I bury my face in my hands and rub my eyes. "I do. I get it."

"Explain."

A small, bitter laugh leaves me—a bitter laugh tinged with sadness. "He remembers everything, Liv. Every single thing about that summer is encased in his memory, and every chance he has, he reminds me." I swallow and look down. "Everything."

"Holy mother of..."

"Yeah." I nod roughly. "He wants me, Liv. Not as his escort or the girl to keep his bed warm."

"Okay, you don't know that for certain, do you?"

I smack the table. "He still calls me fucking Bambi!"

Her silence is telling. Ironically deafening. "Shit."

"You really need to work on getting some stronger cuss words. Shit doesn't cover any situation where Aaron Stone is concerned."

She shrugs. "S'all I got, baby girl. What are you gonna do?"

"Long term? Not a fucking clue. Short term?" I hold up the card I pulled from the nightstand. His card.

"Is that a black Express card?"

I nod. "I've been ordered to go shopping."

"Well, shit. Send something back for your poor model friend, won't you?"

"I don't think I can fit a hunky Australian in a box."

"Plane tickets to said Australian will be fine." She grins. "Look,

I gotta get to work. By the way, you didn't have to pay me back for that call. It's cool."

"Don't be stupid."

"Okay. Monique said your calls will be sorted in two days, so you can call me next time. Got that?"

"Got it."

We end the video call and I close the laptop down. That was as helpful as it was a hindrance. I love her, but sometimes I wonder if having someone who understands anything past a casual hook-up would be a good idea.

The red strapless bra hugs my breasts perfectly, giving them just enough lift above the neckline of the equally red dress I'm wearing. The satin hugs my body perfectly before flaring at my knees in a mermaid-style skirt. It's the sexiest classy dress I've ever worn, and it leaves nothing to the imagination while keeping everything hidden.

I smooth my dark hair back and grab a lipstick from my makeup bag. The fire-engine red color is smooth as I slide it across my lips. I grab the black purse I bought to match the dress with a trembling hand.

Aaron decided to call at four and tell me that tonight isn't just any party. It's a party in his honor. For the man who will soon be the CEO, the boss, the owner of the global whirlwind that is Stone Advertising. "Sorry," he said. "Should have mentioned that."

"You asshole," is what I said. Give a girl some time to prepare appropriately.

For that, I spent an extra six hundred dollars on this dress and hated every cent of it. The temptation to whip out and hand over my own card was almost consuming.

I run my hands along my sides to smooth the dress. But damn, it's worth every penny. Aaron wanted sexy, and sexy is what he's going to get.

"Holy fuck."

His voice echoes through the room and wraps me in a warm bubble of pleasure and smugness.

I turn my face to the side and catch his eye. "Is the dress okay?"

"Okay? You're standing in front of a fucking mirror and you're asking me if it's okay?" He crosses the room and rests his hands on my sides. He drops a kiss to my bare shoulder. "There's no way you won't be the most beautiful woman in the room tonight. If every guy doesn't have their eyes on you the whole time, they need their eyes tested. Shit, Dayton. You look fucking incredible."

I look at the floor and smile.

"No." He cups my jaw from behind and lifts my face to the mirror. "You don't get to look at the floor. Look in this mirror and see how devastatingly beautiful you look."

"Shut up," I murmur. "It's just a dress."

"No. It's the woman that makes the dress. And you? You make this dress something that borders on illegal." He lowers his mouth to my ear. "Tell me I bought this."

"You did. And the shoes." I stick out my foot, which is wrapped in a black stiletto.

"Good. Now I know every part of you, including your clothes, belongs to me. And I'll be thinking of that when every man in the room tonight is undressing you with his eyes. More importantly, I'll be a smug bastard knowing you're leaving with me tonight." His lips brush the nape of my neck. "I'm going to shower and change. Don't move."

I nod. An unexpected emptiness fills me when he releases me, and I perch on the end of the bed, staring at myself in the mirror as the shower starts.

Wishing I could see myself the way he sees me.

I know I'm good-looking. I can pull off sexy and cute and everything in between. But to supposedly look so beautiful that you can devastate a powerful man like Aaron? That's something I've always believed was beyond me.

Until now. Looking in this shining mirror, with my dark eyes and red lips, my face framed by a head of dark brown curls, my body encased in red satin, I believe I'm beautiful.

I believe I'm beautiful enough to be more than just a casual fuck for a guy that can spare a few hundred dollars.

Because that is the essence of my job. It was. It should be. It's supposed to be.

My title is high-class call girl. An escort.

In reality, I'm nothing more than a whore. An expensive one, but still a whore.

And I know that.

But I'm not with Aaron.

I'm something. Someone he's proud to have on his arm and introduce to people. I'm someone he doesn't mind pushing into the public eye as something that belongs to him. Someone he doesn't mind the world knowing about.

That takes me above and beyond the title of whore, escort, high-class girl call.

It makes me Dayton.

The bathroom door clicks as Aaron walks into the room. A towel is wrapped around his waist, soaking up every drop of water that falls down his sculpted body.

I know that body. I know every dip and crevice, and I know what spot turns him on and what makes him groan with pleasure.

And I can't watch when he changes or I might just touch those spots in a moment of impulsive insanity.

Aaron stands in front of me, clad in a tailored suit and bow tie. His fingers wrap around mine and he pulls me to standing. His eyes never leave mine as he tugs me up, and they only do when he stands behind me. Then they leave me for a handful of seconds until our gazes meet again in the mirror.

"Never doubt it," he murmurs, running his hands down my arms to mine. "Never doubt your ability to walk into a room and stun every man into wanting you."

I swallow and let him link his fingers through mine.

"Never doubt the way you walk into a room and make every man in there want you. And never ever doubt how beautiful you are to me. Not even for a second."

"You and I see different things," I whisper.

"You see things jaded by what you believe." He rests his chin upon on my shoulder. "I see the raw truth of you. I see that you're the most beautiful woman in the world, and I'll spend as long as I have by your side convincing you of that."

A long moment passes as we stare into each other's eyes in the mirror. A long moment that seems to be everlasting. That makes me want to cocoon myself in his arms and not go this damn party tonight.

"We should go," I say softly. "You can't be late to your own party."

He chuckles. "I suppose not. I could always blame it on you, you know."

"Try it, Mr. Stone, and I'll be forced to publicly kick your ass."

"It's really quite dangerous to call me that, you know."

I back into the elevator with my lips curved. "Why, Mr. Stone? Have you had a change of heart about your name?"

He pins me to the back wall of the elevator with ease. "Why yes, I have, Miss Black. Surely you haven't forgotten the way my fingers feel while they're stroking inside your beautiful pussy?"

"No." I wrap my fingers around the lapels of his jacket. "I was just reminding you."

"Believe me. There's no way I could forget you squeezing around me as you came." He touches his lips to mine, his voice lowering and turning huskier with each word until it's a low hum that vibrates through my body. "No fucking way."

My breath catches. This man is irresistible. "Are you going to behave tonight?"

"Around you? Impossible." The elevator doors open and he pulls me into his side. "Especially when you're wearing a dress like that. That bright red against your gorgeous skin makes me want to fuck you in ten different ways."

"Only ten? I can think of more," I whisper in his ear as we enter the room.

"Enough," he snaps, his voice raw with sexual need.

Over the next twenty minutes, I'm introduced to more people than I'll ever remember. Gorgeous Australian women and their high-flying partners. Single men with eyes that rove over my chest. Women who eye me with jealousy and disgust. Investors and workers in the business.

I let their looks and quiet comments go over my head. By now, I'm a pro at it. By now, they're mere whispers in a world of screams. By now, they're as commonplace as a kind word.

Nothing in my job is easy.

The Australian models signed with Stone Advertising's agency are here, tall and lean and gorgeous. Some are on the arms of men equally as beautiful. Others are with slightly older men, and the rest are alone, their eyes stalking the room for someone who can support them when their modeling days are over.

And those eyes are on Aaron. Some fleeting glances. Some blatant stares. Some coupled with fluttering eyelashes and pouting lips.

I hate every single one.

I hate that I hate them.

I excuse myself for a moment, and a server directs me to the restrooms. The room is suffocating. The whispers and stares I usually ignore are all encompassing, making my head spin and my stomach turn. Things that shouldn't matter do. Things that shouldn't bother me do. Because of Aaron.

Because I care about him, and the way people view me when I'm connected to him matters. It matters for his reputation as a man and a CEO.

And right now, all I can hear is the not-so-quiet mumbles asking who I am and wondering how I 'bagged him.' I'm remembering how dangerous this world is—where money is no object and no price is too high for information—and how stupid it is to lie.

Yet again, I'm protected by Mia Lopez.

I pat my cheeks and apply some more lipstick, more to pass another few measly seconds instead of walking back out there. My eyes rove over my face in the mirror. I'm just as beautiful as the girls out there. I don't look out of place or as if I'm playing dress up from Mommy's closet. I look like I belong in a dress that costs as much as I earn in a day.

Taking a deep breath, I leave the restroom and enter the party. Aaron's standing by the bar now, leaning lazily against it, completely surrounded by models. *Of course.* I suppress my eye roll.

He looks up as I approach and shoots me a dazzling smile that eclipses any look he's given the models. He straightens and holds out his arm. I step into his side and ignore the cold looks being shot in my direction when he touches his lips to my temple.

"Everything okay?" he asks.

I nod. "Fine. I just needed a moment."

His lips twitch. "Dayton, let me introduce you to the girls. This is Kirsty, Jay, Maria, and Lola. They're our top Australian models, and I expect we'll be seeing one or two of their faces on some billboards when we head into the city later this week."

"Isn't the Marielle makeup campaign running now?" Maria asks.

"I believe so."

She beams at him. "Then you'll definitely see me. You'll have to let me know what you think of it."

Ugh.

"I'll make sure to do that." He smiles politely. "Ladies, if you'll excuse us, there are a lot of people to see tonight. I'm sure I'll see some of you again this week."

"Looking forward to it!" one of them trills to our backs.

And that right there is why I chose fucking over modeling. God forbid I'd end up all dried up at twenty-five when the next big thing came along, begging any hot, rich guy to take care of me.

"Not a fan of the models?" Aaron murmurs in my ear, pulling me outside.

"Oh, yes. I loved them. Can you tell?"

He laughs. "I imagine they feel the same way."

"I'm sure we'll be braiding each other's hair in no time." I roll my eyes.

"I like it when you're jealous."

"I'm not jealous. I might look it, but I'm not."

"You're a terrible actress."

"I take offense to that, Mr. Stone."

His eyes darken, and he runs his thumb along my jaw. "I take offense to you not being jealous."

"So we're both offended. Gee, aren't relationships *great?*"

His lips curve as his thumb tugs on my bottom one. "If you're not jealous, you won't mind if I go and buy one of those girls a drink, would you?"

The thought makes bile rise up my throat. "No." I swallow it down. "Go ahead. I think Maria would be very accommodating."

A low laugh leaves him. "Jealous. I knew it."

"I'm not—"

He touches his lips to mine tenderly. "Don't worry," he says against my mouth. "I've barely taken my eyes off you all evening."

"I should hope not. You shouldn't be looking at other women when attending a party with your girlfriend."

"Fuck the ruse, Dayton. Whether you were here with me or not, I'd still be eying you like a sex-starved teenage boy all night. Don't tell me you haven't seen the way men, married or not, are staring at you?"

*Nope.* Felt it, not seen it. "I don't notice that stuff. Besides…" I run my finger down his jacket. Time for a little honesty. "I might be too busy looking at someone else to notice."

"Who am I kicking out?"

I laugh. "Can you kick yourself out of your own party?"

"Shall we try it?"

"Aaron. You can't just leave your own party."

"Sure I can. I have an early start tomorrow. I can use that as an excuse." His lips are soft against mine. "Come on."

"I can't believe you're doing this."

He grins over his shoulder and leads us to the manager of the Sydney office. "Mr. Marks. I'm afraid Dayton and I are going to have to leave early. I have an early start tomorrow. I'd love to stay longer, but my schedule is full this week."

"Of course! Such a shame, but we'll see each other in two days, correct?"

"Yes—to discuss the incoming contracts. Thank you for organizing this. It's been a wonderful evening."

The two men shake hands, and Mrs. Marks pecks my cheek.

"I do hope we'll get to see each other this week, Dayton. This evening's meeting was far too short."

"I agree. Perhaps I can convince Aaron to bring me along to the shoot later this week." I wink at her.

Aaron squeezes my waist. "I think you could convince me to do just about anything, Day." I smile. "Goodnight, everyone."

We step into the elevator and Aaron presses the button to go up. He slides his hand from my waist to my hip and curves me into him. I've barely grasped his shoulders when his fingers are in my hair and his mouth is covering mine. His tongue forces itself between my lips and sweeps across mine, making me whimper at the sudden onslaught.

Shivers snake through my body and I arch into him, a primal instinct taking over. I feel his kiss everywhere, feel it reverberating through my body in tingles and aches and shots of pure lust. It tightens my stomach and clenches the muscles in my pussy, and when he breaks the kiss, I gasp for air.

"What the hell was that?" I breathe.

"That was what I've been wanting to do all night." He takes my bottom lip between his and sucks gently as he pulls me into the suite.

He leaves me standing in the middle of the room. I kick off my shoes and let my eyes follow him as he enters the kitchen and pours a glass of wine. He puts it in my hand and smirks down at me.

"I'm going to shower." Aaron backs out of the main room into our bedroom and pauses by the door. "Before I do something crazy."

Something crazy? As opposed to dragging me around the world and kissing the ever-loving shit out of me at every opportunity?

Do we have different definitions of the word?

The sound of the shower running reaches my ears, and I slowly bring my gaze up. Something crazy. He wants something crazy?

I'll give him fucking crazy.

# Chapter Ten

I place the glass on the kitchen side and follow his footsteps. My dress falls from my body as I undo the zipper, and I slink out of my underwear, leaving a trail across the floor to the bathroom.

Without thinking, I push open the door. The glass surrounding the shower is steamed, but not enough to keep Aaron hidden from sight. I drink him in greedily.

Broad shoulders. Toned biceps. Washboard abs. Tight ass.

It's the same body I remember but so different. It's older. More mature. More confident, defined, powerful.

I pull open the shower door and he jolts. "Dayton? What are you doing?"

"Shh." The door clicks shut and I hold a finger to his lips. "Don't ask me questions I can't answer."

I curl my hand around his neck and pull his face to mine. His hands slip over my body at the touch of our lips. They move slowly, exploring every inch of me and caressing like he's committing it to memory in case it never happens again. Each touch becomes more frantic, more urgent, and I feel his cock get hard against my thigh.

I slide my hand between us and wrap my fingers around his hardening length. Slowly, I stroke him, feeling him get harder and harder with every movement of my fingers.

"What are you… Ah—"

"I told you to shh."

I squeeze his cock lightly and step back. My lips travel from his jaw and down his neck, following the path of the water running in rivulets down his body. His stomach tenses beneath my kisses as I touch my mouth to each of the muscles there.

My tongue tastes his skin as I trace it along the V muscle, stopping an inch above his bulging erection.

"Dayton," he grinds out.

I look up into heavy-lidded, dangerously dark, seductive eyes. Shivers course through my body at the intensity in his gaze despite the heat of the water, and when his jaw tics, my lips twitch in response. He clenches his hands into fists at his sides when I drop to my knees and kiss the base of his cock, my eyes still on his.

"Fuck." The word leaves him in a tortured hiss, his restraint obvious.

I relish the small rush of power that flows over me from knowing that I'm affecting him this way. Knowing that I'm affecting him so much that he closes his eyes as my lips travel up the length of his shaft delights me. The realization is instantaneous—right here, right now, I'm completely in control. I have control in a way I haven't for two weeks, and I'm going to make the most of every second Aaron Stone is at my mercy.

I swirl my tongue around the end of his cock and lick away the tiny bit of pre-cum that escapes. My fingers are wrapped around the base of him, and I run my tongue along his length several times, teasing him, delighting in more heavy breathing from him. I take him fully into my mouth and he growls my name in his throat—a raw, primal sound that rests and settles inside my already-wet pussy.

His hand fists my hair as I grip his hip and pull him deeper into me. My cheeks hollow as I give one long, slow, hard suck that makes him groan loudly. I control my smile and suck again, this time faster, moving my head and flicking my tongue around him. He tightens his grip on my hair and tugs a little, making my scalp sting. I gasp at the sharp, unexpected feeling and wrap my fingers around him tighter.

My hand moves with my mouth. Covering all of him. Milking all of him. Playing all of him. He's big and he's beautiful, and the tiny drops of cum falling from the end of his cock coat my tongue and throat as I swallow them down.

"Fuck, Dayton." My name is a heavy, deep groan. He reaches down and takes my hand from him. "All of it. With your mouth. I want every last bit of my cock in your mouth."

His words make my pussy clench. I relax my throat and push forward until my lips wrap the base of his cock. I suck extra hard as I pull back, and my tongue has no sooner touched his head than he's pushing me back down. I slide my hand from his hip to his ass and smack it lightly.

"I'm in charge here, Mr. Stone. Not you." I link our fingers, both hands, and hold them to the sides.

"Jesus." He breathes heavily, and I can tell he's close. His cock is harder and swelling, and a small bit of cum spurts from him.

"Come for me, Aaron," I murmur, my lips brushing against the end of his cock. "Hard."

He does. My lips wrap around him and he comes instantly, hot spurts hitting the back of my throat. I suck him until he's dry, swallowing every drop and savoring the rich taste of him.

He pulls me up and against him harshly. His lips take mine roughly, slowly tapering off to softer, tenderer kisses.

"Fucking hell, Dayton," he whispers, cupping the back of my head. "I was wrong earlier. You in that dress isn't the sexiest thing I've ever seen. It's you on your knees in front of me with your red lips wrapped around my cock."

I smile against him. "You wanted to do something crazy."

"Mmm. I like your crazy." He slips a hand down to my pussy and runs a finger along it. "You're wet, gorgeous. Is that for me?"

My lips part and I nod. *Crap.*

"From sucking my cock?"

"Uh-huh."

He slides two fingers inside me easily. "So very wet." He kisses along my jaw. "And you still resist me. Why, Dayton? Wouldn't you rather this be my cock inside you right now?"

He brushes my clit with his thumb. Holy…

"Wouldn't you rather I be holding you against his shower door and sinking deep into you? Fucking you hard and fast?"

I drop my head to his shoulder and part my legs slightly, breathing more heavily than a moment ago.

"It's tempting. I could pin you against this wall right now and fuck you until you scream my name. Or I could hold you there and lick every last bit of your wetness up with my tongue. How about that?"

I cry out as pleasure begins to build inside me, but I can barely feel his fingers working me. It's his words. They're making me think of what could be and how he could make me feel.

"I'd hook your legs over my shoulders while I run my tongue along your wet slit. You'd shudder and tremble and beg me to stop, but I wouldn't. I'd lick you harder and faster until you came all over my tongue. And I bet you taste just as sweet as you used to." He drags his teeth along my bottom lip.

I hold on to him tightly, my nails digging into his skin as he brings me closer to the edge. As his fingers sink inside me, his thumb pushes into my throbbing clit. I gasp and push my naked, wet body against his solid one. I writhe against him until he brings his mouth to my ear and whispers, "Come for me, Dayton. Hard."

He presses his fingers deeper and pushes my clit harder and I come apart on a blissful high. Pleasure threads through my body, making my legs tremble. I am wholly consumed with the feelings flooding my body.

"Fuck," I mutter into his chest. "I didn't plan that."

Aaron's chest vibrates as he laughs. "If you think you're going to suck me off and make me come that hard without getting the favor returned, then you can think again." He runs his hands over my body. "Come here."

He lathers soap in his hands and rubs it over my body before reaching for the shampoo.

"Turn around."

"I can wash my hair," I grumble.

"I know," is all he says before he runs his fingers through my hair and works the shampoo in. His fingers moving against my scalp is relaxing and comforting and—

"You always used to love washing my hair." The words are soft. Unsure.

He falters in his movements. "You remember."

I swallow back a sudden lump of emotion. "Yep. I had a fight with Mom. She didn't want me to get hurt by you. Because she didn't get it. So I ran to you and you spent half an hour in the bath, sitting behind me, just washing my hair and listening to me talk."

"And then I held you while you cried because you felt so bad for yelling at her."

I close my eyes. "Then I dragged you to meet her properly and convinced her it didn't matter if I got hurt because I loved you. And the love was worth the pain I knew would follow when we parted."

Aaron washes the shampoo from my hair, and when it's completely clean, when I think the conversation is over, he runs his fingers through it.

"Was it? Worth it?"

"I don't know."

I hear the scrape of metal as the dark curtains are spread open, filling the room with bright sunlight.

"Good morning," Aaron says in a voice that's way too happy.

"No it isn't." I burrow beneath the covers. "Go away."

He laughs and tugs the sheets away. "I have coffee."

"I don't care. It's too early."

"I told you I had an early start."

"Yep. *You.* You have an early start. Not me."

"Wrong."

I narrow my eyes at him. "What do you mean, wrong?"

"We both have an early start."

"But you said—"

He leans forward, smirking. "I didn't say anything about a meeting or work, did I?"

Did he? No. Crap.

"So you left that party early why?"

"Because this is the only day this week without a meeting or a goddamn party, and I want to spend it with you."

I prop myself up on my elbow. "And what if I have plans?"

"With who?" He raises an eyebrow in amusement.

"With myself."

"Stop being ridiculous. Drink your coffee, get up, and get ready."

I sit up. "Is that a request?"

"It's a demand. Fucking do it."

I grin at his retreating back and grab the coffee, sipping slowly. I kind of love it when he does that. When that demanding, powerful side of him I see so clearly when he's turned on creeps into everyday life.

"I'm not waiting all day, Dayton!" he yells into the room.

"You didn't say I had to drink the coffee fast!"

"We leave in ten minutes." He pokes his head around the door. "So it's the coffee or your looks."

"You woke me up with ten minutes to get ready?" I jump out of bed, totally disregarding the fact I'm only in underwear, and run to my suitcase.

"No."

I look straight into his amused, smirking face.

"You have half an hour. But it was worth it to see you in that lace."

"You're an asshole, Aaron Stone."

"You should see me in the boardroom." He winks and I shake my head. I can fully believe it.

I unzip my suitcase and stare at the masses of clothes there. "What am I supposed to wear?"

"Whatever you want to wear."

I fake a gasp. "No *demands?*"

"Don't fucking tempt me, Dayton."

I laugh quietly and grab a dress. It's fun pushing these newfound buttons he has—even if I've only nudged a few of them. These are sides that were suppressed when we met, things I only ever got a glimpse of. But maybe that's a good thing. Maybe if he'd been this powerful, then I'd have run a mile.

Funny how the thing that probably would have scared me then is very thing that makes me so attracted to him right now.

"And don't even think about taking that lace off," he calls through when I hook my fingers in the side of my panties.

"Does it matter? You won't be seeing it."

"No." He appears in the doorway again, his eyes hooded. Shivers assault my body. "But that doesn't mean I can't imagine you in it and fuck you in my mind all day."

He goes as quickly as he appeared and my jaw drops. So what if men fuck me—physically and mentally—all the time? None of them have ever been quite as blunt about it as Aaron.

"Close your mouth, sweetheart, or I might be tempted to fill it for you."

"Jesus Christ!" I pull my dress over my head and storm out of the room. He's leaning against the small bar in the corner, a shit-eating grin on his face. "Did you swallow an erotica book or something?"

"I warned you I'd be fucking you in my mind. That includes your mouth."

My cheeks heat.

"Are you blushing?"

"No! I don't blush." Or I shouldn't. I'm a fucking call girl!

"You're either blushing or you're having an orgasm right now. You have the same look on your face. Glazed eyes, lips parted, cheeks flushed." His eyes flick over my features. "And if you're having an orgasm, I'm better than I thought. Or you just really love the idea of sucking my cock."

I ignore the sudden clench of my pussy and point at him. "You, sir, are an arrogant bastard."

He smirks. "Go and get ready, Dayton. We're leaving soon."

I show him my middle finger and stalk into the bedroom. There isn't a chance in hell I'm about to let him know just how much I *did* love having him in my mouth.

It was the power, the knowledge that, for five minutes, Mr. I Don't Ask, I Tell was completely under my control. He was at my mercy for as long as my lips were wrapped around him and his hips were jerking into my mouth. His actions were completely controlled by me until the moment his cock swelled and he filled my mouth with his release.

That was it. Not the way he groaned my name and tugged my

hair. Or the way he kissed me after as if he were starving.

It was the power.

Yep. I'm going with that.

When I step back into the main room, he throws a beach tote at me. "Put a bikini in that."

"So much for not taking off the lace," I throw over my shoulder.

"You can take it off when I say you can take it off."

Fuck that.

I pull my dress over my head and change from my underwear to my bikini, shoving the lace into my bag. I wonder how long I'll get away with this one.

"Ready?"

I nod, and Aaron takes my hand in the elevator. Neither of us says a word on the way down, but I know when he curves his lips to one side. He pulls me close to him the in lobby.

"Nice try," he whispers in my ear, reaching up to my neck. He tugs on the pink string, freeing my bikini tie, and I gasp. The top slips down, the halter neck of my dress not tight enough to keep it in place, and my nipples brush against the soft cotton of my dress.

"You..."

He grazes my earlobe with his teeth. "Asshole? I know. It's a nice view from here though."

I jab him in the side with my elbow. "How am I supposed to tie it back up?"

We step into the dry Australian heat and a black BMW pulls up. Aaron opens the passenger-side door.

"I suppose you can do it in here."

I glare at him and get in the car. He pauses after getting in, his eyes focused on me.

"I'm not tying up the fucking bikini with the valet staring at me like he's never seen a woman before." I glance at the wide-eyed young guy with a tent forming in his pants.

"How awkward for him." Aaron's voice is amused, but I can sense the hint of annoyance he's trying to hide behind a smirk.

I lick my lips. "How old do you think he is?"

"Don't even go there."

"He looks at least twenty. That's totally in my age range."

"Dayton," Aaron growls, flexing his fingers in his lap. "Shut the fuck up."

I sigh and maneuver my bikini back over my breasts to retie it. "I'll keep my thoughts to myself in future."

"You shouldn't be having thoughts like that."

"Why not? I'm single."

He doesn't need to know I don't fuck for pleasure.

"Not on my bank account you're not."

I huff. "Pulling that again, are you?"

"I can have this car pulled over so I can take you on the side of the road if you'd prefer that as reminder."

*Oh my.* "Exhibitionist."

His blue eyes cut to me. "In fact, I couldn't do that."

I shake my head. "Chicken."

One of his eyebrows arches, and we pull into the harbor. "I could fuck you on the side of the road, Dayton, just as long as there aren't people around. I'm much too possessive to let anyone else see the body I did last night." He helps me from the car.

"Perhaps you should blindfold me next time I change then. Lest anyone other than *you* lays eyes on my body."

A grin twitches his lips and he brings them close to mine. "Don't be so fucking difficult."

"Middle name," I murmur against his coffee-flavored mouth.

"No, it's not. It's Lauren." He takes my mouth in a delicious kiss that makes my knees tremble.

"You're being very obvious today, Mr. Stone."

"If you look to your left, you'll see a man on a boat. Blue cap, no shirt, cargo shorts." He ghosts his way to my ear so I can turn my head. "That boat belonged to my father, and now, me. The man is named Joseph, and he's looked after this boat for the last five years. He'll be sailing it today."

"If I didn't know better, I'd have to say your dad is spying on us."

"No, that's my mother." He grins and pulls me over to the boat. "Dad's just the middle man keeping her happy."

"Keeping her happy? You mean you Stone men can be tamed?"

"That's what we like our women to think."

He helps me onto the boat and introduces me to Joseph, a thirty-something man with a physique of a twenty-year-old and the charm of a man who's been around. He brushes Aaron's annoyed look off with a wink to me, telling us lunch will be served at midday.

"Nice guy," I say, watching him go.

Aaron's hand cups my jaw and he turns my face into him. His eyes are dark and his breath hot. "Stop provoking me, Dayton. You know it pisses me off and that's why you do it. I told you before. You don't get to look at other guys when you're with me. You don't get to look at them, think about them, or flirt with them. You still belong to me for a few more weeks."

I want to argue. I want to fight back and tell him to shove his 'you belong to me' bullshit where the sun doesn't shine. But I don't.

"Okay."

He blinks. "Okay?"

I shrug. "Okay."

"No arguments? No fight? No insults through gritted teeth?"

"I can be agreeable sometimes. Not often," I add at the disbelieving look that crosses his face, "but it's been known to happen. And there's no need to look so fucking surprised."

"Do you have to swear so much?"

"Yes." I knock his hand from me and sit back on a sun lounger as we leave the harbor.

"You never used to."

My eyes trace the skyline of the city we're slowly leaving behind. "I never *planned* to, but my job changes people. It pushes your limits and broadens your horizons in what is sometimes the most effed-up ways possible. That's just how it is, and when you stand in front of enough men who only want you for one thing, you accept sex for what it is. Fucking."

"You don't need to talk about yourself in such a derogatory way."

"Why? That's what it is. I don't have sex with these guys, Aaron. We don't make love. We fuck. After a while, you accept your job for the blunt reality of what it is and it filters through into the rest of your life."

"And it jades you."

I glance at him. "No. It changes you and perhaps the way you see the world, but it doesn't jade you. The person that jaded me is me."

He leans back, folding his arms across his chest, and peers over the top of his Ray-Bans. "I don't believe you. Something jaded you."

A small, dry laugh leaves me and I look away. "Sleep with enough men who promise forever to a woman then go away on business while she's sitting at home rocking a baby to sleep and you see how hollow love is. How easily promises can be broken."

Nothing but the sound of the boat against the water surrounds us for an uncomfortable moment.

"Have you ever come between a marriage?"

"I don't know. It's not my job to know."

"That sounds...cold."

I smile wanly and meet his eyes. "Why people hire me is none of my business, unless a reason is explicitly asked for, like with you. Most of the time, the meeting is made and carried through with no questions or information provided to me. Call me cold, call me a bitch, but when I walk into an appointment with my clients, all I want to know is if they have my money and how they want me to fuck them. Not if their wife is sitting at home polishing the silver while he gets what he's obviously being denied."

"What he's obviously being denied?"

The arch in his eyebrow pisses me off, and I raise my own in return.

"If he was getting it at home, he wouldn't need to pay for it, now would he?"

Aaron snorts, and I shift in my seat.

"Are you telling me if you were married and weren't getting it you wouldn't go elsewhere?"

His eyes crash into mine with an intensity that makes my heart stutter. "No. No, I fucking wouldn't. I'd grab my wife, sit her the fuck down, and work through that shit. Whatever it took. If I was committed to one woman, I'd be committed to her and her alone. And if, in the impossible event I was tempted to look elsewhere, I certainly wouldn't pay for it."

"That's ironic, don'tcha think?" I stand and storm back to the cabin.

"Shit. Dayton! I didn't mean it that way." His footsteps are hard against the floor as he follows me.

I lock the door behind me and lean against it. It's more than a bit goddamn ironic coming from the guy *paying* for someone to be by his side for six weeks. Try the absolute definition of the fucking word.

"What way did you mean it?" I yell through the door. "That you don't need to pay for it because you could easily find it for free? That you're too *good* to pay for a hooker?"

He bangs his fist against the door, making it vibrate against my back. "Don't call yourself that. Jesus. Open the door!"

"Fuck no." I cross my arms over my chest, a pang of hurt tightening my chest. I'm surprised by how bad that last sentence made me feel—especially given the situation we're in.

"Bambi, please open the door."

"If you don't stop calling me that, I'm going to order a figurine off Amazon and shove it up your backside."

A muffled sound rumbles through the door and I pause. Is he laughing? He is. What a jackass.

"I'd like to see you try. Now please open the door because I'm sick of shouting at you through it."

I push off the wooden surface and throw myself on the sofa that curves the corner. This is one big-ass boat. "No. I'm mad at you and I don't want to speak to you right now."

He sighs loudly, and I can imagine him running his fingers through his hair. "Okay. I tried asking nicely. Open the door before I kick the fucking thing down."

"You wouldn't?" That sounded more uncertain than I'd hoped for.

"I'll kick down anything that stops me from getting to you."

"If that was supposed to soften me up, you failed!"

Now, if someone could tell that to the flutter in my stomach, that'd be great.

"Open the door."

"No!"

He rams into the door, once, twice, three times. The lock snaps and the door splinters with the weight of his body against it, and he nearly falls into the cabin. I narrow my eyes and fold my arms across my body.

Aaron steadies himself and brushes off his shoulder. "That was unfortunate."

"I'm sure you can afford a new one, what with all the sex you don't have to buy."

"That came out wrong and you know it."

"Actually, you know what?" I stand. "I don't. Do you know why I keep my job a secret? Why I have a second name? My safety aside, I do it because I don't want to live with the stigma of being a call girl. I don't want to be viewed as the kind of person you just made me feel like."

"Day…" He reaches for me and I step back.

"I do it because sometimes, at the end of the day, I feel dirty and cheap enough that I don't need anyone else to weigh in on it."

Aaron grabs me quicker than I can move away and holds me to him. "You're not dirty and you're certainly not cheap."

"Only because you know my price tag," I hiss.

"Wrong," he says firmly. "Because you did what you had to do to survive at a time when there weren't any other options for you. When you were scared and lost and alone."

"And now? What's your excuse for now?"

"Monique became the family you'd lost, and no one likes to leave their family."

And he's right. He's so, so fucking right that I'd probably cry into his chest if I weren't still so pissed at him.

"Thank you for that evaluation, Dr. Phil, but I'm a big enough girl to know that the only opinion of you that matters is your own." I shake his hands off my arms and cross to the kitchenette area.

Why the fuck is there a mini kitchen on a boat? I yank open the cupboards until I find a glass and pour myself a glass of water, draining it in one go.

"If my opinion of you doesn't mean anything to you, tell me why you just stormed away from me."

He's right behind me. My skin is buzzing despite the fact that he's not touching me. I'm completely alive at the mere feeling of his breath brushing across my shoulder.

"I'm a proud person. I don't like to be put down."

"You're a stubborn person, sweetheart." He runs his hands down my arms to my hands, where he slowly links his fingers through mine. "Don't be proud with me. It doesn't wash, and neither does your not-caring bullshit. You don't get to be as in love as we once were and not care about what the other person thinks."

"Seven years, Aaron. Things you care about change a lot in that time."

"I still care about you. That never changed. It never will."

"You care about the person you knew."

"No, I care about the beautiful, stubborn, challenging, difficult woman standing in front of me."

"I think I should be flattered by that, but you lost me at 'stubborn, challenging, and difficult.'"

He chuckles lowly and steps into me. My back curves into his body in response to his touch, a response I neither want nor like. Automatic reactions are dangerous territory.

He runs his nose along my neck, his breath tracing below its path, making me shiver. "I'm calling it in, sweetheart. I know I said I wouldn't, but I am."

"So much for not paying for it."

"I'm not. I pay for you to accompany me to dinners and functions and all the fancy shit. I'm not paying for your body because you'll give it to me freely."

"You sound real sure of yourself, Mr. Stone."

"I can't stand seeing you and not being able to have you the way I want."

He creeps his finger to the hem of my dress and pulls it over my head then removes his own shirt. His bare skin burns against mine, and his hands flatten on my stomach, holding me flush against him. My breathing picks up slightly when his fingertips graze my bikini line.

"Like this. Do you know how hard it is to lie in bed next to you night after night, both of us in our underwear, and not pull you to me? Do you have any fucking idea how hard it is for me to not flip you onto your back and explore your body with my fingers or devour it with my mouth? It kills me, Dayton. I want you so badly my head is clouded with thoughts of you every second of the day, and just the mention of your name makes me hard."

It's not all that makes him hard. I can feel his erection pressing into my lower back through his shorts, tantalizingly hard. Almost as if it's teasing me because it knows I've seen the beauty of it. I've seen it, felt it, tasted it. And I want more.

"Tomorrow night, after the dinner, I'm going to take you back to our suite and I'm going to fuck you the way I've dreamed of since I saw you again two and a half weeks ago. And you're going to let me. You're not going to treat me like your client and fake your way through it. You're going to treat me and respond to me like the man you want beside you and inside you."

"What if I fight you?"

"You won't." He nips my neck then flicks his tongue over the tiny sting there. "Because you know you won't win. I've waited too long, Dayton."

"It hasn't even been three weeks. I've waited longer for a shoe delivery."

He slips his fingers inside my bikini and runs two along my pussy, which has been brought to life by our skin-on-skin contact and his forceful words. I close my eyes at the sweet feeling that hits me when he grazes my clit.

"Seems like I'm not the only impatient one."

I sigh when he removes his hand and watch with widening eyes as he brings his fingers to his mouth and sucks on them, licking off every bit of me.

"And she still tastes like heaven," he murmurs, spinning me so he can kiss me.

"Heaven doesn't have a taste," I argue against his lips.

"It sure does. And it's you." His hands slide into my hair. "You taste like a heaven full of sins, something that's bad but at the same time far too good to give up."

"What kind of sins?" I tease, running my hands down his sides.

"Temptation and greed. Two things that will be my downfall. You're far too tempting and I'm far too greedy to ever stop being tempted."

"Did it take you long to think that up?"

He smacks my ass, and I squeak. "Don't start with me, woman. Now behave yourself and go upstairs before Joseph thinks we're having a morning fuck."

"Is that a bad thing? You said he was spying on us." I grab my dress and saunter out of the cabin, but not before his palm connects with my other butt cheek. "Ouch!"

"I told you to behave."

"Hmph."

He follows me back to the loungers, where two drinks are waiting for us. I pick up my cocktail glass and point to it.

"It's called a Blow Job." He smirks.

"Oh. I like these." I smirk back at him and take a sip.

He eyes me as I set it on the mini table next to me. "I'm aware."

My smirk changes to a grin and I lie back on the lounger, pulling my oversized glasses over my eyes. "Aaron?"

"Dayton?"

"I'm still really mad at you."

His throaty chuckle wraps around me. "I know."

# Chapter Eleven

Crocodile tastes like chicken.

At least to me. Aaron insists that it has its own unique taste, but it definitely doesn't. Why we couldn't eat something normal for dinner—like octopus or squid or something—I don't know.

Not to say I don't like crocodile. I do. I'm just not in a hurry to eat it again.

Aaron leans back in his seat and brings his martini glass to his lips. His eyes rove over my face and settle on my lips as I lick my spoon clean. I run my tongue over the cold metal slowly, and I purposely keep my eyes focused over his shoulder.

The longer he stares at me, the harder it is to keep my eyes from his. His gaze is strong and compelling. It spreads warmth and tingles over my body, especially when I know that his eyes are darkening the way they are now. It's *how* I know. When his lids get heavy and the electric blue of his eyes changes to a hue close to indigo, the intensity that hits me increases. When he looks at me the way he is now, his gaze penetrates my very core.

I look down at the table, tracing the swirls of cream in my bowl from dessert with my eyes. His quiet laugh reaches me and I drop my spoon.

"Still mad at me, sweetheart?"

"Of course I am. I'm *always* mad at you. Extra mad today."

"Look at me."

I shake my head.

"Dayton. Look at me."

My traitorous eyes look up at his sharp demand. He reaches across the table and takes my hand. His fingers are rough and warm, and try as I might to focus on the feeling of them threading through mine, his gaze holds me captive.

"Are you still mad about what I said?"

"Yes."

"And hurt?"

"I'm not—" I pause at the tightening of his jaw. "Yes. Okay, yes. It hurt."

He flips our hands over and rubs lazy circles on the inside of my wrist. "Why?"

"It doesn't matter."

"It does. Talk to me." He tightens his grip on me when I try to pull away.

The young girl who brought out our food returns and silently takes our empty dishes. We stare at each other the whole time, an uncomfortable feeling brewing in my stomach. I don't talk about feelings to anyone except Liv. Ever.

"Talk to me, Day," he says in a softer voice once we're alone on the deck again.

I tug my hand from his and stand, moving to the edge of the boat. The sea air hits me, wrapping me in a warm, salty embrace, and I inhale deeply, my eyes closed.

"It's because *you* said it." My voice is quiet yet strong enough to travel to him. "In fact, it's not so much what you said. It's how you did. When you said you 'certainly wouldn't pay for it,' you said it in such a disgusted way it made my skin crawl."

His hands cover mine on the railings, and he leans his forehead on my shoulder.

"It made me feel dirty, like you'd demeaned me. In that moment, you could have thrown me into a pile of pig crap and I would have come out feeling cleaner. And yes, it hurt because it came from you. Never mind the situation we're in. It's not something I ever would have expected you to say."

"I'm sorry." He drifts his lips across my shoulder blade. "I really am. I'm so fucking sorry."

I shrug the other shoulder. "It doesn't matter. You've said it now."

Aaron wraps his arms around my waist and turns his face into my neck, and I flash back to Paris. *Standing at the top of the Eiffel Tower... Holding me this way... Whispering that he loves me...*

"It matters to me. Do you think I like paying for you? I don't. It goes against everything I believe and I fucking hate it. So much. I just..." He sighs, his breath warm against my skin. "When you walked into the hotel and sat in front of me, I remembered everything. Looking at you was like being catapulted into the past again, and when you left a few hours later, I couldn't let you go. All those times I'd thought of you and wished I could find you, and I finally had. Somehow you'd ended up in front of me again and I knew without a doubt I couldn't just go on this trip and leave you there."

"You didn't have to do it that way."

"I know. Believe me, sweetheart. I know. But you wouldn't have come with me. You would have fought me."

My lips curl slightly. I would have. There's no way I would have followed him on this crazy trip if I hadn't been forced into it.

"And I couldn't let you walk." He presses a kiss to my collarbone. "Not again."

We stand in silence for a long while, our bodies together and his chin on my shoulder, just staring out to sea. The endless blue sea and perfectly clear turquoise water stretches for miles around us, the gentle breeze teasing my hair. The gentle bobbing of the boat is barely noticeable now. I feel Aaron sigh against my cheek.

"Do you ever wish we'd done it differently?" I ask.

"What?"

I look down at the water beneath us and whisper, "Leaving. Paris. Do you think back and wish we'd tried to make it work long distance instead of walking away?"

The tightening of his fingers into my stomach tells me what I need to know before he answers. I slide my hands along his arms until I'm holding myself as tightly as he is.

"Every day," he whispers back. "And I've wished it every second of every day since you came back into my life."

*I wish it too,* I want to say. I wish we'd looked at what we had and realized it was more than a boy and a girl having a whirlwind romance. I wish we'd stared into each other's eyes in the airport just after he'd caught up with me and promised each other we wouldn't give up.

I wish we'd both had the courage to hold on to us.

We're in Paris again, strolling along the Champs-Élysées hand in hand. I'm laughing at something he said, my free hand covering my mouth to muffle my hysterical giggles. He grabs me around the waist and dips me back, staring into my eyes for a tantalizingly long moment before, finally, he lowers his lips to mine in a sweet kiss that promises everything…

I roll over and rub my eyes. Jesus. I stretch my arm out and hit a box instead of the body I was expecting. What's the time?

The clock reads eleven a.m., and I sit bolt upright. *Eleven a.m.?*

The last time I slept this late I was sixteen and faking being sick to get out of school. Really, I'd been partying the night before and was just too hungover to get up.

I slide out of bed and pad into the kitchen in my underwear. Sun filters through the large windows, and I lean back against the side as the coffee machine works its magic. Within minutes, the scent of freshly brewed coffee reaches my nose and I turn and grab the mug.

The Sydney skyline stretches out before me, the Opera House standing proud in the distance. I want to explore this city some more, beyond the shops and the harbor to everything else. The tiny cafés and bars no one but the locals know. The quiet spots where you can forget about everything and just watch the world pass you by.

The bar Liv works at is much like that—a quiet little place on the corner nobody really knows. With its view of the piers and Elliot Bay, it's one of my favorite places ever. A glass of wine and book in the corner is pretty much my favorite way to chill out.

I hum the tune of *The Way I Loved You* by Taylor Swift and walk back into the bedroom. My eyes fall on the box when I put my coffee down, and I tilt my head to the side. My curiosity is spiked, incredibly so. I jump onto the bed like a little kid and pull it onto my bed. I shake it.

No sounds.

I frown and pull off the small envelope tucked beneath the ribbon.

*Dayton,*

*I'm in meetings all day and can't get away until dinner tonight. I'll meet you in the function room at 6:30 I'm so sorry. I wish I could be there sooner.*

*I took the liberty of buying you a dress and planning your day. I feel like a complete bastard for what I said yesterday, and this my way of making it up to you.*

*At 11:30 head to the spa on the floor below us. There you'll get a massage, a manicure and pedicure, and anything else you want. I scheduledit for you, and you alone. But don't be too long—a hair stylist is meeting you at the room at four, and so is a makeup artist.*

*I want you to do nothing but relax today. I'm so, so sorry for what I said yesterday.*

*Aaron*

*PS. - There's coffee in the machine.*

*PPS. - I might have hidden two boxes in the suite. Good luck finding them*

*PPPS. - If you make a mess, you're cleaning it up.*

*PPPPS. - I'm kidding. (Not really.)*

I shake my head, a stupid grin on my face, and open the box. Inside, I find another hastily scribbled note.

*I wasn't lying about what I said yesterday. Tonight, you're mine.*

*I'm sure you have some underwear in your suitcase to match this dress. If not, the personal shopper my mother uses here is coming with the hair stylist with a trunk full of (hopefully) lacy things. Pick whatever you want. Actually, pick it anyway. NO ARGUMENTS, woman!*

This time I roll my eyes. But hey—I'm not turning down underwear. Fuck shoes and jewelry. Underwear is the most important part of an outfit. Sexy panties and a bra that makes the girls look good are all a woman really needs.

The pink tissue paper makes me itch to rip it open. But it's wrapped so carefully and perfectly, I slip my finger beneath the seal and tear it off gently. I'm shaking as I open it. Crap. Why am I shaking?

I grasp the shoulders of the dress and stand, holding it up in front of me. The turquoise lace falls in a sleek line until flaring out roughly where my knees will be. The layer beneath it brightens the color, but the pure lace of the long sleeves shows the intricate weave of the material.

It's perfect.

The kind of dress I would have picked.

The kind of dress I've always wished would be bought for me.

I lay it back on the bed carefully, mindful of creasing it, and grab the note again. He mentions two more boxes... I frown and spin. There's nothing out of place in the bedroom.

I walk through the whole suite, checking each room for boxes, until my perusal is disrupted by the clock catching my eye. Shit! It's almost eleven thirty! I run back to the bedroom, throw a dress over my head, and fly into the elevator.

It reaches the next floor down in no time, and when the doors open, I'm greeted by a girl about my age—give or take ten years and a few Botox injections.

"Miss Black?" she asks.

"Yes."

"Follow me. Mr. Stone requested you have your massage first." She waves me over her shoulder and leads me into a separate room. "You can change and I'll bring you a drink to enjoy until your massage therapist arrives" She hands me a white fluffy robe. "What would you like? Mineral water? Fresh juice? Champagne?"

I ponder this. Champagne? At noon? Can I do that?

Is it acceptable in a spa?

Oh, who cares?

"Champagne would be perfect. Thank you."

She smiles and nods before slipping out of the door. I strip and lie on the massage bed, my head spinning. There are a lot of ways for a guy to say sorry, but this is one of the best.

The girl arrives with my drink, and I take a seat while I wait for the therapist. If this is teaching me anything, it's that Aaron Stone knows how to treat a woman. That is, when he's not being demanding with those dangerous fuck-me eyes.

Hell, who am I kidding? I'm not a prude. I love that.

The massage therapist enters the room and introduces *himself.* Him? Isn't this how porn movies start?

This won't go down well with Aaron... But I could have fun working this in my favor.

I'm a bitch and I shouldn't even be entertaining these thoughts, but I am. I love it when that protective side comes out and he challenges me with his darkening eyes and ticking jaw. When he grabs me and pulls me into him then kisses the living crap out of me...

"Oooh!" I cry when Jason, my therapist, hits a knot in my back. I can almost hear his smile as he gently begins to work it out.

Aaron would be steaming mad right now. Another guy putting his hands on me while I'm on his time? Holy shit. I know he said he's going to fuck me tonight, but this is a ticket to a *real* fucking.

I shouldn't even be thinking this—how much I love the feel of his lips or his touch or how much he'd hate this.

God, I've fucked a masseuse, and it was fucking wonderful until he stuck it in me. The guy had hands like a god but a dick like a virgin.

Over the next hour, Jason works out every knot and kink and bend in my muscles, teasing each one into a completely relaxed state. *God.* He massages my calf. Can I get him transported to Seattle? He's good.

"We're all done here, Miss Black," he says quietly, crossing the small room. "Dana will be waiting for you when you're ready for your pedicure."

"Thank you, Jason," I sigh. "That was great."

"You're welcome."

He shuts the door, and I take a few deep breaths before standing. I encase myself in the robe and pull out my cell, my lips quirking in a troublesome smirk.

I just had my massage. Thank you.

Aaron's response is immediate. Good. I hope you enjoyed it.

I did. He did a wonderful job.

HE?!

I slide my phone back into my pocket and skip out of the room. In the corner of the main spa area is a woman sitting in front of a foot spa. She's surrounded by all the items she needs for a pedi.

"Dana?" I inquire, moving forward.

She stands with a beaming smile, crow's-feet snaking from her eyes. "Miss Black. Please, take a seat. Mr. Stone requested that your toenails match your dress. Madeline will be along shortly to do your manicure, but until then, it's you and me."

I sit back in the plush, white leather seat. "Thank you."

The girl that greeted me places a glass by my side. "Sorry for the wait, Miss Black, but I thought you might like your drink cooled."

"That's perfect." I take the glass. "Thank you."

Dana takes my feet, and after a cleanse, she begins the usual pedicure procedure but with more precision and care than I've ever experienced before. I feel relaxed and spoiled within an inch of my life, and when Dana applies the bright polish, I see that the color matches my dress perfectly.

My cell vibrates in my pocket, interrupting our conversation about the differences in Australia and America, and I pull it out to see Aaron's name on screen. Dana looks up.

"Please do answer." She smiles.

I return her gesture and hold it to my ear. "Hi, baby!"

"He? What the fuck do you mean he?"

Oh, he's mad. Really mad.

"He, as in Joseph. I thought you'd like to know he did an amazing job."

"I requested you only had females tend to you." His voice is strained and tight. "Especially for the massage."

"Relax, honey."

"Another man had his hands all over your body and you're telling me to fucking relax? You're lucky I'm not hauling my ass down there and switching hotels right this second."

"You're overreacting," I state. "Maybe there was no one else available."

"Overreacting would be coming down there and punching that sonofabitch."

I roll my eyes. "Jesus, Aaron. It was a massage. That you booked, I might add."

The line crackles as he takes a deep breath. "You're right. I just hate the idea of some other guy having his hands on you."

"It was a good massage." I'm taunting him, I know. I can't help it.

"*I'll* give you a fucking good massage, woman. Don't you worry about that," he growls. "Now get off the phone and do that relaxing shit I organized before I piss you off."

I smile. "Goodbye, Aaron."

"The foyer. Six thirty. In that dress."

"You got it, lover boy." I hang up and roll my eyes a second time at Dana's smile. "Men."

"I feel ya, sweetie. I feel ya."

# Chapter Twelve

I swear that everyone standing in this room has their eyes on me. Running their eyes down the length of my body, admiring the dress that hugs it like a second skin. Flicking their gaze across my face, taking in my natural makeup, staring at the curve of my eyelashes. Combing my perfectly styled hair, which is clipped over one shoulder the way I requested for Aaron's benefit. Examining the diamond necklace glittering around my neck and the matching bracelet at my wrist from the boxes Aaron hid beneath the sofa cushions.

But they're not. There's only one set of eyes on me—and if there are more, I can't feel them. The only ones I'm aware of are bright blue and belong to the incredibly handsome man clad in a suit, leaning against the wall. His gaze is drinking me in unapologetically and sparking lust in the pit of my belly.

I let my eyes rove over him in the same manner. Brashly. Obviously. Appreciatively. And, shit, do I appreciate the sight of him. The dark grey suit tailored to him that makes his eyes pop and the stark white of his shirt against his tan skin makes him a vision. A very sexy, very confident vision.

He looks away for a second when he excuses himself from his conversation. His eyes are back on me the moment he strides toward me purposely, like he's not willing to let anyone get between him and me. As if he can't be in the same room as me without needing to be next to me.

He stops in front of me and rests a tender hand at my side. "You look beautiful."

"You picked the dress," I say softly. "Thank you."

"No." He curls his fingers around my neck and pulls me closer to him. "Thank you for wearing it. Really, you look incredible."

I run my fingers down the front of his dinner jacket. "You brush up pretty good yourself, Mr. Stone."

He pulls my lips to his. "I know." He kisses me slowly and sensually, each touch tingling through my body. "God, I wish we could skip this," he murmurs, nuzzling his lips into my neck. "I want you out of that dress more than I wanted you in it when I saw it."

I smile. "Obligations, sir. Come on. Aren't you going to introduce me?"

"No," he says seriously. "You're all mine."

"Aaron," I scold, tapping his chest. "How many of these people are spying on us?"

He laughs. "Probably half of them, but I don't care. Don't you think sneaking off before dinner would give my parents something to talk about?"

"You're so bad."

"Bad for you, Bambi."

"What a charmer." I grin and kiss him quickly. "Behave. Everyone's sitting for dinner. Let's go."

I walk and he stops me. "One thing."

"What?"

"Did you use the personal shopper?"

I look down and smile. "Do you need to ask?"

"Do we really need to do dinner?"

"Yes."

"That's a shame." He pulls out my seat and places his lips by my ear. "Because I'm already thinking of all the ways I can take your body tonight."

I swallow my gasp as he sits next to me and introduces me to the others around the table. The Australian boss and his wife, the modeling director and wife, and the head of advertising and his girlfriend. Pretending I care is a challenge when his words are ricocheting around my mind and adrenaline is flooding my body.

Getting through this dinner with his hand resting on my thigh? That's another challenge altogether.

I spend my appetizer silent, listening to the quiet hum of conversation around the table, and it isn't until Aaron nudges me while we're waiting for the entrée that I realize I'm being spoken to. And that I've been looking at him.

"Gosh, it's adorable," Mrs. Modeling Director's Wife gushes, holding her hands to her chest. Oh, God. I hate the gushers. "Dayton, you must tell us the story of how you met. I'd simply love to hear it."

Murmurs resonate around the table, and my throat tightens. That day is seared into my mind and my heart no matter how I try to forget it. It's one of a thousand memories of that vacation that have locked themselves inside my body and refuse to leave. And telling the story, actually telling it, instead of having a gentle reminder from Aaron, makes all the memories come to life again.

"Oh." I look down and smile. "It was such a long time ago. I'm not sure I remember."

Aaron laughs. "Don't play that card, woman. You know I was the one who tried it on."

I glance at him and pretend to fake a sigh. "Fine."

Mrs. Modeling Director's Wife's eyes twinkle.

"It was the summer before my senior year of high school and my parents had taken me to Paris for two months. My father had business to do with an old friend, so they decided to turn it into a vacation. The last time I was there, I was just a child, so it was if I were seeing the city through fresh eyes.

"We'd been there for around ten days when I finally made it to the Eiffel Tower alone. I'd been there with my mom several times, but she was always in a rush to go somewhere else. It was my chance to really enjoy it." My lips quirk, and Aaron slides his hand into mine. "I was standing in front of the tower, completely awed by its size and beauty, when someone came up behind me. 'Beautiful, don't you think?' he asked. I was holding a coffee and jumped so hard I nearly spilled it over both of us."

Giselle, the girlfriend of the head of advertising, sighs and leans forward. "Do you remember how that felt?"

I raise my eyes to hers, my heart pounding at the memory. "Do you remember how it felt when you saw your first love for the first time?"

Aaron's fingers tighten around mine.

"I do. How did it feel?"

"Like the world had stopped," I answer quietly. Silence lingers for a moment, and I speak again. "Of course I agreed with him. The tower is beautiful. He handed me his sweater so I could wipe the coffee from my hands and laughed at me." I turn my face to Aaron's, my lips curving to one side. "'Oh, you're talking about the tower,' he said. 'I was talking about you.' I blushed and he practically dragged me to a nearby café to replace the coffee he insisted he'd made me spill, and the rest is history."

The three women all smile widely, their eyes full of that mushy, romantic stuff only Aaron has ever made me understand. The stuff that makes your heart go boom-boom and your lungs go clench-clench.

"It's true," Aaron agrees as the entrées are placed in front of us. "In fact, I think if she'd refused to get coffee with me, I would have slung her over my shoulder and poured a cup down her throat."

"You're so romantic, baby, I can barely stand it."

He laughs and brushes his mouth across my knuckles. "I'm trying to tone it down, sweetheart. Can you tell?"

"Not at all." I roll my eyes to the amusement of the rest of the table. I pull my hand from his but he tightens his grip. "Aaron? I need to eat."

"So eat one-handed." He holds up his own fork.

I stare at the fish on my plate. "I don't think I can."

"I told you I couldn't let you go again. Now, after hearing you tell that moment, *our* moment, as if you're living it all over again? Nothing could tear me away from you."

I swallow and take my fork with my other hand, hoping to god no one else will say a word to me through this dinner. If they do, I might just burst into the tears that have been hiding since I saw him again.

I get my wish. The rest of the dinner is full of business talk, and true to his word, Aaron never lets my hand go. He rubs his thumb over the back of it, brings it to his lips, and presses it to his cheek repeatedly.

"Dayton?" Giselle looks to me.

"Yes?"

"I'm going for some air. Would you like to join me?"

No. But the look in her eye, a knowing look, tells me that I should whether I damn well want to or not. I grasp my wine glass and kiss Aaron's cheek.

"I'll be back soon."

"Take your time." He pats my butt.

Giselle leads me onto a balcony that stretches the length of the hall. We're the only people here, everyone else still engaged in conversations around their respective tables.

"I think it's a universal belief, you know."

"I'm sorry?"

She lights a cigarette and leans against the ornate gates keeping us safe. Her dark eyes hit me with an understanding and knowledge only a few people have.

People like me.

"That call girls don't fall in love."

Her words vibrate through my body.

"How do you…" I flatten my hand against my stomach.

The smile that curves her lips isn't the malicious smirk I expect. It's gentle and kind. "How could they? How could they fuck any number of men a day and still go home to their boyfriends or husbands and have a normal relationship? Where would the trust, the belief, the honesty of love be?"

It dawns on me, washing over me in a warm flood. "You were one. Before."

She nods. "Before Mick. I was the call girl you are. Highly desired, highly paid, highly respected. I gave my agent the biggest cut and took the most home. Falling in love was something reserved for the novels I lost myself in at the end of every day."

I approach the railing and lean next to her. "I think we all do that."

"We all need some hazy dreams in our blunt reality."

My head jerks in a nod. "I agree."

The question burns in my throat, and I want to ask with every part of me. So I do.

"You gave it up?"

She takes a long drag. "Yep. Six months ago. Mick hired me last year to be his date for his sister's wedding and his company for the night." Smoke leaves her mouth in a white, billowing cloud. "And he kept hiring me, randomly it seemed, until I was with him more nights than not. He was taking me to dinner, to shows, everywhere. After three months of it, I asked him what the hell he was playing at. And he told me he was falling in love with me."

"And you were falling in love back."

"I couldn't not. I left him that night thinking about my options. He'd made it clear he couldn't have a serious relationship with me as long as I was doing my job. I had to ask myself if I valued my job or love more."

"And you picked love."

"I picked love." She grinds the cigarette into an ashtray on the wall and drops it in before turning to me. "Dayton, call girls *do* fall in love. We fuck hundreds of men without an ounce of emotion, but that doesn't mean we're not capable of it. We're still human, and we still have hopes and dreams."

I snort. "How many call girls do you know who have fallen in love?"

"Just one. Just me."

"Then why are we having this conversation?"

"Because above anything, call girls are masters at the art of pretending. We pretend every day, to other people, and occasionally to ourselves. And you, my darling, are pretending so hard you almost believe yourself."

"I have no idea what you're talking about."

Giselle takes my hand and leads me to the door. "Just because you're not falling doesn't mean you're not in love."

She pushes the glass door open and we sit back at the table without a word.

Every time I'm at an event like this, I look around the room and wonder how many of the guests are call girls. How many of them have been hired for the same reason as me. How many are smiling and pretending to know everything about their handsome, rich date.

Usually, I know. Usually, they're easy to pick out.

But Giselle has caught me. Somehow she sees me for who I really am and has called me on it. Somehow…she knows and she understands.

And now I'm on edge. Apprehension is prickling at my skin, making my hair stand on end and shiver. If she can tell, how many other people are here who are call girls who can tell? How many can see right through the façade I hold each day?

Dessert dishes are cleared away, mine only picked at. Aaron turns in his seat to face me and gently cups my chin in his hand.

"What's wrong?"

"Nothing," I lie, wrapping my fingers around his. "Do you want another drink?"

"I'm fine." His eyes narrow. "Dayton?"

"Give me a second." I kiss his hand and stand. Music begins as I cross the room to the bar and take a deep breath.

No one ever knows.

What if she says something?

Fuck.

Everything could be over in a second.

"White wine please," I tell the girl behind the bar.

"Dry, medium, or sweet?"

"Medium."

Giselle appears at my side. "Make that two."

I look away.

"Dayton. I apologize if I've made you uncomfortable."

"You have." I straighten. "Are there any others here?"

"Two. One is just starting by the way she's been wringing her hands all night, and the other is too star-struck by her client to do anything."

"How do you know?"

"My ex-agent is my best friend."

I smile as two glasses are put in front of us. "Charge it to the Stone account," I tell the bar girl. "Both."

She nods and disappears.

"Thank you," Giselle says. "Normally I wouldn't have said

anything."

"About knowing or now?" I shoot her a wry smile.

"Both." She returns it. "But I just got a grilling from the boss, so I thought I'd better come apologize."

I glance over to the table and find Aaron's eyes fixed on us. I laugh into my glass. "Don't worry. I'm just not used to anyone knowing."

She places a hand on my arm. "I didn't tell you for some fucked-up reason or to freak you out, I promise. I just…" She sighs. "I see how he looks at you and how you look at him. The way you told the story of how you met… Jesus. There's so much between you it's impossible to ignore."

"He's my client." I drag my eyes from his to hers. "If I could have, I would have run ten thousand miles when I saw him again. Believe me."

"I do." She laughs. "I believe you completely, and I know we just met, but I'm asking you for something."

I narrow my eyes. "What?"

"Believe," she replies simply. "Disregard everything you've ever been told about your life and believe in something beautiful. Something that's staring you in the face every time you look into that goddamn lovely pair of blue eyes."

I chew on my lip and turn back to those eyes. "Believe in what?"

"Love. Always believe in love."

# Chapter Thirteen

"We're going." His husky voice breathes hot air across the back of my neck.

"It's still early."

"Turn around."

I spin and rest my hands against his chest.

"Now tell me," he whispers, bringing his face to mine. "Do I look like a give a fuck?"

"No."

Aaron's hand snakes around my waist. "Then let's go."

He leads me through the hall and we aren't stopped once. No goodbyes, no excusing ourselves, none of the usual bullshit that comes with leaving a business dinner.

"No goodbyes?" I mutter.

He spins me into the wall of the elevator and presses his lips against mine. "I'm going to be inside you within the hour and you're worried about saying goodbye?"

My breath catches in my throat.

"Hmm?"

"No. Not worried," I squeak.

He takes my mouth firmly in a way that makes my body melt beneath him. I'm molten lava, hot and gooey under his touch, easy molded and teased into pure, red-hot desire.

I want this. I want this so fucking badly my body aches with the sheer pressure of it. I want—I *need*—his body lying over mine as he sinks his cock deep inside me and fucks me with the same intensity he kisses me with.

I want to remember how it feels to be desired for me.

Aaron pulls me into the suite, both our breathing heavy. "Leave it. All the client bullshit, all the money, and all the obligations. Leave it in the motherfucking elevator and tell me you want me." His eyes sear into mine, lighting my whole body up. "Tell me you want me to fuck you so hard the only thing you'll be able to scream by the end of the night is my name."

Everything clenches. I can't breathe and I can't think and I can't hear anything over the pounding of my blood through my body.

"Say it!" he growls, pulling me closer.

"I want you!" I whimper. "Fucking hell. I shouldn't but I do. I want you."

"How badly?"

"Don't push it."

"How fucking badly?"

"So bad that if you don't kiss me right this fucking second I might hit you!"

His lips attack mine with a delicious desperateness I feel in every fiber of my being. The raw need I feel as his tongue sweeps mine spreads through my body and tugs at the most intimate part of me. My nipples pebble inside my bra and my fingers work the buttons on his jacket with ease. I slide it over his shoulders.

"Want me or need me?" he breathes against my mouth.

"Shut up and take it off before I rip it off."

"You forgot something." He unzips my dress.

"What's that?"

"My name."

I pull back slightly. "I'm about to rip your shirt off, *Mr. Stone.* Are you okay with that?"

"Not really."

I tear it apart, buttons popping. "Tough shit."

He laughs, his bare hands spreading across my back, and plunges his tongue into my mouth. My back hits the wall with the force of him against mine, and I swear to fucking god I'd climb on him if I could.

His lips caress mine and his tongue explores my mouth like I'm an undiscovered cave ready to be exposed of my secrets. My dress slips over my shoulders and he helps it along the way, kissing my neck and easing the lace away until there's a pool of turquoise at my feet.

I run my fingers down his body, our panting breaths mixing together, and rest my fingers on the buckle of his belt.

"Hell no." He takes my hands away and holds them to the sides. "Don't you remember what I said?"

Yes. I remember. Every muscle in my body tenses.

He chuckles against my neck. "I'm going to taste you now, Dayton. And I'm going to take my sweet fucking time exploring every bit of that beautiful cunt."

His lips ignite a blazing trail down my neck and collarbone. I sink my fingers into his mass of dark hair and revel at the sensations flooding my body, feeling like a virgin again.

The tingles, the nerves, the incessant ache—it's all so new to me, so unrecognized, feelings that have been buried for seven years.

The feelings that have been buried since him are now alive again. For him.

He makes his way down my body, my breath catching with every tender kiss against my skin, until he reaches my hips. He slips a finger through the string of material there and runs it along, his knuckles brushing my core.

"I like these. I hope you asked her for more than one pair."

He rips them from me before I can ask why.

"Nope. Just that one."

"Order more." He breathes the words over my tender flesh that's crying out for his touch. His mouth, his hands, his cock. I don't care anymore. My body is screaming for him from every pore, begging for him from every curve.

Aaron runs his hands up my thighs and hooks them over his shoulders. I flatten my hands against the wall at the feeling of hot air across my clit.

"Please."

He squeezes my ass. "Are you begging?"

"No."

He runs his nose up the inside of my thigh and stops before he hits the apex, before he hits the part of my body desperately needing him.

"Are you begging?"

"Yes. I'm fucking begging you!"

His tongue slides along me slowly. I arch my back at the pure pleasure that shivers through my body. God. One stroke of his tongue and I'm flying somewhere else, especially when he flicks the tip of it into my pussy, stretching it upward.

"Fuck," he moans, his tongue still against my aching core and dragging along me. "You taste amazing."

The pressure he applies to my clit sends waves through my stomach. I moan out loud and he licks along me repeatedly, leaving no part of me untouched by his hot tongue. I writhe against him with each stroke of his tongue, each one bringing me closer and closer to the edge.

He holds me to the wall with his hand, pinning my hips, and frantically circles his tongue against me. My clit swells and I throw my head back, unable to control the cries leaving my parted lips or the shuddering of my body.

"Dayton," he growls against my opening and presses his thumb to my sensitive clit. I fall apart, deliciously, deliriously, hovering somewhere unearthly as pleasure hits me full force.

I come back to now slowly, my head buzzing and my body on fire, and feel the head of him resting against my opening. I can feel the wetness I'm spilling over him and the way he's rubbing his cock against it. He does it for so long. Too long. It feels like he's been hovering against me for hours.

"For the love of God, Aaron," I pant. "Just fuck me already!"

His cock slides into me with ease, stretching me and filling me. I shudder around him, my muscles clenching at his sudden invasion, and his lips brush mine.

"You asked for it."

One hand holds my hip and the other grabs the back of my head. He pounds into me relentlessly, each time going a little deeper and hitting *that* spot a little harder. Our skin is slick against each other's, coated in sweat born of a frantic orgasm and the raw need for a release.

Each stroke of him inside me makes me tighten, and I grasp his hair tighter. I grasp it and I curl it around my fingers and I tug at it. My forehead hits his shoulder as he thrusts into me relentlessly. Tears build behind my eyes at the pure power of him, the desperate way he moans my name a trigger for my own building orgasm.

I hold back. I need him inside me. I need to feel him connected to me and indulging in me. I need to feel every single fucking part of his body against mine as long as possible.

Every part of him is sacred to me.

"Stop fucking holding it back," he hisses into my ear. The husky undertone forces my muscles to tighten around him and I squeeze his cock. Hard. "Fuck. Dayton. Come. Now!"

I throw my head back and let it build into me with each

relentless pound of him inside me. He grabs my jaw and tugs my face down.

"Eyes. Look at me."

My eyes open but flutter back closed at the overwhelming hit of the beginning of an orgasm.

"Open your eyes!"

I force them open and stare into a pool of dark blue passion.

"Don't you dare close them. I want to see you and feel you come." He pushes into me deeply.

"Fuck," I mutter.

"Hard. Come hard or not at all. Got it?"

I nod.

I get it.

He picks the pace up again. My eyes stay on his, the intensity of his gaze only increasing the pressure in my body. It builds and builds, shaking my muscles and making my heart pound and panting all my breaths until finally.

Finally.

His name leaves my mouth in a desperate scream. My pussy clenches around him until he groans my name into my shoulder. I milk him for everything he has, taking everything from him until his body is limp against mine.

Heavy breaths coat his body the way his does mine. My legs ache as the orgasm subsides, and I want to drop them, but I don't want to lose the feeling of completeness I have with him inside me.

Like he knows, he kisses me and pulls me from the wall. I hug him to me as he walks, each step another jolting thrust inside me. He lays me back on the bed.

I refuse to let go. He doesn't say a word.

He lowers himself on top of me and spins us to the side. His arms go around me and he pulls me into his body.

I snuggle in, still riding a high from the intense orgasm that just racked my body, and fall asleep with him still inside me.

A murmur of "Good morning" and a thumb brushing across my cheek stirs me. I stretch out and let my eyes flutter open. Aaron stares back at me with curved lips.

"Good morning," he repeats.

"Mmm." I roll onto my side. "No it isn't."

"Any morning after a night like last night can't be bad." He runs a finger down my side. My bare side.

I yank the covers up to his deep chuckle. "Go away. Do you know what time it is?"

"It's ten in the morning."

"What are you doing here?"

He stands and holds up a finger. I frown when he disappears from the room and stare at the door. What the?

Oh.

He fills the doorway, black slacks resting low on his hips and shirtless, a mug of coffee in one hand and a plate of food in the other.

"Is that for me?" I ask, my eyes tracing the lines on his stomach.

God, he's so beautiful. I desperately try to find a scar or spot or mole or *something* on his body, but there isn't one. Just a chest and a stomach that have been sculpted by someone who knows women so well they probably created the vibrator too.

My eyes drop to his hips and the clearly defined muscle that dips down, the very muscle my tongue has run along, catching water droplets and eliciting groans from the pink lips I just know are pursed in amusement.

"Is what for you?"

"Both," I mutter. Wait. *That wasn't supposed to come out.* I shake my head and meet his eyes. "The food. And the coffee. Definitely those."

He grins and crosses the room, placing the coffee on the nightstand and the plate in my lap. Mmm. Bacon, eggs, and toast.

I make a mental note to check out the gym facilities here. Maybe tomorrow.

"They are for you."

"Thank you."

Aaron leans forward and touches his lips to mine, tugging on my bottom lip as he pulls away. "And so am I. I'm all for you, baby."

"That's my word."

"Baby?"

"Yep."

"Are you using it?"

"Right now?" I chew some bacon and he nods. "No."

"Then I'm using it." He sits on the end of the bed and watches me as I eat. "You don't use it nearly enough."

"What? 'Baby?'"

"Yep."

"That's because I don't need to use it all the time. I only need to use it when I'm being your girlfriend, and that's only when we're in public."

Something glimmers in his eyes. "I'm changing it."

I pick up my coffee mug and hide behind it. "You can't."

"Of course I can. As you so often remind me, I pay for the privilege of you by my side." Disgust filters in his voice, and I know it's at the 'paying for me' part. The annoyed twist of his lip that disappears as quickly as it appeared tells me that.

"So you do."

"That means I can change the agreement at any time. And I'm changing it now."

I'm not going to like this. Or at least, I'm not going to want to like it.

"Go on."

He crosses the room and pulls a shirt on, pausing before he buttons it and glancing at me. I keep my expression blank. Damn.

"You're now to act as if you're my girlfriend at all times. Even if we're alone."

*I knew it.* I click my tongue. "Is that right?"

"Yes. I don't think you're believable enough as my girlfriend while we're in public. You need more practice."

"Funny." I put my plate on the nightstand with my mug. "You didn't seem to think I needed practice before, and especially not when you were dragging me out of the room to fuck me last night."

I stand and wrap the sheet around my body. I hate that he gets to me so easily.

I know what he's doing. He's playing a fucking game with me, and I should have seen it coming. I should have known the second he got his way and fucked me that everything would change.

Because that's how it works, isn't it? Sex is the game changer. It's always been the game changer, and right now, it's just changed the game into something I don't want to play at all.

"Dayton, I believe this is where you agree to what I'm asking."

"Oh, you're asking now?" I hug the sheet to me. "Should I feel special?"

He rubs a hand down his face. "Stop being unreasonable."

"Unreasonable? You wanna know what's unreasonable, Aaron? Unreasonable is hiring your call girl ex to pretend to be your girlfriend for six weeks then fucking her and suddenly deciding she has to act as your girlfriend *all* the fucking time!" I put my hands on my hips. The sheet falls to my waist, exposing my breasts, and he draws in a sharp breath.

Almost immediately, the charge in the air changes from annoyance to sexual. It's strong and it's compelling, and as he takes a step closer, I move back one. No, no. Any closer and I'll do something I'll regret later.

"You're right. It is unreasonable."

"I'd believe you more if you said it to me instead of my tits."

He fights a smile and looks at me. "It's unreasonable and I don't care."

*Ex-fucking-cuse me?*

His long stride covers the kitchen in seconds and he drops his palms on the island in front of me. His eyes are hard, the lusty determination there making me swallow.

"I didn't ask you for an answer, Dayton. It was a rhetorical question. I *am* changing the agreement. You *will* act like my girlfriend at all times. You'll act that way until you drop your call girl-client bullshit."

"Fuck you."

"You'll act like it until you believe it." He pushes off the island and grabs his tie, knotting it and sliding it into place. I grit my teeth and watch as he grabs a jacket and briefcase from the sofa.

He doesn't look at me until the elevator doors open. When he does, his stare hits me with such an intensity that I almost step back.

"I've never been reasonable where you're concerned, Dayton, and I'm not about to start now. Understand that. And the next time you say 'fuck you' to me, that's exactly what you'll be doing."

He steps into the elevator and the doors close with a swish. I grab a clean mug from the side and throw it across the room. It collides with the door and smashes, white china falling over the carpet.

Fucking self-entitled, controlling, demanding fucking bastard.

# Chapter Fourteen

I think I might move.

My love of water has always kept me in Seattle. The Bay has kept me grounded close to a place full of happy memories from years gone by, but I've never really loved the weather.

I'm thinking Sydney has everything. It has water, a harbor, hot weather, and beaches. It's like California and Seattle all rolled into one beautiful little package. Even if it does feel like I'm standing on the surface of the sun again.

A drop of sweat rolls down my back. Okay—maybe it's a little *too* hot.

I pull out my cell, now armed with international messaging and calls, and send a picture of the harbor to Liv. She replies immediately with a picture of her raindrop-covered window and a great big *Fuck you*. I laugh, and when the device buzzes in my hand, I smile at the sight of her name.

"Let me call you back." I hang up before she can argue and redial.

"What the hell?"

"International calls. I'm not paying your damn bill again."

"Screw the bill. I'm wondering why you're sending me a photo of fucking boats and not hot shirtless dudes surrounded by sand and sea."

No one can say Liv's priorities are skewed.

"Because I'm at the harbor and not the beach," I reply. "How's my house?"

"Your house is fine, but your plant died."

"I don't have a plant."

"Yeah, you do. I think your aunt bought it when you moved in."

"That was three years ago."

"Well, no wonder it's dead. I chucked it in the trash."

I shrug. Me and plants don't go well. Evidently. "Are you working today?"

"I'm always working. My agent is MIA again. I need to fire his fat ass."

I nod in agreement although she can't see and walk along the harbor, keeping my eyes on the softly bobbing boats. "Did you go on that shoot I organized?"

"Yes! I haven't seen the finished pictures yet, but the originals looked good."

"Of course they did. You're gorgeous." An idea flits through my mind. "Hey, is Darren really not getting you any work?"

"None. The last job was six weeks ago."

I flinch. Ouch. She might work at a bar full time, but her wages only cover her bills—and that's barely. The cash she gets from modeling is what keeps her going.

"Why don't I speak to Aaron?"

"About me?"

"Why not? Stone Advertising is modeling too. I bet he could find you a job or two."

"Great. And Darren will get his cut for doing jack shit."

"No he won't. You've been around long enough to negotiate a deal. I bet Monique would even do it. I know it's a different kind of thing, but she knows her stuff, Liv."

"So fire Darren and then what? Be agentless? No one would touch me."

"No, do one job for Stone and you'll be able to get an agent. A decent one."

"That's a big risk, Dayton. A big-fucking-ass risk."

I sigh. "Think about it, okay?"

"Mmph. Okay. I have to go to work now. Talk soon?"

"Yeah. Bye."

That conversation didn't last nearly as long as I'd hoped. I leave the harbor and walk into the city. My glasses cover my downcast eyes, and I yearn for a pair of jeans and a sweatshirt with pockets I could shove my hands in.

What am I doing?

If I had any sense, even an ounce of it, I'd run to the hotel. I'd run and I'd pack and I'd jump on the next plane back to the US. I'd run from the situation that's gradually building around me. The one I knew could happen. The one I promised myself wouldn't. The one that changes everything.

The building that houses Stone Advertising comes into my peripheral, and I stop in the middle of the sidewalk. People mill around me, sidestepping to avoid me and running across the road. Flagging cabs. Laughing with friends. Normal things.

I stare at the tall building. Aaron's in there somewhere, probably in a meeting or sitting at stupid long table and watching as hair-flicking, eyelash-batting, chest-pushing, gorgeous girls parade in front of him and present him with a fat portfolio of them wearing barely anything.

Something that feels an awful lot like jealously curls in my stomach, and I walk down the street. I wrap my arms around my waist and walk until I find a tiny, tucked-away restaurant.

The low lighting is counteracted by the rich laughter of the staff when I walk in. Three guys and two girls—too many for this empty place—are all laughing like they'll never laugh again. One of the girls is bent at the waist, holding her stomach as her giggles peal out of her.

The eldest guy shushes them and looks at me. "Can I help you, ma'am?"

"You can." I smile. "I'm looking for a place to hide that has good food. Know anywhere?"

"As it happens, I do!" He steps forward and bows exaggeratedly. "Follow me."

He leads me to a table in the back corner. The bench is covered in bright cushions, the table adorned with an equally bright cloth. He hands me a menu, and I open it.

"What do you recommend?"

"I own the place. I recommend everything." He winks. "Would you like a drink?"

"Do you have white wine?"

"Do I have white wine? Of course I have white wine." He rolls his eyes in a decidedly campy way.

"Well, could I have a glass, please?"

"You can have a bottle, darling. Hold it right there." He scuttles away and returns moments later, a glass in one hand and a bottle in the other. "Here. Try this."

I take the glass from him and smell it. Fruity. Sweet. Not my usual taste, but okay… "Oh my god!" I stare at him. "That's incredible. How can something that smells so sweet be a medium dry?"

He leans forward and crooks his finger. "Don't ask me, honey. I just sell it. But it goes wonderful with our mussels. The fish mussels, not the babies you see hiding beneath my shirt."

I laugh as he pats his thin arm. "Then I'll have the mussels."

"Yes!" He fist pumps the air and turns, pointing a finger at the other staff. "I told you!"

I raise my eyebrows, his infectious happiness making me smile.

"I'm sorry. We had a bet over who could sell the mussels first."

"You set me up!" I gasp.

"I'm sorry!" He takes my hand. "Gosh. Have whatever you want. Here. You can even have me. My bum is peachy." He wiggles his hips.

I think I found my new favorite place.

"I want the mussels," I reply, patting his arm. "Really."

"Done. Ella, tell Barry we need a mussel dish. And not his muscles—he can keep those." He slides in opposite me and leans in. "Believe me, there's nothing nice about those overcooked muscles of his."

I smile.

"So. Who are you hiding from?"

"Tom!" A girl—Ella—appears from the kitchen and scolds him. "You can't ask people personal stuff like that!"

Tom rolls his eyes. "Oh gosh, El. If she doesn't want to tell me, she won't. Talking helps, girl."

She turns soft brown eyes on me. "Just tell him to piss off. He has no boundaries."

"It's okay." I run my thumb along my glass. "I'm hiding from my boyfriend."

"Oh no," Tom sighs dramatically. "It's always the men, isn't it? I'd tell you to be gay like me but I realize that contradicts my last comment."

Ella sits too. "Tom, if she was gay like you, she'd be into women."

"Like you."

"Precisely."

So I'm sitting in a restaurant in Sydney, Australia, telling a gay man and a lesbian how I'm hiding from my boyfriend who isn't really my boyfriend.

There's something I never thought I'd say.

Tom knocks on the table. "You tell us everything."

"Do you make it a habit to have this conversation with everyone that walks through the door?" I ask with a wry smile.

"Of course I do. Why ask questions if you don't want to find anything out?"

I'll concede that point.

"So why are you hiding?"

I bring my glass to my lips. "Because he's an asshole."

Ella nods sympathetically. "There's a reason I'm not into them."

"Nothing wrong with arseholes," Tom counters.

"Enough." Ella points at him. "What's your name?"

"Dayton."

"Tell me everything."

And I do. Even as my mussels arrive—which they help me eat, leading to another order, a plate of fries, and a second bottle of wine—I talk. I tell them how we met in Paris and agreed to leave it behind. I tell them how we 'met randomly one night when he was in the city' and he 'convinced me to come with him' around the world. How he drives me crazy and makes me happy and blows my body up with every feeling imaginable all of the time.

And I tell them how I'm so very, very scared of what it all means.

"You must care, right?" Ella licks her fingers. "I mean, how often do you agree to go on a trip around the world with your ex-boyfriend?"

"That's right," Alana, the other girl, agrees. "And it's written all over your face. You love him."

Jared, one of the guys, throws a fry at her. "You can't just tell people who they love, Alana!"

She throws him an evil look, and Ella leans into me. "They're in love denial."

I nod. "Ah. He kind of has a point though."

"Just don't tell her that."

I nod again.

"So, darling, what are you going to do?" Tom asks, cutting through Jared's and Alana's sniping.

"I'd like to know that myself."

My head snaps up. Aaron's standing in the doorway, his sleeves rolled up and his tie and jacket discarded.

I sigh into my glass. "Of course he'd find me."

"Is that Aaron Stone? Stone Advertising?" Ella whispers. "We've been trying to get them to work with us for ages."

Tom whistles before I can answer. "Is it hot in here or is the heat wave playing havoc with my hormones?"

I close my eyes and swallow my laugh.

"Dayton? Are you going to answer the question?" His voice cuts through me like a knife.

Ella nudges me and I look at her. "Yes, it is."

"Holy shit, girl. I don't even like men but he might just turn me."

Aaron's jaw visibly clenches. "Not that question."

"Oh, what am I going to do?" I look at my glass. "I'm going to sit here with my new friends, drink wine, and bitch about what complete and utter dickheads straight men are."

Jared and the other guy, Ollie, cry a protest. Alana throws fries at them.

"Or you're gonna get off your pretty little ass, get in the car waiting outside, and come back to the hotel with me."

"I think I'll go with my option, thanks."

"I wasn't asking you, Dayton."

"You were telling me, right?" I finish my wine and stand, staring him down. "Because you get to do that. You get to tell me to do whatever the hell you want without considering how I might feel about it, don't you?"

"You've had too much to drink." His voice is controlled but his eyes betray his shock at my words.

"The only person who decides that is me. I still have that, or are you telling me that too?" I grab my purse and look at everyone around the table. "I'm sorry. It was great to meet you guys, but my asshole says it's time to leave."

I dig my hand into my purse for some cash, but Aaron throws some bills down before I can.

"I can pay for my own dinner."

"And you're not going to." He takes my upper arm in a strong grip and nods to everyone. "I'm sorry about this. That should cover the bill. Have a great night."

I'm pulled, open mouthed, out of the restaurant and into a waiting black car. I snap my jaw shut when he slides in next to me with a slam of the door.

"Back to the hotel, Martin."

I fold my arms over my chest, my head feeling a little fuzzy. Maybe a bottle of wine to myself wasn't the smartest idea I've ever had, but I'll blame Aaron for that. He makes me need to lose myself.

And not in a good way.

Tension bounces between us on the drive back to the hotel, and when we arrive, he all but carries me into the elevator that will take us up to our suite. Still, he doesn't say a word, but the ticking in his jaw tells me just how pissed off he is.

I kick off my shoes inside the suite and chuck my purse onto one of the sofas. No words leave him as I walk into the bathroom and strip off my clothes.

Who the fuck does he think he is? Coming in there and dragging me away like that? What gives him the right to do that?

Oh, that's right. He owns me because he spends his endless amounts of cash on my time. I forgot about the part where I'm supposed to appreciate that gesture.

I scrub my hair and body under the hot spray of the shower, and once I'm clean, I get out, still angry. I'm so angry I can barely fucking think straight.

I towel dry my hair and let it fall around my shoulders and onto the fluffy hotel robe I'm wearing. Argh!

Aaron's sitting on one of the sofas when I leave the bedroom, leaning forward. A beer bottle spins between his fingers, and the wine glass clinks against the side when I set it down.

"I don't think you need any more."

I pour a glass, ignoring his comment, and set the bottle back in the fridge. *Fuck you. Fuck you, fuck you, fuck you.*

I'm being childish and there isn't a single part of me that gives a fuck.

Control is how I live my life, how my days unravel, how I keep sane. I control every single aspect of my life, aside from client preferences. But I'm still free to go where I wish, see who I wish, do whatever the frigging hell I want.

Now? I have no control. All I can control is what I wear each morning, and he can take that from me as easily as he's taken everything else.

"Dayton."

I walk past him. Or I try to. He grabs my hand and pulls the wine glass from it. I hit him with narrowed, angry eyes and yank my hand back.

"What?"

"You're being ridiculous."

I take a deep breath but the bitter laugh escapes me anyway. "I'm being ridiculous? You woke up this morning and decided I should spend every second of my day being your girlfriend. Then you looked for me and dragged me from a place I was comfortable and relaxed in to bring me here, so don't you fucking stand in front of me all righteous and tell me I'm being ridiculous."

"Go to bed. Go to bed and sleep off however much wine you've consumed, and we'll speak in the morning."

"No, we won't." I shake my head. "We speak right the fuck now or the only person I'm speaking to tomorrow is the airline!"

His body goes rigid. Frozen. Still. "What?"

"Oh, you're finally listening to me? Is that what it takes to get my feelings heard, huh? A threat to leave?"

"You're not going anywhere."

"Aren't I? Are you going to stop me?" I spin and he grabs my waist.

"You're not going anywhere," he repeats through gritted teeth.

I shove his arms from me and walk backward. "Then instead of telling me what to do, you're gonna shut the hell up and listen to me!"

"Dayton—"

"Don't Dayton me. Don't Dayton me, sweetheart me. Don't fucking Bambi me!" I point at him. "For the last twelve days, I've done everything you've asked, everything that's been expected. I've put up with your unreasonable demands and your requests disguised as demands and I've been the perfect fucking girlfriend, but I'm done. Unless you listen to me right now, I'm fucking *done!*"

He inhales slowly and runs his hand through his hair. I stare at him, my chest heaving, and wait for him to argue.

"This is because of this morning, isn't it?" His voice is gentle. Soft. Caressing.

"It took you long enough to work it out." I snort. "Yes, it's about this morning. What the fuck, Aaron?"

"I…"

I raise my eyebrows.

"I hate it, Day. How you treat me like any of your clients."

"You are my client!"

"No I'm not!" A vein in his neck bulges and he balls his hands into fist. "Fuck. Can you honestly look at me and say I'm just a fucking client to you? Go on. Do it right now. Look at me and tell me I'm just a normal client."

"You're just a normal client."

"Liar! You're lying to yourself and you're lying to me."

I back away. "The past is in the past. Stop bringing it up."

"I didn't. You did that when you walked into the hotel."

"You *hired* me!" I fist my hands in my hair. "Jesus. What did you want me to do? Walk away?"

"I wish you had. I wish you had, but I'm so glad you didn't."

"How does that even make sense?" Shit! I walk forward and grab my glass, taking two big mouthfuls of wine.

"I don't know. Nothing has ever made sense to me where you're concerned."

"Well join the goddamn club!" I put the glass down and lean my forehead against the wall. "Why did you say it? What you did this morning?"

He sighs heavily. "I already told you. I want you to treat me like *me,* not some asshole you don't know in a hotel room."

"And what about me? What if I don't want that? What if I'm better off with you being my client?"

"You don't mean that."

"I do." I straighten and look him in the eye. I take a deep breath and fight the rollercoaster of emotions riding around my body. "You're better off staying my client. I was better off not even coming here."

"Don't say that. Jesus, Day, don't say it."

"Goddammit, Aaron!" I smack the wall. "Are you only thinking about yourself? All this 'do this,' 'do that' bullshit. Are you only thinking about what you want?"

He says nothing.

"What about what I want, huh? What about if it's hard enough being your girlfriend in public? What if that pretense, knowing how pure the real thing is, is too much? And you want me to do that all the time. Have you even thought about how that feels for me? Have you sat back in your expensive suit and your fancy car and considered for just one second how pretending to be your girlfriend all the time might feel? What it would do to me?"

He shakes his head slowly, letting a long breath escape through parted lips. "No. No, I haven't."

"Why not? Do my feelings mean that little that it doesn't matter to you?"

"Don't you ever fucking say that!" He storms to me and cups my face. "Don't ever say that."

"Then listen to me when I say I can't!" I push his hands from my cheeks. "*I can't.* Okay? Do you hear that? It's not that I won't. I can't. Physically, mentally, emotionally, I can't do that."

"Why?"

His blue eyes are full of anger and pain and heat and what once was.

"I can't fall in love with you," I whisper. "Not again. If I have to pretend all the time, I might just do that."

"Is that such a bad thing?"

"Yes!" I find his eyes and hug myself. My voice increases in volume until I'm shouting so hard my throat hurts. "Yes! I loved you before, and walking away from you destroyed me. I nearly didn't survive you, Aaron. You wrecked me! That summer took every part of me and wound it into something so pure and beautiful, and the day I left, a string holding it together was tugged and I unraveled. Falling in love with you and losing that was losing a part of me. I won't do that again!" I close my eyes and swallow back the moisture in my eyes. The tears. "I won't do it again."

His lips touch mine. Firmly but full of honesty. "You don't have to. You don't ever have to walk away again."

"I do. Call girls don't fall in love."

"Fuck call girls. You're not that. Not deep down." He curves his hand around my neck. "Look at me."

I shake my head.

"Look at me. Please."

The desperate tone of his voice makes my eyes open.

"You're not that person. Not really. You're still my Dayton. You're still the girl I fell in love with who was addicted to vanilla coffee and awed by the Eiffel Tower and loved Bambi with an obsession so unhealthy it rivaled mine with you."

I grab his shirt because I have to if I want to stay on my feet. "I'm not her. I can't even remember who she was."

"I can. I never forgot."

"I hate vanilla coffee, the Eiffel Tower doesn't amaze me now, and I'm not obsessed with Bambi anymore."

"You're still my Dayton. No matter what. You've always been mine."

"No, I'm not. I don't belong to anyone except myself."

His lips crash into mine ferociously. I gasp at the sudden assault of his tongue between my lips, and feel all my resistance leave me for a fleeting moment. Then it's back and I'm pushing at his shoulders, shaking my head, and he's shaking his right along with me.

"You can't fight everything," he whispers. "Stop trying."

"I'm not fighting everything. Just you."

"I am everything, Dayton. Open your eyes and you'll see it."

His mouth silences me again, and this time I melt into him fully. His hand cupping my ass and the other holding my head to his means I'm pressed against him, feeling his cock harden against my lower stomach and my nipples pebble against his chest. He kisses me deeply, his tongue sweeping through my mouth possessively.

We spin and I'm lowered back to the sofa. My body sinks into the plush material, and the hand that was just on my behind creeps up and around my body. Aaron's skin is red hot against mine, his lips even more so as they trail a path down my neck. He tugs at the belt holding my robe closed, and the soft towel falls away, exposing my body.

He draws in a sharp breath, sending bolts down to my core, his eyes focused on my hardened nipples. He lowers his head and takes one in his mouth, his tongue rough against my tender flesh. I arch into him, pushing my breast into his mouth, and he turns his attention to the other.

Every muscle in my pussy clenches at the unexpected invasion of his fingers, and I'm pretty sure I moan into his shoulder. The slow, torturous caress of his fingers inside me combined with the tugging of his mouth on my nipple is overloading me with an overwhelming sensation.

Heat swamps me and I buck my hips, pulling his fingers deeper into me. I don't want to come. Not at all.

Not like this.

"Please," I whisper, burying my fingers in his hair. "Please."

He removes his shirt and pushes his pants down. I wrap my legs around his waist at the feeling of his cock resting against my wet opening.

"You just have to be you." He sucks lightly on my bottom lip. "I don't want the call girl Dayton or the fake girlfriend Dayton. Just be you."

"I never wasn't," I whisper into his mouth.

Aaron slips inside me. He fills me so perfectly and stretches me in a way that makes my whole body ache. He moves slowly, driving his hips gently into me, rolling them with each thrust. Each movement hits me in the right spot.

Each kiss, each rock of our hips, each mingled breath, and each flick of our tongues against the other's helps toward the building pleasure in me.

"Aaron." His name falls from my lips after what seems like a forever of him being inside me.

He takes my mouth roughly. "I can't. I need to come. Fuck."

I tilt my hips up and he hits me deeper. "Harder."

"Jesus, I..." His words are lost as he picks up speed, slamming into me. My head spins with each hit. Sweat slicks my skin and I can't breathe.

I can't breathe for the intensity of the release tightening my body. "Oh, god."

"Let it go." He grazes his teeth down my neck. "Fucking hell, woman! Come now!"

He thrusts into me harder than before. I throw my head back as an orgasm swamps my body. Through the pounding in my ears, I hear Aaron yell my name as he empties himself inside me in hot spurts. My muscles clench around him as we come together, both of us riding on a crazy-intense high.

He murmurs against my neck, unintelligible words, and I let go of his back. I run my hands over the spot I was digging my nails into. I swear I had my hands in his hair minutes ago.

"Come here."

Aaron steps out of his pants and lifts me, staying inside me as he carries me into the bedroom. I cling to him with alternate arms as he takes my robe off.

We fall back onto the bed the way we fell on the sofa, and he rolls us to the side. His arms cocoon me in warmth and comfort, and I snuggle my still-shaking body into his.

He breathes heavily, each exhale ghosting across my hair. I tangle my legs with his and kiss his chest.

"I don't care what you say," he whispers in a shaky voice. "To me, you're still my Dayton. You're still my Bambi."

I hold him tighter and squeeze my eyes shut.

I'm afraid I always will be.

# Chapter Fifteen

Aaron rubs his thumb in lazy circles over the inside of my wrist. There's barely been a moment where he hasn't been touching me this morning. Even through the night, he was there whenever I woke—his arm draped over my stomach, his legs tangled in mine, his chest gently rising and falling beneath my head.

Last night has affected him. I can see it in his eyes and feel it in the way he touches me. Since we woke, limbs entangled, he's treated me like I'll break if his gaze is too sharp or his touch too heavy.

Like if he does a single thing wrong, I'll pick up my cell and call the airline.

Just like I threatened.

And I can't deny that I would. I can't confirm it either, though. I have no idea what I'll do if he pulls that crap again.

He's right. He's not my normal client, and I'm not his normal call girl. That means if I have to treat him like someone more, then he has to do the same for me. He can't demand of me and force me to do something I don't want to do. It means I can fight back and argue, and it means he has to sit down and take it.

Just like a real relationship.

The only reason his bank account is still sending money to Monique's is because it's the only foolproof way to keep me here. I won't run on a job, no matter what turns it's taking.

Even if he cut the money, I'd probably stay.

Aaron Stone is my drug. Since the second I met him, he's been a deliciously and frustratingly addictive part of my life. The highs are sky high, out-of-this-world delirious, and the lows are rock bottom, smack-back-into-reality painful. There is no middle ground—there is only one or the other. He knows no middle ground. All or nothing. That's the way he lives, and it's how he loves.

I chose the all before. I took the all and all the bliss and pain I knew would come with it, because back then, the highs were worth every single drop back down to Earth. It was worth it to be so happy. I flew so high I couldn't see the ground.

Now I'm discovering the middle ground he ignores. I know the other side of the coin, and I know it so intimately I could relive that pain right here, right now.

I don't have a choice on the highs now. He makes them happen and pushes them into my path, and he'd continue to do so no matter where I turned. But the lows…

I have a choice for them. I know I do. In reality, I have a choice for everything. I could leave and have nothing. I could leave the middle ground and go back to my tidy, controlled life in Seattle. I could climb out before I sink too deep.

I could.

The problem is that the highs are worth the inevitable lows. No matter what he says, how he tries to convince me, I know what will happen at the end of this. I know we'll both walk away the way we did once before. We have no other choice.

Just like the first time we met, our lives are too different and so far apart that it would never be anything but a train wreck.

The car stops outside a villa-type building sitting on the edge of a private beach. Large, leafy plants surround it, bathing it in shade, and I know where I'll be spending my day.

Beneath one of those plants.

Aaron opens his door and pulls me along the leather seat. I raise an eyebrow at him and he smirks, helping me out of the car. His fingers stay tightly linked through mine as he leads me into the property.

"You can let me go, you know. I'm not going anywhere." I bump his arm with mine.

"Joel!" he calls, ignoring me. "Is everything ready to go?"

"Aye, boss," he replies in a mild Scottish accent.

"Scottish?" I whisper to Aaron.

"We fly our best suited photographers to the location they're needed. Joel is a master at getting the sultry beach shoots, so he's here for this swimwear shoot."

"Who's the shoot for?"

"Marlena Luiz's new collection. She's used us for every single one, and for her advertising, too. She's one of our biggest clients in South America."

"And you couldn't shoot this in her home country?"

"She didn't want it done in Brazil. She requested Australia." He looks at me, his lips curved. "And when a woman like Marlena Luiz asks for something, she gets it."

"You'll have to introduce me sometime," I mutter. "I'd like to know how that works."

"I heard that." He brushes his lips across my temple. "Come on. I'll introduce you to our models."

I slip my sandals off before stepping onto the white sand. The beach is surrounded by rocks and runs straight out into crystal-clear turquoise water. This place is like a little slice of paradise—the places you see as backdrop for shoots like these and wonder if they're real.

"Dayton, this is Reah." He motions to a gorgeous dark-haired girl. She gives me a wan smile and Aaron turns my attention to her companion. "And this is Derrick."

Derrick gives me a thorough once-over. Aaron's grip on my hand tightens, and Derrick's smile falters when he meets my eyes.

"If you were expecting me to be blushing or ready to drop my panties for you, you'll have to do better than that." I give him my own smile. "And for the record, staring at the boss's girlfriend like you want to bend her over one of those rocks and do her from behind isn't the best way to start your day."

"Or your career." Joel joins us. "Hana, can we get some more makeup over here? And Charlee, Reah's hair isn't right. They want waved, darlin', not crimped."

A flurry of activity descends on the models in front of us. Aaron pulls us back into the house, and his lips capture mine the second we're out of view. He pulls the band from my hair and runs his fingers through it, undoing my braid and leaning me back slightly.

"Most other women would have stood there and waited for me to defend them."

I grin and wipe a smudge of lipstick from his bottom lip. "I'm not most women. And I'm definitely not into having a guy who looks like he's just reached adulthood undress me with his eyes."

"*Most* women would be flattered by that."

"He'd probably be able to handle *most* women." I lift onto my tiptoes and drag his bottom lip between my teeth. "He definitely wouldn't be able to handle me."

"You've got that right." Aaron runs his hands down my body and creeps his fingers beneath the hem of my dress. "I could do with another pair of hands to deal with you."

I smile against his mouth and hear a cough from the doorway.

"Not to interrupt, but we're ready to start."

"Thank you, Joel." Aaron smiles at him and winks at me, wrapping his arm around my shoulders. I reach up and wipe his lip again.

"Red isn't your color."

"Oh, it is. It's my favorite color," he says into my ear. "As long as it comes with you, that is."

"Lips or underwear?"

"We'll arrange both."

I grin and ping my bra strap. "I already did."

He drops his arm, bends back, and lifts my dress. I shriek and jump away, shoving my dress back down.

"So you did." His eyes twinkle. "For what it's worth, I definitely like you in red lace."

"Well keep your like to private, please." I swat his arm and realize this is the first time all day he hasn't been touching me. I spin on the sand.

"What the hell are you doing?"

"Being not touched."

He grabs me and pulls me into him. "Now you're being touched. Deal with it."

"Be quiet. They're trying to shoot." I elbow him and spin so he's holding me from behind.

Reah and Derrick look incredible together. Both of them are dark haired and toned, and they have a chemistry that's palpable from fifty feet away. I can almost see it zinging between them, and I tilt my head to the side.

"Hey, are these guys an item?"

"Not that I know of."

"Would it matter?"

"No. We have couples modeling for us all the time. It's actually preferable because they're already comfortable together."

I nod. "I think they're together."

"Are you a matchmaker now?" Aaron teases.

"No." I snort. "I just have a pair of eyes."

"Smartass," he mutters as Reah claps a hand to her mouth and runs up the beach to the house.

"Reah!" Joel yells. "Where are you going?"

Aaron releases me, and I follow him closer to Joel and Derrick. "What's going on?"

"I know as much as you do, boss," Joel replies.

We all look to Derrick and he shrugs. "No idea."

"Do you want me to go after her?" I touch Aaron's arm. "If she's sick, I'll probably be more useful than you all."

He nods, and I turn to the house, jogging up the beach.

"Reah?" I call, walking through the luxurious building.

"Back here," she groans, followed by the sound of retching.

I cringe and open doors until I find a bathroom. "Are you okay?" I wince at my own stupid question. She's bent over a toilet, shaking. Of course she's not fucking okay.

"I had seafood for dinner last night. It can't have been cooked properly," she answers in a hesitant voice.

"Seafood. Riiight." My eyes find her hand clutched over her belly. "So when is this seafood due? I'd guess in about seven months."

Her head snaps around so quickly it'd spin right round if it could. "What?" Wide brown eyes stare at me.

"Seafood. Everyone uses that as a morning sickness excuse. My friend used it on everyone until she used it on me twice in three days." I wave my hand dismissively and perch on the bathtub. "So when are you due?"

"September," she whispers. "I'm nine weeks."

"Does anyone know?"

She shakes her head.

"It's Derrick's, isn't it?"

"How do you…"

"Call it a hunch." I shrug. "When are you planning on telling him?"

"I don't know." Reah flushes the toilet and hugs herself. "I have to go back out there."

I grab her arm. "Honey, you have to go home and see your doctor, not go out on that beach to model in one-hundred-degree heat."

"I need this job." She closes her eyes.

"And I'll make sure you still get paid for it." I'm bluffing. I can't make that happen. "But you need to be honest with Derrick, your agent, and Aaron. Okay?"

She nods.

"Wait here." I sit her in the kitchen and give her a glass of water. Aaron looks up as I approach, questions in his eyes. "She's not feeling great," I explain, nodding toward the house for him to follow me.

"Give me a second," he says to Derrick and Joel. "Reah. Are you okay?"

Her brown eyes flit to me and I jerk my head.

"Um. I have to see my doctor." She looks away from him. "I can't finish the shoot. I'm sorry."

"Are you sick?"

Her hair flies as she shakes her head. "I'm pregnant."

Aaron stops and looks at me. I suck on the inside of my lip and look away. "Congratulations. I'm assuming your agent doesn't know or he would have informed us."

"He doesn't."

"Jenny, call for a car for Reah and have someone make an appointment with her doctor."

A blond girl pauses, looking between the three of us, and Reah smiles wanly. "I ate some bad seafood last night. I need to see him today."

She scuttles off, a phone already attached to her ear.

Aaron turns back to Reah. "Next time the shoot requirements

involve being directly in a heat wave, at least make us aware of the situation so we can cater for your needs. There should be a doctor here right now."

"I'm sorry," she whispers. "I just… I thought I'd be okay."

Jenny enters the room and holds up five fingers.

"A car will be here in five minutes to take you to your doctor. Please take care of yourself." He pats her hand and leads me back outside.

"Well? Where's my model?" Joel asks.

"She has food poisoning." The lie rolls smoothly from Aaron's tongue. "She's going home."

"Great. That's just fuckin' great. How do I shoot a couple shoot with one half of it?"

"Can't you call someone else in?" I ask.

"Not this late," Aaron sighs, pacing. "It's too short notice. If we don't cancel, someone here will have to step in, and there's no one who can do it."

He stops, and both he and Joel turn to me. I know what they're going to say before they open their mouths, and I shake my head.

"No. Oh, no. I'm not a model." I walk backward.

"You have dark hair and an incredible body. You could stand in for her." Aaron cups my face. "Please, sweetheart. If we have to cancel this shoot, Marlena might never use us again. She doesn't do fuck-ups."

"I'm not a model." I swallow. "I don't do pictures, Aaron. I do…you know."

"And you are amazing at it, but now you need to put that gorgeous body to use in a different way," he pleads quietly. "Please."

I glance over his shoulder to Derrick. "And you're happy for Mr. Baby Daddy over there to rub his body against mine?"

"Not at fucking all," he answers through gritted teeth. "But we need this shoot to go perfectly so I'll have to deal with it."

I close my eyes. I'm not a model. I can barely stand taking a picture for my Facebook profile, let alone professional images to be plastered who the fuck knows where. But he's asking so desperately, actually begging me…

"On one condition."

"Anything."

"Reah still gets paid for the shoot." I look into his eyes. "She needs the money."

Aaron nods without hesitation and kisses me—hard—before waving the team over.

What the hell am I doing?

"Please stop looking at me like you want to dribble chocolate sauce all over my body," I snap.

Derrick grins in a way that I'm sure is supposed to be sexy but does nothing for me. "We're supposed to be lusting after each other."

"I think you left the 'supposed' at home." I close my mouth as Joel yells for him to thread his fingers through my hair, pull my head back, and kiss my neck.

Oy vey.

He does as instructed, and I try to play the part, to get into it, but I can't. And when he kisses me a little too enthusiastically, I shove him off of me.

"Do that again and I'm gonna slap it right out of you!" I point in his direction.

"We're done here!" Aaron yells, moving forward. Joel's annoyed cries are drowned out by him. "There's no chemistry. Derrick, you'll be paid in full, but you can go. It's not working with the two of you."

Derrick shrugs, shoots me a wink, and saunters off. What a fucking jerk.

"What are we gonna do now?" Joel shouts. "Two models and a non-model and the only one left is the non-model!"

I put my hands on my hips. "Hey! You forced me into this."

"And you are fuckin' great, but not when you're working with a dick like Derrick," he responds. "I'm just wondering where the hell I'm getting a male model from now."

"You don't need one." Aaron pulls his shirt over his head. "Do you have a second pair of those shorts?"

A girl from wardrobe nods and runs off.

"What the hell are you doin'?"

Aaron puts his arms out. "I'm being your model."

"You're the boss!" Joel and I reply in unison.

"You don't model. You order them around," I remind him.

He takes the shorts from the girl and walks to the house. "Don't model. Not can't. Don't."

Two minutes later, he appears, clad in the shorts the same style as Derrick's, and approaches me. I give him my best 'not impressed' look.

"If I didn't know any better, I'd say you set this up."

"Good thing you know better." He takes my hands and pulls me toward the water. "And now you can relax with me."

He's right. Derrick had me wound so tight I was at risk of snapping, and all because of his asshole attitude.

"Right. Can we finish this shoot now?" Joel calls. "I want you two to be sexy. I want you to have lust—so much lust we'll all leave here thinking you'll be making out in the back of the car on the way back to Sydney."

"I'll do him one better," Aaron mutters, pulling me close to him. "We'll go for so much lust that there will be absolutely no doubt we'll be fucking in the back of the car on the way to Sydney."

The huskiness of his voice combined with his hand curving down my body tugs at every part of my body in sexual awareness. *No problem.* I hear quiet snaps from Joel's camera as Aaron teases my body into various poses, each one sparking desire and need across my skin.

And when he gets onto one knee and slides me along his thigh and drops his lips to my neck, making me drop my head back and tangle my fingers in his hair, that desire goes deeper.

Every part of me hums with wanting him. My nipples harden inside my—thankfully—padded bikini top, and I'm grateful for the sea sweeping over my legs, drenching my bikini bottoms. God knows my core is aching so much, my clit throbbing so hard, my arousal would be evident in minutes.

"I love this," Aaron whispers in my ear, leaning over me, all gorgeous and bronzed and powerful.

"Love what?" I breathe, gazing into his eyes.

He holds the connection for a moment and drops his forehead to mine. "Knowing you're turned on right now in front of all these people. I love knowing I've done that to you, and that even though there are twenty sets of eyes on us, you still can't hold it back."

The sea washes over me, wetting my hair and coating my body in a salty sheen. Another wave comes up, and as it washes away again, Aaron pushes his lips against mine. My head falls back against the sand, my leg bending at his side, and I forget about the shoot.

Forget about the audience, the eyes on us, the expectations from this. All I can feel and see and hear are his lips on mine, his short breaths mingling with my own, and my heart pounding in my ears. I quietly moan into his mouth at the feel of his tongue sweeping across mine.

He pulls back and tugs me up, his breathing labored. My own is heavy and full of want. My body is on fire with needing him, and I have to wonder if he has a switch for it. I don't know how easily he does it, but my nipples are begging for his tongue to circle them and my pussy is practically fucking screaming to be filled by him.

"Holy shit," one of the wardrobe girls cries. "I think *I* need a make-out session in the back of a car. What do you say, Joel?"

Aaron smiles against my jaw.

"Anytime, Annabelle. Anytime," Joel responds, coming closer with his camera. "You two are fucking magical. Ms. Luiz is going to be one happy lady when she sees this."

I smile and rest my nose alongside Aaron's. He opens his eyes and I get lost in a sea of blue, completely captivated in him in this moment. Still with desire humming through my veins.

He runs his thumb along my jaw, and my lips part. I curve my fingers around his neck, and I nearly forget we're not alone.

"Perfect. Hold it there."

I couldn't move away if I tried.

"And we're done." Joel stands and claps once. "Unravel yourselves and come see."

Everyone's eyes are suddenly away from us, and Aaron helps me stand. "You're a natural," he murmurs, kissing me softly.

I smile and shake my head. A towel is handed to me and I wrap it around my body, leaving his arms to find Joel in the house.

He pats the stool next to him in the kitchen as he uploads the pictures to his laptop. One by one, pictures flick across the screen too quickly to see. By the time Aaron joins us, they're all on there.

"Don't need these," Joel grumbles, deleting all the images of Derrick and Reah and Derrick and me. "Here we go. Let's see what we have."

A large image of me and Aaron fills the screen and my jaw drops. It's not bad—far from it. It's amazing. And every one after is even more so. We look so natural, so together, so desperate for one another.

Each hand is perfectly placed, our eyes are connected even

when they're closed, and pure, unadulterated lust is written all over our faces.

"Brilliant. These are brilliant." Joel flicks through them. "It's not often one gets to shoot their boss—in a photographical sense or otherwise—but this? This needs to happen again." He shuts the top down and sighs happily. "You two. Magical. Amazing. Wow."

"Thanks, Joel." Aaron shakes his hand.

"I'm gonna pack up and go and find that Annabelle." He winks and walks back through the beach.

Aaron and I sit in silence until everyone leaves. His eyes burn into me the whole time, doing nothing to expel the lingering arousal in my body. The fierceness in them makes me feel naked, completely exposed to him.

"Get dressed," he orders me. "Our car is waiting."

I take my clothes from him. "No one else is here, are they?"

"We're alone."

Good. I drop the towel and unclip the bra-style bikini top. My body heats at the way Aaron's eyes roam over my body, and I crook my fingers in the sides of the bright bottoms.

"Turn around."

I quirk an eyebrow but do as he says. My back is to him as I bend forward and shimmy the fabric down my legs. I step out of it and reach for my dress, stopping when I feel his hands on my hips.

He slides one around to my front and dips it between my legs. "Still so wet," he murmurs into my neck.

I reach around and brush my fingers across his hard cock. He shudders, and I peel back the wet material clinging to him to touch him. "Still so hard," I respond in kind.

He moves his hand so quickly a cold breeze caresses my sex. "Put your dress on and get in that car."

I pull it over my head and tuck my underwear in my purse. "Sex in the back seat?"

Aaron buttons his pants, his shorts discarded on the floor, and follows me out. He doesn't answer until he opens the door for me.

"No, a good hard fuck that will have you screaming my name by the time we reach the city. Several times over."

I hold my breath until he joins me in the car and closes the partition. The engine rumbles as we pull away from the villa, and I look over at him.

"You left our stuff on the floor."

"The villa belongs to me. They'll be washed and returned tomorrow."

He grabs my thighs and pulls me to him. I straddle his lap, sinking my fingers into his hair as his sink inside me. I exhale heavily at the feeling, our lips meeting.

"Should have you bare beneath all of your dresses," he breathes. "I love how easy it is to touch you."

"Only if you follow the same rule."

He laughs, taking his fingers from me and releasing his erection. His swollen head rubs against me, and he teases my opening by dipping in partially then slipping up to nudge my clit.

"If you'll take me this easily, I'll forget pants every fucking day." Our mouths meet in a feverish kiss and I whimper, pushing down against him.

"There's nothing easy about this."

He eases into me, going as deep as he can, drawing a breathy moan from me, and holds me against him. "This is easy, Dayton, but only because my need to be inside you is stronger than all else. I want to slide down this seat and lick you from below while you ride my tongue, and I want to tease you to your release with my fingers flicking between your nipples and your clit, but I *need* to fuck you." He rocks our hips, stretching me and filling me so deeply there isn't a part of his cock not inside me. "And savor it, because the next time I'll be inside you will be in Italy, and I won't be doing it this way. I'll be spreading you on the bed and devouring every inch of you with every part of me, worshipping you, and I'll be making love to you."

"Oh…"

He kisses my neck, lifting my hips and dropping them back down. Our movements become more frantic, his grip tighter on my hips, mine tugging his hair.

"But right now…" He stares into my eyes, pushing himself right into me. " Right now, I'm going to fuck you until your throat is sore from screaming my name."

And he does. He pounds into me relentlessly until I tumble over the edge, his name leaving me in a series of desperate cries.

And he doesn't stop.

And when he yells his own release, I go again, screaming until I'm sure everyone in Sydney can hear it.

# Chapter Sixteen

Milan. A beautiful city in a country that values love above all else.

I walk around the extensive suite. The outside wall is exactly like the one in Vegas – where it's wall-to-wall windows. I can stand against it, my body flattened against the coolness of the glass, and see the whole of the city. As the sun rises, I can run my eyes along the skyline and see every inch of the gorgeous, romanticized city that surrounds me.

And I do. I lean into the glass being warmed by the sun and flatten my hands, spreading my fingers wide. I breathe in deeply, as if the Italian air creeping in on a breeze through the bedroom window can clear my head. As if the incredible view before me can wash away all my thoughts and replace them with a sense of wonderment and awe. As if I can forget the *feelings* and just enjoy Italy.

If. If, if, if, *if*. Fucking if.

My life has been one big goddamn 'if' since Aaron Stone walked back into it. Everything I planned and everything I thought I knew would happen has been ripped away and torn into a thousand pieces. The certainty I prided myself on has been worn down, stripped back, destroyed. Now everything about me is uncertain.

How I'll feel tonight, tomorrow, next week. What I'll do when we get to Paris. What I'll do when this trip is over. How I'll feel. What I'll want. Where I'll go.

I know none of it and I can't even begin to contemplate it. I never thought I'd see Aaron again, and when I did, pulling away that certainty, he made me his client. I let go of the freedom and ignored my gut. Then he didn't want to be my client anymore, and in one traitorous beat of my heart, I agreed.

I agreed to be us. And that's the problem. Us is so uncertain. Us always has been. Even the first time around, we were uncertain and impulsive and surprising. This time is no different. Each touch, kiss, whispered word… They're all spur of the moment.

I don't like spur of the moment.

A spur-of-the-moment phone call and job are what got me in this emotional fucking mess.

"Sometimes I look at you and wonder if you're really here or if I'm imagining it again."

I turn at the sound of his voice. "Again?"

He rubs his wet hair with a towel and paces to the kitchen. "Teenage girls aren't the only ones who get lost in dreams and wake up wondering if they were real or not. I did that plenty of times after Paris."

"You dreamed of me?" My lips twitch.

"Dreamed of you, saw you in places you weren't, thought I was hearing your voice shout my name across the street." His blue eyes pierce mine. "What? You never did that?"

"Never."

"Liar."

"I didn't!"

He walks to me, his lips twisted in a smirk. "I don't believe you."

"You don't have to believe me." I walk backward, holding my arms up. There's a hint of mischief in his eyes, one I recognize, one that sends promises of forever flooding through my body like they were whispered yesterday. "Aaron."

"Admit it." He stalks me, coming closer.

"There's nothing to admit."

He grabs me and throws me on the sofa. I laugh as he lowers himself over me, eyes sparkling, mouth grinning. "Admit it, or I'll tickle."

"Tickle? Mr. Serious can tickle?"

He lays his fingers at my side in a threat. "Every part of you."

I push at his chest through my laughter, and he makes good on that threat. I squeal and arch my body into him to make him let go. "Crap, stop! Aaron, stop it!"

"Only if you admit it."

"You're a…grown man," I breathe, squirming. "You don't need the validation from teenaged memories to prove our love was real!"

"Yes. I do." He covers my mouth with his in one swift movement, plunging his tongue between my lips. His fingers still, and I bury mine in his hair as he continues a delicious assault of my mouth. "And 'was'? No, Bambi. There's no 'was' about it. When you have a love that runs as deep as ours, it's always alive and very, very real. It doesn't die just because time passes."

I draw in a deep breath. I know this. Of course I do. The kind of love that spreads through your body, possessing and controlling it, doesn't just die. It keeps living the way a broken heart keeps beating.

"Yes," I whisper into his mouth. "I did it. I looked over my shoulder every day hoping you'd appear from behind a tree. I heard your voice whispering my name whenever there was silence, and I felt your touch when no one else was around. And I saw you everywhere. You were every tall guy with dark hair, and I called your name and waited for them to turn, each time hoping it was you." I grip his hair tighter and squeeze my eyes shut.

"And then?"

"And then when everything changed, I stopped wanting to see you but kept living in a hopeful fear you'd walk around the next corner. I needed to see you, but I didn't need you to see me the way I am."

He brushes his thumb across my cheek. "Why?"

"Because out of the handful of people whose opinions mattered, yours was always the most important."

"Then you rounded the corner and I saw you anyway." He softly kisses me again , a touch filled with truth. "And all I see is what I saw then. A beautiful woman with dreams she doesn't think she can fulfill."

"That's because happiness always comes with a price."

He pulls me up and wraps his arms around me. "Lucky for you, I can pay it."

I smile into his chest and shake my head. *You already are.*

"And the price for today's happiness is a coffee, and you're paying." He turns me in the direction of the kitchen area and pats my butt.

I shoot him a look over my shoulder. "What if I don't want to pay?"

His blue eyes twinkle with a lusty mischief. "Then I'll lock you in the suite."

"What exactly will that achieve?"

"I have no idea, but the thought of you being locked in here all day is giving my cock ideas."

I press the button on the machine and lean on the island, my arms squeezing my breasts together. His gaze flicks from them to my mouth and then to my eyes.

"And you can tell your cock its ideas are completely useless considering it'll be with you in a meeting all day. You can lock me in this suite, Mr. Stone, but if any orgasms happen, you won't be a participant. They'll be of my own making."

The mischief dissipates from his stare, morphing into a dark heat that sends shivers through my body. "Of your own making?"

I dip my finger into the sugar pot and lick it off. "I'm quite adept at providing my own orgasms. I've done it plenty of times. I know all the right spots."

He crosses the room in a few quick strides. He flattens his hands against the counter and leans forward until we're barely a breath apart. "Let's get something clear, Dayton," he rasps. "If anyone makes you come, it'll be me. And if I decide you can do it yourself, you'll be doing it while I watch you."

The idea of his eyes fixed on me while I touch myself makes me ache.

"Are we clear?"

I lick my lips.

"I said"—he leans in closer, his lips moving against mine as he speaks—"are we clear?"

"Still a little murky."

His fingers curl around my neck and he holds my face to his. He kisses me slowly. Deeply. Intensely. A ball of need coils low in my stomach, tightening until it's at the very brink of exploding. It hovers there, growing as Aaron's kiss teases and taunts me.

He pulls away briefly before returning to my mouth and dropping a long, lingering kiss there. "My coffee."

I grab the side of the counter until my woozy, heady feeling from him passes. *Holy shit, the man can kiss.* The tongue strokes, the pressure, the twitch of his fingers on my skin…

"Is apparently yours." He shoves his jacket on and pockets his phone. "You," he murmurs, rounding the island and cupping my chin, "have distracted me, and now I'm going to be late."

"Better late than never."

"I told you you're my biggest temptation." One more kiss. "There's a car waiting for you downstairs when you want it. Just call the concierge and they'll bring it around."

"Why on Earth do I want a car?" I frown, watching him cross to the door.

"I'm not locking you in here. Not today," he adds with a wicked grin. "Go and explore. You have the whole day to yourself."

"I don't want it," I respond. "The car. How can I explore if I'm stuck inside a fancy-ass car?"

"You have a point. By the way, I thought you'd say that, so I programmed the concierge's number into your cell in case you get lost. He'll arrange for you to be picked up wherever you are."

"In case I get lost?" I raise an eyebrow.

He winks. "Have fun, Bambi. Oh, and keep your eyes to yourself. I know how you like concierges."

"Gosh, no concierge, no touching myself... Is there anything I can do?"

"Yes. Me. Tonight." He opens the door and walks through it before I can respond.

I blink after him for a second then pour a cup of coffee. The clock reads eight a.m., and I should be tired from the flight, but I'm not. I never really adjusted to Australian time, so being in a time zone somewhat closer to home is sitting right with my body.

I hug the mug and stroll through the suite, my eyes gazing out of the windows. I have a city to explore.

The *Duomo di Milano* is by far the most incredible building I've ever laid eyes on. It stands proudly in the Square, ornately designed spires and window decorating the majestic cathedral. From the huge iron doors and carved archways over each window to the intricate patterns wrapping the building, it's amazing. Just amazing.

It felt like I was standing in front of the Eiffel Tower again, wowed by one of man's greatest creations. I felt the same rush of wonderment and excitement at what I was seeing, and it's something I feel now as I sit outside a small café with the best coffee I've ever tasted.

I couldn't even go in and explore the inside of the *Duomo*. All I could do was stand in front of it and stare at it like a teen girl at a One Direction concert. I may even have wanted to scream in delight at one point, so completely overcome with the beauty of it.

Still, something was missing.

I sip my coffee and watch the Italian people breeze past on the sidewalk. Some are chatting hurriedly into cell phones pinned to their ears, others are linking arms and laughing, and a few are coaxing young children into following them. The fluid, relaxing language surrounds me, and I sigh.

He was missing.

The last time I felt the way I did while staring at the *Duomo* was the day I met Aaron. It was the day my wonderment at something manmade changed into amazement at someone naturally created. It was the day an all-consuming relationship began, although neither of us actually knew it.

I wrap my arms around my stomach and raise my face to the sun as I walk away from the café. How different my life would be if we'd never met... How empty it would be. I'd never have felt the heart-pounding warmth of real love or the heated breathlessness of heavy lust.

I'd never have felt the earth-shattering reality of heartbreak either.

And I wouldn't be here, in Italy, wondering if the way my stomach flips when he walks into a room is a reaction to something I know. Something comfortable. Something familiar.

Or if it's an automatic reaction that will always happen because my body recognizes something I choose to ignore.

I wander the streets in a contemplative haze, those thoughts spinning around and around in my head. Spinning and somersaulting and beating at the corners of my mind. Demanding to be listened to, demanding to be answered, demanding to be known.

The hustle and bustle of the outlet stores outside the *Galleria Vittorio Emmanuelle II* drags me back out of my own mind. Shiny shoes and purses and cut-priced dresses grab hold of my attention and I gravitate toward them. I might not have planned to go shopping, but the concierge recommended this as the best place, complete with the original Prada store.

And a girl can look. And touch. And dream.

Maybe even buy if it can be kept a secret…

I shake my head at the absurd thought. Aaron would have a fit and burst the seams of his suit if he found that out—and I have no doubt he would.

The tiny stores are full of designer apparel. The only difference is the price—and it's a big difference. A black knee-length dress with a pink patterned flirty skirt catches my eye. I run my finger down the seam and pull it out.

I nibble on the inside of my lip. It's gorgeous. My size. A dress that could be dressed up or down depending on the occasion. With the pink heeled pumps across the store…

It's a Paris kind of dress.

Taking a deep breath and refusing to linger on that last thought, I hold it to my chest and find the pink shoes. They're my size, and there's no way I can't not buy them. This is one of the crazy little 'fate' moments Liv mutters about that I've never believed in.

Mostly because she talks about love and fate. This is shoes and fate. Totally different ballgame.

I take them to the counter and the olive-skinned girl behind it beams at me. I ignore the way my stomach rolls at the cost and reach for my card.

But it's not mine I find. There's a black American Express card with a bit of paper wrapped around it.

*I know you too well.*
*A*

A smile wins out over the pursing of my lips, and I hand her that card—begrudgingly—since mine is nowhere in sight. *That asshole…*

I leave the store with a small smile, despite being caught. I'll let him have that simply because I have no other choice, but he's not getting away with it that easily.

You're sneaky, Mr. Stone. Nice move.

I tuck my cell back into my pocket and enter the *Galleria. And holy crap!* Is there a place in this city not completely shrouded in beauty? The glass ceiling stretches high above me, and I'm surrounded by the elite shops, old and at home in this Italian city.

Prada looms before me, and there's something magical about knowing I'm standing in front of the very first store. Chanel might be my preference of label, if only because of the country in which it started, but Prada is a close second.

My feet pull me toward the store like a moth flies toward a light. There's no hesitation… Wait, can I fit anything else in my closet? Or my suitcases? Never mind. I don't plan to buy. I plan to look and touch and dream.

I think this over and over. *Look and touch and dream. Look and touch and dream. Look and touch and dream.*

Yep. I will behave, especially since I don't have my card. As much as Aaron—and Monique—says that he has to pay for everything, I disagree. The strong, independent woman in me balks at the very idea.

Clothes. Everywhere. Shoes. Purses. Coats. *Dresses.*

Oh. This store is like a little slice of heaven set in a very large pie.

"*Mi scusi, signora,*" a gentle voice says from behind me. "*Sei Signora* Black?"

My eyes widen, and I turn to face a young blond-haired woman. "I'm Miss Black, yes, but I'm afraid I don't speak Italian."

She beams. "No problem. We have a message for you from *Signor* Stone."

I think my eyebrows just met my hairline. "You do?"

"*Si.*" She nods. "He ask that we tell you to purchase anything you like and charge the account."

Of course he did. Why wouldn't he? And more to the point, why wouldn't he have an account at Prada?

"Right." I laugh uncomfortably. "Please don't think I'm being rude—that isn't my intention—but how did you know it was me?"

Her smile widens a little. "He send us a picture this morning."

Of course he fucking did.

"He say you're very important to him."

I'm gonna kill him.

"Well, thank you…" I glance at her tag. "Adelina. I'm just here to browse, so I won't be needing Mr. Stone's account today."

"Well, um, *Signora* Black, he ask you don't leave without something."

I take a deep breath and note the wringing of her hands. She's clearly new and not cut out for this job.

"Okay. Could I speak to your manager?"

She nods and disappears in the back of the store. What the fuck? Is this real? Walk into a random store and get told I *have* to buy something on someone else's account?

I pull out my cell and open the unread message.

Surprise…

Surprise? I'll give you a fucking surprise next time you're naked and turn your back! I fire the message back, and the response is immediate.

Enjoy Prada… Their SS14 collection is beautiful.

Asshole.

I shove it back in my purse in time to notice the tall, dark-haired woman approaching me. She's as thin as a stick and pinches her lips when she looks at me. I know exactly what she's thinking— I'm not what she expected.

God forbid anyone with a couple of extra pounds on their ass should walk into Prada and ask for the manager.

"*Signora* Black, how can I help you?" The manager clasps her hands in front of her stomach.

I meet her mildly disapproving look. Friendly lady. "Adelina here has just informed me I'm not to leave without a purchase on Mr. Stone's account. Is this correct?"

"*Si*. He called this morning and was very specific."

"I understand. Do you have somewhere I can go to call him in private?"

She nods and leads me to the staff area at the back without a word. She pauses at the door and looks me over, her dark eyes calculating. "Forgive me for saying so, but you aren't what I expected."

"Excuse me?" I spin, but she's already gone.

If it's really about the ass thing, she could do with a candy bar or two.

I dial Aaron's number and hope he picks up. I don't have any of the office numbers—I don't need them. I don't usually have to call him to chew out his ass about this kind of crap.

"Find anything nice?"

"In Prada? So far all I have is a shy sales girl and an absolute bitch of a manager who has a vendetta about the extra three pounds on my ass."

His laugh warms my annoyed body. "I like those extra three pounds."

"That's where you're supposed to say, 'Extra pounds? What extra pounds?'" I snort. "That's not the point. I'm not allowed to leave without buying something?"

"Oh, good. They told you."

"Uh, yeah, they told me, and I'm pissed."

He says nothing, a heavy silence lingering between us.

"You don't get to do that, Aaron." And it clicks. "Holy shit. You told the concierge to send me here, didn't you?"

"No. I merely suggested it in case you should ask what's worth seeing. Telling you was his choice, Dayton."

"Don't blame this on the concierge with the nice ass."

"Watch your mouth, woman."

"Then don't piss me off." I grit my teeth. "What if I don't like anything here?"

"Then you can buy the fitted black dress."

I'm not even going to think about how he knows a specific item. "It sounds like you've already decided for me."

"It's reserved for you."

"You're a presumptuous bastard, aren't you?"

"She's learning." He chuckles. "Get the dress."

"No."

"Get the fucking dress, Dayton. End of discussion."

"And if I don't?" I click my tongue.

"I'll arrange for it to be delivered to the hotel tomorrow. You may as well save me the trouble since you're there."

I exhale loudly and rub my temple. "Controlling isn't a good look on you."

I hang up and drop my phone into my purse. Again. I'm like a jack-in-the-box where he's concerned. The Jack is my temper and he's the lever, winding and winding and winding until I snap.

"I'll take the black dress Mr. Stone reserved," I say through a tightened jaw. Fucking asshole. I'll make him pay for this—and not in money.

"*Si.* He has fabulous taste, *Signor* Stone, does he not?" the manager questions as she wraps it in tissue paper in a box.

"Excellent." I fake a smile. "What did you mean a moment ago? I wasn't what you were expecting?"

Silently, she puts the lid down and slips it into a bag. "The dress is charged to *Signor* Stone's account. I'm sure you will look wonderful, *signora.*"

"What did you mean?" My voice is harder as I push it.

She gives me a smile, one lined with the bitchiness she hasn't hidden since she approached me. "Forgive me. It was a slip of the tongue."

She disappears, leaving me staring after her in confusion.

I stir when the bed dips next to me.

"Shh." Aaron's breathy whisper caresses my cheek. "It's me."

I yawn, rubbing my eyes. "What time is it?"

"One a.m."

"You're late."

"I know. I'm sorry." He pulls me into him.

He wraps his arms around me. My body is flush against his, and I snuggle into his hold. Our feet tangle together and my hands wrap around his arms. Warmth spreads through me at the touch of his lips on my head, and I smile.

"What are you doing?"

"Holding you. That's all."

I move deeper into his touch. "I'm still mad, you know." I yawn again.

"I know, Bambi. I know." He buries his face in my hair. "Sleep now."

# Chapter Seventeen

Tingles shoot through my body. I roll onto my back, open my heavy-lidded eyes, and stare into a pair of bright blue ones.

"Hi."

"Hi," Aaron mutters back, dropping his face to mine. His lips sweep across mine softly but firmly, and he sinks his fingers deep into my hair.

"What time is it?"

"Six." He drops kisses along my jaw and onto my neck.

"Early."

"Mhmm." He continues his downward journey with his mouth, pausing at my breasts. He cups one with his hand and runs his nose along the side of it. "Beautiful."

The tingles turn to a simmering heat when he takes my nipple in his mouth and rolls his tongue around it. His teeth graze it and he sucks lightly, easing the sting, and moves to the other. I push my head back.

"Is this how you wake a girl up?"

"It's how I wake you up." He flips on top of me and his large erection presses against the lace at my core.

The simmer turns to a boil, blood pumping through my body at a lightning speed. Desire floods through me at the feel of his lips on my skin and his thumbs ghosting over my hardened nipples. My hips push into him, my body craving him and the inevitable release he'll give.

"I forgot how impatient you are in the morning." He licks a slow trail from my breastbone to my panty line, his tongue dipping into my belly button as he goes.

"I don't like being... Oh, shit!"

I gasp at the fleeting touch of his tongue hitting my clit through the lace.

"What were you saying?" His nose brushes along the inside of my thigh, and he bends my legs. He hooks his finger in the side of my panties and pauses before moving them. "Hm?"

"Saying? Who was saying anything?" I crook my neck and look down at him. Air fills my lungs at my long, needing breath. Fuck. Aaron Stone's face between my legs is about the sexiest thing. Fucking ever.

"Good girl."

He moves the lace and runs his tongue along my pussy in one long, caressing sweep. The sensations fly everywhere as he takes up a slow assault with his mouth. The deep, probing movements of his tongue and lips are akin to the way you'd give a leaving lover a final kiss. They're long and slow and...

A moan echoes around the room. I shudder when he slips his tongue up me, and my muscles clench involuntarily. His muffled groan follows the moan I know came from me.

"You can't do that, Dayton," he says and closes his lips around my clit. He sucks hard, pleasure filling my body. "It makes me think about being inside you too much."

"Not a bad thing," I breathe, closing my eyes.

"Soon." He probes my thighs with his fingertips. "Look at me."

I crane my neck up, my lids heavy from the constant flooding of pleasure. They drop, and Aaron pinches my ass.

"Keep your eyes open. I want to watch you come on my tongue."

*Oh, sweet fuck.* His words send my body into overdrive, and it isn't long before he's holding my hips down. I find his eyes after he snaps my name for a third time, and looking into them is like being held captive. I couldn't fight it if I wanted to, but looking at him, I know I was wrong. There is something sexier than Aaron Stone's face between my legs.

The sexiest thing in this fucking world is his face between my legs while he explores me with his tongue.

I explode with that final thought, and he works me through it. He doesn't pull his mouth from me until I'm done and my hips are still again.

He pulls my legs up, lifts me, and pushes us up the bed. My back rests against the headboard, and he holds me above him as he frees his cock from his boxers. He fills me in one swift movement, and I throw my head back at the sudden stretching of my channel.

My muscles wrap around him tightly, holding him inside me, easing with each gentle thrust of his hips. He fills me so completely and pushes me to the absolute limit of what I can take that bringing me to the edge is so easy. So quick.

And he's so in tune with my body that when he feels me getting close, he distracts me with his mouth.

"Not yet," he says into our kiss. "You're not allowed."

"Controlling bastard," I gasp, my body trembling with the force of holding back.

He laughs and pushes deep into me. A string of swear words leaves my mouth, and I clamp down on his cock. Fuck if I can hold this back any longer.

"Dayton," he grinds my name out, his thrusts gaining speed. "Hold it!"

"I can't!" I yell. My head is rocking side to side and my whole body is locked in tension. I can't hold it. Not anymore.

I meet his thrust with my pussy muscles as tight as I can make them and slam down onto him. He yells his release as my orgasm finally rockets through my body, my limbs trembling in a blissful rush. I feel him come inside me in hot spurts, and I feel his hands at my hips holding me to him.

"Jesus," he breathes, burying his face into my neck. "Really couldn't hold back, could you?"

I shake my head. "And I wasn't going alone."

His lips touch my skin. "No. You weren't."

He wraps his arms around my body, and I hook my feet together behind his back. He's still hard inside me, and as I sigh into his hair, I'm struck by a barrage of overwhelming feelings.

Of fulfillment. Of happiness. Of belonging.

Of completeness.

"Shower," Aaron orders, moving back and pulling me with him. He carries me into the bathroom as I'm laughing into his shoulder and gets in the shower before turning on the water. Ice-cold water sprays over us and I scream, squirming to get away from it.

His laugh washes over me the way the warming water does. "Just a little cold water, Day."

"Put me down now," I sigh, pressing my hands on his shoulders.

Aaron shakes his head and pushes me against the wall. "I'm not done with you yet." He rocks his hips against me. His cock hardens immediately and hits *that* very tender spot with his next thrust.

"Again?" My fingers find his hair again and wind themselves in it.

"Oh, Dayton. If you think I'll ever get enough of you, you're sorely mistaken."

"But we just—"

He silences me with a kiss as demanding as the thrusts of his cock inside me. "I love it when you come. I love the sounds you make and the way you feel. If I could spend all day playing with your body and making you come, I would. So now, when I have the chance to make it happen again, I'm going to."

I cry out at a long, slow ease into me.

"I'm going to send you into a crazy fucking oblivion every chance I get because I need you to know what you do to me. You take me over until there's nothing left but you." His grip on me tightens as his hips move faster, his gentle thrusts of earlier now hard pounds. "This is what you do to me, Dayton. You make me fucking crazy."

I pant at his frantic movements, my breath mingling with his, and stare into his eyes as I feel a third orgasm build inside. "Take me there." I seal my lips over his. "To that crazy fucking oblivion."

He does. I fall apart in his arms yet again, his release seconds behind me, and collapse against him. After a minute of languid kisses he pulls out of me, leaving me with the same sense of emptiness that always accompanies that action.

We wash each other in the shower, something more intimate than I'm ready for but so right in this moment. He massages my head as he works in the shampoo and threads his fingers through my hair as he strokes conditioner through it.

He dries me with a towel and wraps me in a robe before leading me back to the bed. I pull the covers and smile sleepily at him.

"You really know how to wake a girl up."

"So you've said." Aaron smiles and rests his nose alongside mine.

"Yeah, I mean it this time." I grin, brushing the backs of my fingers along his cheek. "Did you say it was six in the morning?"

"It was. Now it's past seven, and I have to get ready. I have a meeting at eight."

I accept his gentle kiss and nod. "When will you be back?"

"Not until late again. I'm sorry I'm leaving you to see the city alone."

I shrug. "It's okay. I actually enjoyed it yesterday, barring obvious things. I'm sure I can find something to do today—without any suggestions from the concierge." I give him a pointed look.

He laughs and pulls on some pants. "What were you thinking?"

"I don't know. I was going to decide when I woke up, but I was distracted by someone."

"Oh, well. What about an art museum? I lost you in the *Louvre* more than once."

He really does remember everything.

"Maybe. Where do you recommend?"

He raises his eyebrows.

"I thought we'd cut out the middle man. I know how you hate concierges, especially ones with nice butts."

"Should I be offended you're mentioning the concierge's ass after fucking me?"

"Passing comment." I snuggle beneath the covers. "Well?"

"*Pinacoteca di Brera.* Call me when you want to go and I'll have a car take you. It's a few miles from here." He stills before knotting his tie. "Concierge cut," he adds on a mutter.

I grin. "You sounded like an Italian when you said that."

"Said what? *Pinacoteca di Brera?*"

"Yep. Oh, wait. Let me guess—you speak Italian as well as French?"

He buttons his jacket and looks at me with sparkling eyes. "*Si.*"

"Of course you speak the two most romantic languages in the world." I roll my eyes.

His deep laugh comforts me and he walks to the bed. He bends down, placing his lips near my ear. "A language is only romantic if you believe in romance itself," he whispers. "And I do."

"Maybe I do."

"*Forse il tuo forse non è sufficiente quando i tuoi occhi mi lasciano senza fiato e il tuo tocco mi fa sentire vivo. Non quando l'amore che abbiamo avuto è bollente sotto la superficie. Non quando sono così pronta a permettere al mio amore per te di consumare me ancora una volta.*" He kisses my cheek and strolls from the room.

"What does that mean?"

"When you get there, I'll tell you."

The door closes on his words, and I close my eyes on a huff.

If I had enough energy to get up, I'd throw another mug at him.

I sit back on the plush sofa and prop my feet on the coffee table. The *Pinacoteca di Brera* art museum is a full day out for someone like me—someone who can meander casually through endless hallways of paintings for hours. Surrounded by both natives and tourists, I was lost in a sea of awed eyes and bored yawns.

The paintings should have taken me away. The crowds that walked the hallways with me, alive with hushed chatter, should have pulled me into the environment in its fullest, but they didn't. The pictures didn't give me a wondered escape from reality. All I could think of every time someone yawned was Aaron.

The way he used to grab my hand and fake one, begging to leave the *Louvre*. The way he used to grumble in my ear as I dragged him from room to room. The way he used to groan whenever I asked to go back.

And the way he always, always used to go with me, even though he hated it.

I'm lonely.

I'll admit it. Being here with him but not having him around is harder than I thought it would be. This is what I wanted. I wanted to spend as little time with him as possible to protect my heart and keep my sanity intact. But now that I have it, I don't want it.

I want him to sigh in my ear and mumble in a bored tone as I gaze longingly at a picture. I want him to wrap his fingers around mine and pull me through the gallery quickly. And I want him to stop my yelling at him by silencing me with a kiss.

I want everything I can't have.

Everything that's addictive and beautiful and inspiring. The things that make you wake with a laugh and fall asleep with a smile. The tender touches and knowing glances and inside jokes. I want the random skips of my heart and coiling of my stomach, and I want the butterflies whenever he walks in the room. I want to give myself over fully to the feelings I'm burying, the feelings I'm not ready or strong enough to take and accept.

I want to give in to the love simmering deep in my bones—the very same love that will consume me and possess me. The love that will lead me to obsess and be obsessed over. The love that never really went away, despite the distance between us.

I want to give in to the world-rocking, leg-trembling love that ignites as easily as our lust and flares as easily as our passion.

I wrap my arms around my legs and lean forward on my thighs, resting my chin on my knees. The city looks duller somehow with those thoughts. The spark has been taken out, and the hazy magic that astounded me when I first gazed out of these windows has cleared.

Milan is beautiful—it always will be—but when you're in turmoil, the ugliness of it dulls that. It taints the refreshing feeling the city gives you.

I exhale slowly, a deep sigh full of confusion and the craziness in my mind. Night falls, and I lie back on the sofa, endlessly tracing the skyline with my eyes.

"Oh, Day." He brushes a thumb across my cheek, pausing for a long moment before lifting me into his arms.

I curl into his body, gripping his shirt, and sigh. "You're back."

"I'm back." He lowers me onto the bed and carefully peels my dress from my languid body. I slide beneath the covers, my eyes still closed, and wait for him to join me.

The bed creaks as he does, and I reach for him instinctively. He pulls me into him and I rest my head on his shoulder, tilting my face into his neck.

"Good," I whisper, fighting my yawn and cuddling in. "I missed you."

He kisses my forehead and tightens his grip on me. "Not half as much as I missed you. *Tu me manques.*"

# Chapter Eighteen

After a third day of being alone in Milan, albeit inside an exclusive spa having my every whim tended to, I'm shrouded in a sadness that shocks me. These are the longest hours Aaron's worked since we arrived in Vegas. Will they ever end? Or is the norm until Paris?

I sit up in bed. The covers pool on my lap, leaving my bare breasts exposed, and I look around the room. Aaron's shirt is discarded on the chair in the corner, and I pad across the thick carpet to grab it. It hangs from me, the hem skimming the top of my thighs, and the material isn't quite thick enough to hide the bright blue of my underwear.

Aaron's voice drifts through the half-open door, and I walk to the doorway. He's sitting on the sofa, his head ducked. His cell is attached to his ear, and his other hand is rubbing through his hair in agitation. The tension is flying from him, and he shakes his head vigorously when I silently pass behind the sofa to pour a cup of coffee.

My hand hesitates over a second mug, and when he growls an angry, "No!" down the phone, I pour a second.

"You have my father's number. You cope without us here every day."

Silence.

"Jesus. Call Fabio if you have to. He's the boss of the fucking Milan office."

I place the mug on the table in front of him, and he glances up at me. My lips curve into a small smile, and I drop my head. He grabs my hand before I can step away and I look back at him.

"I told you," he says firmly, his eyes on mine. "I'll be unreachable today. Anything urgent goes to my father…"

Unreachable?

"I'm your boss before I'm your friend, Ric. You were given this job as a favor, and I can just as easily take it away. You got into this contract mess. I've done everything I can to help you. You'll have to contact the legal department and see what they can do, and failing that, contact my father. I'm incommunicado until ten a.m. tomorrow."

I raise an eyebrow.

"Deal with it. Today." Aaron hangs up the phone and takes my coffee from my hand. He sets it on the table before pulling me onto his lap and burying his face in my neck. His nose runs across my skin as he breathes in deeply. "You smell good."

"Yeah, I'm sure Eau de Morning will be a real hit."

"You're wearing my shirt." His fingers skirt along the tops of my thighs.

I shrug. "Couldn't find anything else to wear."

Aaron pulls back. His eyes meet mine. "What's wrong?"

"Nothing. I'm fine." I move to climb from him but he holds me tighter.

"You're not moving until you tell me what's wrong."

Everything. "Nothing."

"Is it because we've barely seen each other for three days?"

*Yes.* "No."

"And you miss me?" He moves my hair from my face.

I snort. *Yes.* "No. What makes you think that?"

His lips curve at the edges. "Because, Dayton, I came back at midnight and found you asleep on the sofa."

"Maybe I lost track of time."

"And when I carried you to bed, you told me you missed me."

"I was delusional. Totally under the influence of sleep." I pat his cheek and get up.

His sigh follows me to the bedroom. "Sometimes it's hard to believe the amount of bullshit that leaves your mouth."

My jaw drops and I spin. "Excuse me?"

"Don't pretend you don't know what I'm talking about." He stands and stops in the doorway, leaning against it. "For once, Day. For once since you walked back into my life, can you just be fucking honest about the way you feel instead of hiding it under the persona you take when you go to work? I don't give a fuck about that side of you or what your agent thinks you should do or how you should act. I care about what you're keeping inside and fighting against."

I clench my hands into fists and stare him down. Trying to pretend in front of someone who sees all of you is like trying to look through a brick wall.

"Fine," I say softly. "You wanna know?"

"Yes. I want to know everything."

"When this whole stupid trip started, I promised myself it wouldn't go the way of Paris. I have a job that takes over my life. God knows I don't need anything else to do that. I was supposed to be Mia every second of the day to keep you away from Dayton." I run my fingers through my hair. "But I forgot how very *you* you are. I forgot how charming and seductive and wonderful you can be, and everything I was supposed to do got pushed aside. You tore apart all my meticulously laid plans. You ripped apart the control I have over my life and threw me back to a time where being impulsive was beautiful, not reckless. And damn it all, Aaron. You made me remember how love feels—how our love felt.

"And now I'm standing here, eighteen damn days into what was supposed to be a job for me, wondering when shit got so real. I can't look at you without wanting you. I can't touch you without needing more and I can't kiss you without feeling like I'm seventeen and head over heels in love again. Fuck. I want you and I don't even want to! I didn't even want to spend any time with you. I hoped you'd work all the time and we'd barely see each other, but that didn't happen."

"Until it did."

"Until it did." I sit on the bed and put my head between my knees, clasping my hair at the nape of my neck. "And then I realized I didn't want that at all. I didn't—I don't—want to spend three days barely seeing you and I don't want to explore all these places by myself."

"Why?" He crouches in front of me and rests his forehead against mine as I look up.

"Because yet again you're so far under my skin I couldn't even burn you out, you bastard."

He tilts my chin up and secures his lips over mine. "I'm yours. All day and every day."

"Until you put on your suit and I'm left here again."

"You're always with me, Dayton. No matter where I go. Even when we left Paris, you were still with me." His fingers curl around my neck. "But today I'm leaving the suits here. Today is for you."

"Really?"

"Really. Didn't you get that from the call just minutes ago?"

"No," I mutter. "I was too busy being kind of mad at you."

Aaron laughs quietly. "Bambi, you're always mad at me."

"It's not my fault. You make me mad." I run my thumb across his soft bottom lip. "You're really not working all day? At all?"

"Not at all."

I smile against his mouth. "I sound like a lovesick teenager."

"It's a good look. Keep it."

I smack his chest and laugh, getting up. *No, it isn't.* Feeling anything wasn't the plan, much less letting him know of them. But it's happened now. I broke and shit got real and it's done.

He knows that a part of my heart is beating for him right now. I know it always has.

"What are those?" Aaron looks at my jeans in disgust.

"Uh, pants?"

He reaches across and snatches them from my hand. "Dress."

"I was trying to."

"Wear a dress, Dayton."

"I much prefer you less demanding."

"I much prefer you when your mouth is occupied by mine instead of spouting your smartass shit, but we can't always get our way." His amused blue eyes find me, and I click my tongue. "Put a dress on."

I put my hands on my hips.

"What now?"

"You can't tell me what to do. You're not my client, remember?"

His jaw tics and he swallows. Ha! He knows I've got him. I can almost see the wheels in his brain turning as he thinks what to say.

"Please."

I stop. "Did you just say please?"

"Please wear a dress."

My mouth stretches into a grin. "Why, Mr. Stone, are you *asking* me?"

"Take the request and do it before I throw you on this bed and fulfill my cock's request."

I grab a red dress from the closet and sigh. "Even when he asks, he still demands."

He grabs my waist and kisses my shoulder, reaching for a polo shirt. "You make me kind of demanding."

"I kind of like it." I grin teasingly and clip my bra.

Aaron zips up my dress for me. "I'll remember that the next time you moan at me."

My smile widens until my cheeks burn, and I back into the bathroom. "Haven't you realized? I usually moan *because* of your demands."

His chuckle follows me into the room, and I grab my brush. "Keep that up, woman, and my cock's demand will become a requirement!"

I roll my eyes as I slick powder onto my cheeks. I have no doubt that will happen. He means what he says, and his threats are always disguised promises. If he says he'll do it, he'll do it. Regardless of the consequences or what anyone else thinks. It's definitely one of his best and worst qualities.

"No smartass comment?" He appears in the door.

My mascara wand hovers above my lashes as I glance his way. And at the bulge in his pants. "No. I told you before. I can be amicable."

"Does that mean you'll stop being mad at me?"

I zip up the bag and lay my hand on his chest. "Oh, Aaron. I can't do them both at the same time. It's either amicable and a little mad or mad and a little bitchy."

He captures my mouth in a kiss and sucks lightly on my bottom lip. I feel it right down to my toes, and they curl against the tiled floor.

"You're something else, Dayton Black."

"I know."

*Via Montenapoleone*, the largest street in the Rectangle of Gold, is where our car stops.

I look across the back seat at Aaron and tap my foot to an invisible beat. My eyebrow arches in question, and he smirks at me.

"We're here." He gets out of the car and opens my door for me. My heels click against the sidewalk as I join him on the street, and I jab at his chest.

"What is this?"

"This? It's the *Via Montenapoleone*, one of four streets that make up the Rectangle of Gold, or the *Quadrilatero della Moda*, home to the most expensive and exclusive stores on the planet."

"Now who's being a smartass?" I knock his hand from my cheek. "You know how I feel about this."

"About what?"

"You spending money on me. I can buy my own stuff."

He leans in, putting his mouth close to my ear. "And I can get myself off, but that doesn't mean I should."

"Nothing alike." I narrow my eyes. "I don't want you to buy me stuff."

"Who said I was buying you something?"

"I wasn't born yesterday, Aaron."

He sighs and cups my face. "Indulge me, Dayton. If I want to spend my money on you, then please let me."

"Please again." I turn my face into his hand and kiss his palm. "I don't have to like it, do I?"

He brings my mouth to his. "I'd like it if you enjoyed it a little."

"Okay." I brush a kiss to his lips. "But this is me being amicable with a lot of mad."

"You're going to let me spend money on you?"

"God, I'll regret this, but yes."

"And you won't look at the prices."

"Hey, now."

"That wasn't a request."

My mouth twists. "I won't look at the prices."

His eyes light up as the words leave my mouth, and it's that that makes me realize how important this is to him. How much he wants to spoil me and shower me with the expensive things hiding behind the glass windows that surround us.

So I allow him to drag me from store to store, and I let the sales girls tug me from rail to rail. I find myself in endless fitting rooms surrounded by expensive, well-made clothes, trying each outfit on and adding them to piles.

Yes. No. Maybe.

And I keep my word. I don't look at the prices. Somehow.

Until we're standing in Alaia and the dark-eyed girl hands me a red, figure-hugging dress that flares to the floor halfway down the thigh. The lace that wraps around the waist, snaking up to the bust, leaves me with no doubt that Aaron picked this.

It's red and it's lace, after all.

"How much is this?" I demand quietly, pulling my gaze from the garment.

"*Scusate, signora,*" she replies softly. "*Signor* Stone requested you not see the price."

"Of course." I take a deep breath. "What if I try it on? Will you tell me?"

She hesitates.

"He said I couldn't see the price. Not that I couldn't hear it." *Sneaky, underhanded Dayton…*

She briskly nods once and swiftly pulls the door closed behind her. I remove the cream dress and hang it back up before turning my attention to the red vision in front of me. I have no idea how to squeeze my ass into it—or even where I'll wear it. Nope. No idea.

Still, I shimmy and shake until it's hugging my curves. The zipper at my side slides up easily, and I flick my hair back from my face and look in the mirror.

Oh.

Oh, fuck.

Every woman has a dress—just like they have a wedding dress—where it's it. It's the real shebang. This dress is that for me. It's my dress. Made for me, almost.

The sales girl knocks before entering the room. Her eyes widen as soon as she looks at me, and she covers her mouth with her hand. She nods repeatedly.

"*Si, si! Bella!*" She clasps her hands in front of her stomach.

"Thank you." I smooth the material at my hip. "And the price?"

She reels off a number without picking up the tag, and I balk. What? Did I hear that right?

On a dress?

You fucking what?

"Are you kidding me?" I cry at Aaron, storming from the dressing room. "Really? Forty thousand fu—freaking dollars on a dress?"

He turns to face me so slowly that I see his expression transform. His lips part as his gaze runs down my body, eating me alive in the middle of this store. I feel every brush of his eyes across me as if he's touching me. It's so real, so intense, so desperately filled with awe, and my body heats despite the incredulous feeling flowing through it.

Those blue eyes filled with heat and amazement and never-ending tenderness find mine. "Bag everything on the 'yes' pile, and when Miss Black is changed, add this one too."

"You are not buying this dress!" I protest as the girls on the floor all nod. They pause at my words.

"Non-negotiable," he throws back.

"Aaron!"

His eyes harden briefly. "*Non-negotiable.*"

My chest heaves with my sharp breath. He's not budging. I don't want to argue, but I don't want to give in either. This…whatever this is between us is the most infuriating and challenging thing ever.

If you don't count trying *not* to fall in love with Aaron Stone.

"Fine." The word leaves me between gritted teeth. "*Fine.*"

I reenter the dressing room and peel the dress off with more calm than I feel. A lot amicable and a little mad? A whole lot fucking mad is more like it. He just can't help himself. He just can't not piss me the hell off.

I stand by idly as he hands over his card without blinking. Forty thousand on a dress? No problem. He may as well have bought me a car for that.

I'd probably be less annoyed at that. At least that would get used regularly.

It's not like this dress is fit for a run to Whole Foods, for the love of fucking God!

"So much for amicable." Aaron grabs my hand and swings me into him when we leave the Rectangle of Gold.

"I was perfectly amicable until you pushed it. In fact, I was a fucking delight, complete with icing and a cherry on top."

"That mouth will get you into trouble one day."

"I'm lucky I've gone this long."

He leans his face in, and his eyes search mine. "Just make sure it doesn't get you in trouble with me."

"What are you going to do? Spank me?"

"Don't go giving me ideas, Dayton," he says into my ear, his hot breath crawling across my neck. "The thought of the sound of my hand across your obstinate, tight little ass is far too tempting right now."

I lick my lips. I didn't expect him to say that, and my desire agrees. The thought of it is tempting. Very tempting.

"You only get to do that when you fuck me."

His lips curl against my skin. "Then isn't a great big fucking shame I plan on making love to you tonight?"

I pull back. "You told me the first time we had sex here would be making love. We already did that."

"No." He opens the car door and sits me inside. He slides across the seat and ghosts his fingers along the back of my neck into my hair. "That was because I couldn't keep my hands off you. Tonight will be because I want you to go to sleep knowing I've explored every single inch of your body with my fingers and my tongue. Tonight will be because I want you to go sleep knowing every part of you belongs to me in the most obsessive way possible."

"I don't belong to anyone." I finish on a gasp. His fingers are snaking up the inside of my leg, dangerously close to hitting the apex of my thighs.

"You're my obsession, Dayton, and I won't stop until I'm yours. I won't give up until you belong to me the way I belong to you— wholly." He traces his tongue along the seam of my lips and his finger along my panties. "I won't give up until you believe every word of what you said to me this morning."

"Why?" I whisper. "*Why?*"

His lips curve against mine like I should know the answer. "Anyone who makes me feel the way you do isn't someone to give up on. She's the person you chase until forever ends and keep even longer."

A lump forms in my throat. How do you reply to that? I don't know. Every coherent thought except 'I don't know' has left my mind, and I press my lips to his.

I don't need to ask how I make him feel because I know. I see it when he looks at me and when someone says my name, and fuck it all, I see the very same thing when I look in the mirror and think of it.

It's that goddamn irresistible love we both carry for one another. The only difference is, he's embracing it where I'm fighting it. He's accepting it and basking in it and using it to spur him on. But me? I'm pushing back. I'm not giving in because I know how it hurts.

And I can definitively say I would not survive walking away from him a second time.

And we both know that's what will happen when we touch back down in Seattle in three weeks.

I banish that thought and let him fold me into his arms. "Now what?"

"Now we go for dinner."

# Chapter Nineteen

Aaron stares at me across the table. His eyes are calculating yet soft at the same time, and the smirk teasing the corners of his lips is disconcerting.

Sometimes I can read him as easily as my favorite romance novel. Other times it's like trying to get into a crime story where the only romance is the detective and his job. He guards his thoughts and emotions as easily as he lets me see them. I definitely prefer seeing them.

Especially when he looks at me this way. Stripping me bare with his gaze, tearing down any all resistance to him. Like it's possible to fight for longer than a few days…if you're lucky.

I'm not lucky.

"Stop looking at me like that." I stare into my wine.

"I'm thinking."

"About what?"

"About you. About us." He takes my hand across the table and threads his fingers through mine. "About how very crazy you drive me."

"Crazy good or crazy bad?" I raise an eyebrow, bringing my eyes back to his.

"Depends if you're feeling amicable or not."

"Kind of."

"Then right now it's crazy good." He pulls my hand up and brushes his lips across my knuckles. "But we know how easily that will change."

"I think we're good. As long as you don't piss me off again." I shrug.

He laughs and helps me stand. His fingers brush some hair from my face with a gentle touch. "You are the only woman I know who hates having money spent on her."

I smile. "That's probably because the women you know are all under the impression they need a man to look after them."

"And you don't?" He holds my cardigan as I slip my arms into it.

"I don't need *a* man, no." I glance over my shoulder as we leave the restaurant.

He sweeps me into his arms in one long, elegant movement and tilts my head back with his fingers in my hair. "You need *this* man."

"Need is a strong word," I protest into his kiss. "Don't go and say something that'll ruin the crazy good, baby."

His lips curve against mine as he dips me back. I open my mouth to protest but he covers it with his own, his lips taking me prisoner and making me swallow what I was going to say. He kisses me fully without a care for the fact we're in the middle of the street and there are people around us. Passionate, tender, meaningful movements of his lips against mine make me grab the collar of his shirt and hold on for dear life.

He rights me slowly, sucking on my bottom lip with each peppered kiss against it. I clench my legs together. He knows that's the sure way to turn me on. It's like my bottom lip is connected to my core. Suck it, kiss it, graze it with your teeth and instant desire is ignited in me.

"Aaron," I scold quietly, slightly out of breath. "We're in the middle of the street!"

He smirks. "Look around you, Bambi. Do you see anyone pissed off?"

He's right. There's no eye-rolling or huffing as they move to the side. Just smile upon smile.

"This is Italy. They're in love with love. I think it's a requirement to kiss like that at least once every time you visit."

"I don't believe you."

"I can make it one. It can be our own personal requirement." He leads us through the streets and I roll my eyes.

"Of all the things you could pick, you pick that."

"I already chose all the things you're thinking of. I simply haven't told you yet."

"Yeah? Like what?"

He spins me into him. "Like tonight you're mine, completely and utterly, and you still will be after you're done screaming my name."

"The screaming is a requirement?" My breath catches in my throat.

"It doesn't matter if I require you to scream or not, Dayton. We both know you will anyway."

"Confidence is a good look on you."

"I'm a confident guy." He pulls me in front of him and we walk, his hands on my hips. "So much so, I can guarantee if I dipped my fingers inside you right now you'd be ready and waiting for me."

"There's a fine line between confidence and arrogance, Mr. Stone."

He breathes hotly into my ear. "I'm only arrogant when it's the truth."

I want to squirm my hips and clamp my thighs together, but that would be giving him what he wants—the knowledge that I *am* ready for him.

"Now you're getting in this boat, and as we travel around the city, you can sit opposite me and wonder about all the ways I'm planning to make your body tremble beneath me tonight."

I close my eyes as I take a seat. He knows exactly what he's doing to me. He's playing my body and my desire in a way that means I can't stay out of the game. Every step further into my lust brings me closer to loving him, and he knows that. He's impulsive and playful when he wants to be, but when he wants something, he plans so carefully I have no choice but to go along with it.

He did it in Paris and he's doing it now. If I believe him, that his love never faded, then I have no doubt that this trip was to make me fall in love again.

And he's using my body against me. My body, which responds to even the briefest ghost of a touch from him, is the pawn and my heart is the prize.

It works. Because I am sitting across from him, my eyes tracing the sharp line of his jaw and the curve of his gorgeous lips, wondering what he's thinking. My skin is humming with the many possibilities of what he could do to me. He's at his most seductive and determined tonight, and I know that whatever it is will take me to another dimension.

The last time we made love, we were young and crazy in love, guided by instinct and the thought that it would be the last time we'd ever see each other.

Now we're both older, more experienced, and Aaron's infinitely more skilled.

He leans forward. "What are you thinking?"

"I'm thinking I'm ready to go back to the hotel."

My lips mirror the curving of his. "You're impatient, aren't you?"

"Hey." I kiss his neck and let my mouth rest by his ear. "When you're promising in not so many words to sink deep inside me and make me come so hard I see stars, how can I not be?"

"You're putting words in my mouth, Dayton." He wraps his hand around my neck and turns his face to mine. "And ideas in my head."

"Did you not say that? Oops."

"If you want to see stars, sweetheart, all you have to do is look up."

I meet his eyes, which are shining brightly in the dark. "They're beautiful, but I prefer stars of your making."

He trails his fingers down my cheek. "Then it's a shame you can't see what I see every time I look into your eyes."

I kiss his fingers, and the words slip out. "I can," I whisper. "I see the same thing in yours."

Our lips linger together.

"*Mi scusi, signore? Si può fermare la barca, per favore?*" Aaron taps the guy controlling the boat on the shoulder. His eyes widen and they exchange a few sentences in fluent Italian before the boat stops.

Aaron gets out and lifts me onto the sidewalk, setting me down gently in front of him. "*Grazie,*" he says to the guy without taking his eyes from mine.

The car that took us into the Rectangle earlier today pulls up next to us, and I raise an eyebrow. The smirking man in front of me just winks and motions for me to get in.

"What did you say to him?"

He pulls the divider closed and hits me with a heated gaze. "I asked him if he would stop the boat. He asked me why—we still had half an hour left—and I told him I had a beautiful, irresistible woman waiting for me to take her back to our hotel and make love to her."

My lips part. "Aaron! You didn't!"

"We're off the boat, aren't we?"

"I can't believe you—"

He silences me for a second time with his kiss. His large hands wrap around my waist and slide me across the seat to him, and he lifts me onto his lap. My head spins at the dizzying sensation of his tongue searching my mouth, his fingers probing my thighs, and his thumbs massaging circles up the insides of them.

Everything pools downwards, warming in my lower belly and settling into a desperate ache in my pussy. My hips rock against him and his erection rubs against me. I whimper into his mouth.

"As much as I'd love to pull my cock out and have you fuck me in this car, that's not what we're doing tonight." My hips move again and he holds them down, away from his. "Easy, Day. When I've laid you out in front of me and rediscovered every part of your body with my mouth and made you come, then you can fuck me."

"Holding you to that," I mumble, climbing off him as we arrive at the hotel.

Aaron clasps my hand and guides me into the hotel with long, purposeful strides, and the concierge waves for his attention.

"*Signore* Stone! *Signore* Accorsi call for you."

His efforts are dismissed with a waved hand. "He can wait. His call is not important tonight." And he sweeps me into the elevator behind him before the concierge can say another word.

Tension and anticipation rocket between us. He doesn't look at me, and the only part of our bodies that's touching is our hands hanging between us. I take a deep breath and see the twitch of his lips from the corner of my eye.

I want to spin into him. Grab his collar and pull those damn smirking lips to mine and kiss the cockiness out of him. I want to rip off the shirt and run my fingers over his stomach to his pants then slide my hands inside and touch him.

The suite door slams with a deafening sound, and Aaron finally meets my eyes.

"Bedroom," he demands in a husky voice. I throw my purse on the sofa and walk into the bedroom with him right behind me.

"Stop."

He clasps the top of my zipper and slides it down my back, and his fingertips brush my skin as they travel down. I shudder and exhale loudly and simultaneously, anticipation coiling in my stomach as he touches the bow on my underwear.

"I still prefer red," he rasps into my neck, sliding my dress over my shoulders. His hands never leave me as they guide the dress down my body, gliding over my waist and hips and legs. He reaches around me and unclips my bra, pulling it off with the same gentleness he did with the dress. "Lie on the bed."

I do as he says, my breathing increasing in speed and intensity, and prop myself up on my elbows when he bends in front of me. He kisses down my leg to my ankle and slides my shoe off before doing the same to the other side.

"*Sei così fottutamente bello che fa male.*" He takes my mouth softly with his and slowly guides me up the bed. When my head is on the pillows, he guides his hands along my arms to my wrists and holds them against the headboard above my head.

My body responds to him instantly, easily. The desire that's been building all day consumes me, and the heady feeling makes me lose myself in the sweet stroke of his tongue across mine.

"*Così bella,*" he murmurs, his teeth grazing my bottom lip. He sits up and I move to sink my fingers in his hair, but I'm trapped.

He's tied my wrists to the bed. With his tie.

"I told you… Tonight is mine. I can't explore you and pleasure you the way I want unless you're not touching me."

I want to argue and fight with him, but the lust that fills his eyes as his gaze travels across my nearly naked body stops me. Instead of annoyance, red-hot desire wraps around me and I give in to him.

My heart pounds at the slow, reverent way he kisses his way down my neck and across my collarbone. Everything about the way he's touching me is sending me into overdrive and making me push my body into him.

I don't care if I can't touch him or if he wants to take this slow.

I need him now.

His name falls from my lips as he leaves my breasts and kisses a pattern down my stomach. He slows down when he's hovering above my panty line, and instead of continuing his descent, he kisses from hip to hip. His hands, flat on my stomach, prevent me from pushing myself into him.

"As long as you're doing that, I'm not going further."

The threat is real and I immediately still. He chuckles and brushes his nose across the lace covering me.

"I love the way you smell," he murmurs, his lips brushing the top of my thigh. He peels the material down my legs and throws it to the side. "Bend your legs."

I meet his gaze when he covers my knees with his hands and pushes my legs open. I watch as he drags his eyes from mine to my lips, over my breasts, and settles them on my exposed center.

He inhales sharply and leans down again, his arms circling my thighs and holding my legs apart.

"Please, Aaron." I drop my head back, eyes closed, at the excited tensing of my muscles.

"And I love the way you taste. You taste fucking perfect." He touches his tongue to me and explores slowly, leaving no part of my core undiscovered by him.

He licks and he tastes and he sucks, each glide and sweep lifting me higher and higher. I pull at the blue tie holding my wrists captive but it doesn't work. I can't move them, and I can't push my hips into him the way I want to.

He has me here, still, completely at his mercy. I have no control, no power. All I have is pleasure and heat and—

An intense orgasm that has me writhing on the sheets, desperate to grab on to something, and a tongue working me feverishly through it. Then he's gone and I'm aching for his touch all over again.

Aaron kisses his way back up my body to my mouth and wraps my legs around his waist. He's naked, his skin soft against mine, and he rubs himself along me. He's teasing me, proved by the way he pushes the top of his cock inside me only to pull back out. He does this over and over, and it pushes me to the edge and I snap.

"Fuck, Aaron! Now, please!"

He bends his forehead to mine, grabs the back of my head, making my eyes open, and pushes into me. I moan at the sweet feeling of him easing in to the hilt, stretching me even as my muscles clamp around him.

His thrusts are slow and deep. His hips rock and circle, making sure he hits every spot inside me. He kisses and touches me, never faltering in his relaxed, easy tempo.

It feels like forever passes until I feel a second orgasm build, balling up into an exquisite ball of tension, waiting for the right moment to explode and shatter me.

And my hands are free.

"Come," he whispers in my ear, his voice strained.

He suddenly picks up speed and pounds into me. I grab his shoulders and tilt my hips up, taking him even deeper as the ball begins to unravel inside me. My head thrashes, his name falling repeatedly from my lips until I go.

I clamp down on him and vaguely hear him shout my name into my ear with a string of curse words through my scream.

He kisses my cheeks, brushing away a wetness I only recognize as my tears. I shake my head into his shoulder and cling to him, using all the strength left in my body to stop him from leaving.

"Bambi," he whispers, rolling to the side.

A tear drips onto his skin. Bambi... Him coming to the hotel... Me answering the door in Bambi pajamas... Him taking me to

Disney the next day just because of the little deer, my favorite Disney character…

"Please don't cry."

I squeeze my eyes shut to stop the tears and shudder in his arms. That memory, that very one from the first weekend we spent together just days after we met, is the one I blocked out and refused to acknowledge because of what that day signified. It marked the day my teenage heart started to fall for the beautiful, confident guy I met by chance.

Now it means something else.

It means I broke the rules.

I always would. There was never any other way out of this. When loving someone is as easy and natural as breathing, there's no way not to. No way to break the fall.

I don't want to love him so completely that it consumes me… But I do.

God, I do.

Every single part of me is irrevocably in love with Aaron Stone.

# Chapter Twenty

"There's a car waiting for you downstairs, *Signora* Black."

"There is?" I question the concierge down the phone.

"*Si*. From *Signor* Stone. He says you must go now."

"Uh, okay. I'll be five minutes. Wait, wait!" I call. "Go where?"

"He didn't say."

"Fantastic. Thank you." I put the phone down and run my fingers through my hair.

I'm wearing nothing but his shirt, my hair looks like birds nested in it overnight, and I may as well have swapped faces with a panda. Fucking hell.

I wrench a brush through my tangled locks and kick through my suitcase for a dress. I lift a new floral one out and onto the bed with my toes and grab a wipe to clear my face of yesterday's makeup. Thank god for being a woman and having the power to multitask.

I button my dress with one hand after pulling underwear on and apply my mascara with the other. Shoes. Purse. Phone. Check.

The bell boy opens the car door for me, and I thank him, sliding into the sleek vehicle. The driver says nothing to me as he pulls away and into the busy midday traffic. I sit back in the car, chewing my bottom lip, and wonder what could be so wrong that Aaron would throw me into a car without telling me anything.

What if something is wrong? What if this guy is taking me to a hospital somewhere where I have to try and get past nurses by speaking in a mix of Italian and broken English to see him? What if he's had a car crash or something?

But this is his car.

But still.

Oh god.

I slap my hand over my eyes. *Shut the fuck up, Dayton.* Love obviously makes me a little neurotic and a whole lot batshit crazy.

The car pulls up outside a tall glass building proclaiming Stone Advertising above the large doors. Aaron's standing in front of it, his eyes on the sleeve he's playing with. Some guy in a suit opens my door.

Blue eyes meet mine as I leave the car, and I raise my eyebrow. "Care to explain why you've pulled me down to your office on short notice?"

"I need your help to select some images."

"Are you kidding me?" I stop in front of him and poke his solid chest. "You pulled me down here without any kind of message to pick some damn *photos*? Do you know how crazy I just went in the car?"

Evidently, he doesn't care—not if the grin tugging at his lips is anything to go by. He pulls me into him. "Why? Were you worried about me?"

"Yes," I answer honestly.

He smiles as he kisses me. "I'm sorry. I'll send your friend the concierge with a hand-delivered message next time."

"Probably not a good idea. I wasn't wearing anything when he called."

His step falters as he pulls me into the elevator. "Nothing? At all?"

"Well, I was wearing your shirt, but other than that—nothing.

He would have had quite the sight if he'd hand-delivered a message."

"Forget the hand delivery. The only person who gets to see you in my shirt is me." He pulls me past a receptionist with wide eyes and leans in. "She has a crush on me."

"Of course she does. I mean, she only works in a building where it's not uncommon to see hot male models walk in and out every day. Why wouldn't she want the boss?"

"Behave, Dayton."

"You know my thoughts on that word."

He eyes me sharply and takes me into a large office with a perfect view of the *Duomo*.

"I think I just found my new favorite place," I say softly.

"Ric!" Aaron snaps the name of the guy he was talking to yesterday and follows it up with a string of Italian. The guy I assume is Ric brushes it off and crosses the room to me.

"*Signora* Black, it is a pleasure to meet you." Ric kisses my hand. I meet Aaron's hard eyes over his shoulder.

"And you, Ric. I've heard a lot about you." *Liar, liar.* Make the guy feel good.

"All good, I hope?"

"From what I've been told, there's no way it can't be."

"Can we get on with this?" Aaron asks in a tight voice. "These images need be back in Donna's hands by five tonight so she can pick the absolute finals. Not to mention you have a lunch date with your wife."

God, I love jealous Aaron.

I join him at the desk and look at the images spread out. "And why do you need me?"

"Bella, the person who usually picks these out, is off sick today. On a normal day, we'd put them back until she's back in the office and spin a line about a fault at the printers."

"So why don't you?"

"Because Donna is fashion royalty, and you give her what she wants hours before she wants it. Which means we have approximately forty five minutes to pick twenty images and courier them across the city to her office." Aaron rests his hand on my back. "And we need a woman's eyes on them."

"This 'working for you' thing is becoming a habit, Mr. Stone." I sigh and lean forward. "What am I looking for?"

Ric passes me a pad of paper with a brief description on—thankfully translated to English. From the rambling paragraph, it's obvious to see that Donna wants images that show the class of her designs but are still sexy.

"Move." I hit Aaron in the chest with the pad and he steps back. Ric moves before I have to say anything, and I wink at him before giving the images my full attention.

Almost kiss. Hand on the thigh while leaning back. Hug from behind, his lips bent toward her neck. Her mouth parted and his thumb on her bottom one.

On and on they go, a never-ending stream of photos that are all the same yet so different.

"Here." Aaron hands me a brochure. "This is her usual."

"These aren't sexy-classy."

"What?"

"Sexy-classy. That's what she wants. Teasing images that have the sexiness to appeal to the younger generation but still carry the class to attract the older ladies."

Both men stare at me. "Why didn't we get that?" Aaron asks Ric before turning back to me. "Keep this up and I'll hire you."

The irony of his words makes my lips twist, and he realizes what he's said at the raise of my eyebrows. And there isn't a single thing he can say to take it back.

Slowly, I turn my attention back to the table and the images staring at me. Those three words... A careless slip of the tongue.

Something that's said every day without any repercussions. Something you'd say teasingly to your girlfriend.

Something she'd accept with a laugh instead of a pang to her chest.

*Because,* a lingering voice reminds me, *he did hire me.* And that's the only reason I'm here now. I can love him all I like, but I'm still a call girl.

And the little pangs like the ones I'm feeling are the very reason we don't have relationships.

I flick through the images I've chosen and hand them to Aaron. "Here. They're the best ones."

His eyes search mine, and I know he caught the hitch in my voice. "Thank you. Ric, have these sent out and on Donna's desk by the time she gets back from her lunch. Go and meet Francesca early. I'm sure she'll appreciate the help baby shopping. Send her my love."

"*Si. Grazie,* Aaron. I will." Ric looks at me with warm brown eyes. "It was pleasure to meet you, *signora.*"

"And you, Ric." I smile after him.

"Tell Rosa to hold all my calls on your way." Aaron shuts the door and twists the lock. "Day—"

"Don't." I laugh and turn to gather the remaining pictures on the desk. "It slipped out, right? There's nothing odd about joking to hire your girlfriend who happens to be saving your ass." I flatten my hands against the thick wood and drop my head. "Well, maybe it is if the only reason she's here in the first place is because she's hired to be."

The lump in my throat is too big to swallow, and I try several times before it goes. I step away from Aaron when he reaches for me and walk to the windows.

"I pushed that aside because you asked me to, but no matter what happens, no matter how real this is, it's only happening because I have to be here. We can't ignore the fact I'm only here because you're paying me to be."

"What if I stopped it? Called your agent and cancelled it? Would you stay, or would you go?"

"Don't ask me that," I whisper.

"Would you call her and leave? Stop doing it so you *could* stay?"

"I said not to ask me that!" I snap, turning. "I don't know, Aaron. *I don't know.* What I do is my life. It's all I have."

"You have me, Day. You know you do."

I close my eyes. "Because I'm paid to. That's always going to be the bottom line."

He cups my face. "So quit. Quit and stay with me."

"I—"

"Model. I'm not asking you to sit at home cleaning and cooking and making babies, for fucks sake. You love your independence, and I love that about you. I always have." His nose brushes mine. "You're a natural in front of the camera. Give up all the call girl bullshit and stay with me."

"I can't have this conversation right now." I cover his hands with my own and pull them away.

"Then when's the best time? When we're back in Seattle and you can run?" He circles my wrists with his fingers, stopping me from moving away. "This conversation was always going to happen, and there's no better time than right now."

*Yes, there is. There's always a better time. Preferably one where I'm not still reeling from the realization that I'm madly fucking in love with you and I'm still technically your whore.*

"I need to think, Aaron. I can't just make decisions like that. I'm not impulsive. There has to be a plan. I have to know what I'm doing and where I'm going."

"Jesus fucking Christ, Dayton. I just told you. Leave Monique. Model for us, and live with me."

"Three weeks! We've been 'together' three weeks and you're

suggesting I live with you? Now that's how to scare an independent girl off."

He looks to the ceiling. "Fine. Don't live with me. Just leave and be with me."

"It's really not that simple."

"I never stopped loving you. Not even for a second. It doesn't get much simpler than that."

My heart pounds in my chest. "And if that's true, then you'll respect my need to think things through. The only people I've truly cared about for five years are my aunt and my best friend. You can't ask me to throw everything away and jump into something without knowing it's the right thing to do."

He exhales heavily and wraps his arms around my shoulders. "Fine. I don't like it. Not a fucking bit. But I respect it."

I sink into his body and wrap my arms around his waist, laying my head on his chest. "Thank you."

"Just… Do you have any idea how hard it is waking up next to you every morning and wondering if this is all we have together? The time I'm forced to pay for?"

"Yes. I ask myself the same thing every day," I whisper painfully.

His grip on me tightens. "Then for god's sake, woman, find an answer before you kill us both waiting."

"I'm trying. I'm really trying."

"Don't ever doubt that I'd wait forever for you, but that doesn't mean I don't want to know right now." He kisses the top of my head. "And if this is all the time we have, don't ever doubt that I won't stop until I have you. If I have to pay for you until you're absolutely, completely mine, then I will."

"Don't be stupid."

"There isn't a price I wouldn't pay for you, Dayton. Money has no value when the thing you desire is priceless."

# Chapter Twenty-One

"Beautiful, don't you think?"

I smile as Aaron's arms circle my waist, my eyes fixed on the Tower standing before me. "It is."

"Oh, you're talking about the Tower." He curves his lips against my cheek. "I'm talking about you."

I shake my head and turn my face toward his. "You've been waiting to do that, haven't you?"

"I have no idea what you're talking about."

My fingers link through his, and I turn my attention back to the Eiffel Tower. There are no words to describe the feelings running rampant through my body in this moment. Being back at the place it all started, with him, is surreal. It's been so long, but it really does feel like yesterday he was pulling me to the coffee shop around the corner to replace the one he made me spill.

"At least I'm not covered in coffee this time."

Aaron laughs and steps to my side, keeping one arm firmly around my waist. "I didn't mean to frighten you."

"Sure you didn't. I believe you."

"Whether I did or not, it remains the greatest success in pick-up fuck-ups."

"Pick-up fuck-ups?"

"Where it all goes wrong but still works. At least, that's what Joey, my nineteen-year-old cousin, tells me."

I roll my eyes, but I'm laughing. "Can I ask you something?"

"Always."

"What did you think when you saw me for the first time?"

I stop and look at him after a long moment of silence. His eyes are set on me, clouded with that memory and full of tenderness, and his lips are curved on each side.

Slowly, he reaches out to push my hair from my face. "I remember sitting on the grass, working on something for my father, when you walked past. You were humming to yourself. You couldn't have been more in your own little world if you'd tried to be. You walked past and I watched you, and I remember the exact moment you truly looked at the Tower.

"You just...stopped. Your eyes flicked over it until you'd seen every last inch and your lips parted like you'd never seen anything that incredible before. And it was as if the whole world stopped, just for that moment." He trails his fingers down my cheek and cups my jaw. "I couldn't let you leave without speaking to you. If we'd only ever exchanged a few words, that would have been good enough. But I had to talk to you."

"Why? I was just a crazy American girl amazed by the Tower, just like thousands of others that pass through here every year."

"I was as amazed by you as you were by the Tower. Just like you had to see it, I had to speak to you."

I touch my lips to his gently. "I'm glad you did. Most of the time, anyway."

"Most of the time?" He smirks when I shrug in response then sighs. "Come on. I made reservations for dinner."

"I'm not exactly dressed for dinner." I look at my light blue dress.

"You look perfect. No arguments." He pulls me down a long, winding street, and I flash back to our first date.

The one after he replaced my coffee. The proper one.

"Aaron?" My smile creeps into my voice. "Are you taking me to that little sandwich shop we found?"

"It's not really dinner, I know. But it was the first thing we ate together in Paris and it doesn't seem right we go elsewhere tonight."

*Holy shit.* "Are you trying to make me swoon with your incredible ability to recall all the firsts in our relationship after all these years?"

He turns to me outside the quaint sandwich bar and smirks, his eyes flashing lustfully. "You remember the hotel."

*Of course I remember the hotel.* I lost my damn virginity in it. In our *suite,* for fuck's sake.

"Oh, I remember. Nice move there."

"It wasn't that bad." He pulls me into the building before I can respond and rolls off our orders. My club sandwich, on multigrain bread, with extra cheese and lettuce. His BLT, holding the lettuce and doubling the bacon and tomato. Some things don't change at all.

We step outside, our sandwiches in his hand, and I pick the conversation back up.

"You have to be kidding, right? It was hardly earth-shattering," I remind him, thinking of the first time we had sex. You know all those romance novels where the first time doesn't hurt and it ends with a mind-blowing orgasm? Yeah, they're called fiction for a reason. They're bullshit.

"Day…" He can't help the laugh that escapes him, and I fight my own.

"Fucking hell, Aaron. It hurt so badly I cried for like half an hour. I spent the next two days walking around like I'd shit myself. I couldn't close my legs!"

When we get in the car he's hired for us, he's still chuckling to himself. "If you must know, it wasn't exactly great for me. Making a woman cry during sex is a definite hit to the ego."

"It wasn't bad sex. It was just painful sex. *Very* painful sex," I add at his pointed look.

So painful it makes me want to cross my legs at the memory.

"It wasn't my fault, Dayton."

"Hey, did I say it was?" I prod him in the arm. I know it wasn't his fault. He did everything he could to make it perfect for me. "I just didn't realize you were so big. If I'd have known, I'd have run a fucking mile to find something closer to the size of a tampon to break me in."

He raises his eyebrows. "I'm offended by that. Especially since it was actually your fault."

"Excuse me?"

Aaron leans across the car, his eyes darkening as his face nears mine. "If you weren't so tight, it would have been a lot less painful."

"And that right there is the only time in my life a man has ever complained about my vagina." I tap his nose.

"Oh, you'll find no complaints here. That was merely an observation." He leans in farther and captures my bottom lip between his teeth. I shiver. "I happen to like your tight pussy very, very much."

Said tight pussy clenches.

"Mhmm," I mutter as he tugs on my lips and sends an ache to my clit. "Aaron?"

"What?"

"You're squashing my sandwich."

He pauses then pulls back. I grin at him and shrug a shoulder as the car stops. *Just in time.*

"This isn't going the way I imagined," he mutters in the elevator.

"Join the club. I imagined you'd be as charming as our first date, but clearly your cock has overtaken that part of your brain."

"Charming... Sexual... Is there a difference?"

"Yes, unless you're being sexually charming, in which the two merge together. And you definitely are not," I clarify, opening the door to the penthouse suite of the Paris Stone.

"It doesn't matter what I'm being. I'm still going to be fucking you by the end of the night."

"I'm not sure how I feel about fucking you in a hotel your uncle now owns."

"There are no cameras in the penthouse." He steps up behind me and breathes on the back of my neck. "So we have free rein, and since this week is all about us, I plan on taking you on every. Single. Surface."

My breathing stops and my brain is flicking between the 'all about us' and 'every single surface' while it decides which it wants to address first.

"All about us?" I spin. "Explain."

He strokes his thumb down my jaw and hands me my 'dinner.' "What explanation do you need? This week belongs to us, Bambi. No work. Just me and you."

"I don't get it."

"We fly to London in a week. Then after seven days there, we fly back here for a further week in which I will be working."

Six weeks.

Five cities.

"You mean...every day...you're going to be here?"

"Every day. From the moment you open those gorgeous brown eyes until the minute you shut them again."

It makes so much sense.

I step away from him and toward the balcony doors, dropping my sandwich on the table as I go. I push the doors open and step outside. "Why?" I ask, knowing he's right behind me. "Why aren't you working this week?"

He steps behind me and pushes his chest into my back. His hands rest on either side of mine on the railing. "How can I? How can I be in this city and not see you everywhere I turn? I've been here so, so many times in the last seven years, and every time I was haunted by my memories of you. You were—you *are*—everywhere.

"This city... Dayton, it belongs to us. Regardless of the time that passes, Paris will always be ours. That's why this week is for us. For you. Shit, for me. I need to be in the city and be reliving memories instead of being haunted by them."

I swallow. "You planned this, didn't you? That's why..." *You bought me.* I pause, unable to say the words. "Six weeks, not five. You knew all along this would happen."

"No, Day. I didn't know. I hoped, but I never assumed. Not a single day has passed that I haven't hoped to look in your eyes and see what I feel reflected back again."

I turn and wrap my arms around his waist. He embraces me swiftly, his face in my hair, breathing me in, his arms tight around my body. I sniff.

"You're a real pain in my ass, Stone, ya know that?"

"You've been a pain in my ass since you ruined my sweater by wiping coffee off your shirt." He kisses my head and releases me.

"Oh, don't even go there!"

I stretch out my muscles, aching from a night of being pinned to the bed by a certain strong-willed, demanding businessman, and sit up in bed. The silence of the suite is broken only by my breathing, and I look around for any signs that Aaron is still here.

His watch is still on the nightstand, his turned-off cell still lying next to it and yesterday's clothes still resting on the chair in the corner. The only indication of his being anywhere but here is the absence of a robe on the back of the door.

I climb out of bed and slip my own robe on. I'm ready to leave the room when I notice a bright pink Post-it note stuck to the door.

*You have no idea how beautiful you look when you're sleeping.*

My lips twitch, and I pull it down, holding it to my chest as I leave the room. A soft breeze floats in from the open balcony doors. I spin on the balls of my feet and stop at the view before me.

Aaron's sitting at a cast-iron table, sipping a tall glass of orange juice, a spread of French breakfast foods before him. My lips part slightly, and he turns to look at me.

His eyes flick from mine down to the slip of paper in my hand. "It took you long enough to find one."

"What?"

He stands and pulls a second chair out from the table, gesturing for me to sit. I oblige, and when he reseats himself, he places a *pain au chocolat* onto the plate in front of us. He's ignoring my questioning stare. I can tell by the smirk playing on his lips and the amusement dancing in the depths of his gorgeous blue eyes.

"Well?" I push.

"Eat your breakfast."

"No. Not until you explain yourself."

He raises his eyebrows. "Dayton, eat your breakfast. I'm not explaining anything until you do so."

I mirror his facial expression. "Fine." And I walk back into the bedroom.

"What are you doing?" He follows me.

I grab my lipstick from my bag and stroll casually into the kitchen. I open the trash can and hold it over it.

"What *are* you doing?"

"See this?" I pull off the cap and twist it up, showing him the red he loves so much. "Speak or it goes."

"You're threatening me with your lipstick?"

"Promising you, buddy. Promising you."

"I'm not your fucking buddy, Dayton. I'm your man."

"You're whatever the hell I want you to be if you want me to suck you off while wearing this ever again."

He pauses and runs his tongue over his bottom lip. "You're serious, aren't you? You're threatening me with lipstick and blow jobs?"

"Quickest way to break a man is to take away his favorite thing."

"You're my favorite thing."

"Did I miss that? No red-lipped blow jobs and no me." I point the lipstick in his direction. "Now talk."

Our eyes meet and he stares me down for a long time. I purse my lips. I'm not fucking budging. I want to know what he means about these Post-it notes. I 'finally' found one?

He crosses the kitchen and takes the bright square from my fingers. "This is one of many notes I've left you."

I say nothing.

"I've left one for you every day since we arrived in Vegas."

"Why didn't I find them?"

"You never wanted to find them."

"This one was obvious. It was behind my damn robe!" I put the lipstick on the counter, and he runs his eyes over his own words. "What happened to the others?"

"I kept them."

This surprises me. "Why?"

"Because I hoped that one day you'd be ready to read them." He takes my hand and places the note back in my hand. "But you are now."

He disappears. I watch him go and watch the empty space that joins the main room to the bedroom until he reappears, a stack of small, brightly colored squares in his hand. "*Forse il tuo forse non è sufficiente quando i tuoi occhi mi lasciano senza fiato e il tuo tocco mi fa sentire vivo. Non quando l'amore che abbiamo avuto è bollente sotto la superficie. Non quando sono così pronta a permettere al mio amore per te di consumare me ancora una volta.* And in French. *Peut-être que ce n'est pas assez quand tes yeux me laissent à bout de souffle et votre contact me fait me sentir vivant. Pas quand l'amour que nous avions est en ébullition sous la surface. Quand je suis prêt à laisser mon amour pour vous de me consumer à nouveau.*"

"What does it mean? Tell me. Please."

He hands me the notes. "Read them first."

I take them and flick through. My heart pounds a little harder and my breathing hitches a little more and tears fill my eyes a little quicker at each one.

*True love is never letting go, despite all the odds being against you. I never let go.*

*Two thousand, seven hundred and seventy four days. That's how long I waited and wished for you.*

*I look into your eyes and see everything I've always wanted. Everything I've wanted since I realized the coffee you spilled on your shirt matched the shade of your eyes perfectly.*

*I love it when you smile at me—really smile at me. I can almost pretend you remember as much as I do.*

They go on and on, telling me everything he's never said aloud and some things he has, like the repetition is necessary for me to believe it. Either way, these notes are everything I never wanted to hear. Everything that would make me fall again.

"You said maybe you believed in romance. And I said maybe isn't enough when your eyes leave me breathless and your touch makes me feel alive. Not when the love we had is boiling beneath the surface. When I'm so ready to let my love for you to consume me again."

Air fills my lungs with one short, sharp inhale, and I fall into him. The Post-its scatter on the floor around us, but I don't care. All I care about is burying my face into the chest of this man I've loved since I knew what love was and wondering what the fucking hell I'm going to do.

I cling to the back of his robe. "Why didn't I find them? *Why?*"

"I wanted you to look," he whispers into my neck. "I wanted you to look for something that was so glaringly obvious to me. Something you were oblivious to."

"How was I supposed to find them if I never knew?"

"I don't know. Jesus." He cups the back of my head. "I've done a whole lot of fucking hoping since you walked into that goddamn booth, Dayton. I hoped every morning you'd find them, and when each night you hadn't, a little bit of that hope died."

"That's why you wanted to drop the call girl stuff."

"No." He pulls back and looks me dead in the eye. I've never seen his gaze so hard and determined. "No. I wanted you drop that bullshit because that's not who you are to me. You will *never* be that person to me. I accept it, but I know you better."

"You know me from years ago."

"No. I know the woman who lies about loving Bambi and being amazed by the Eiffel Tower. I know the woman who hides her emotions behind a barbed-wire fence because it's what society expects of her. And I know the beautiful, passionate, playful woman hiding behind that fence." His words wrap around me in a blanket of comfort and security. "And that's the woman I'll take."

I know those words. I know what they mean. *Him or my job.* A choice. An ultimatum.

And not an unfair one.

Also not one I'm going to respond to right now.

# Chapter Twenty-Two

*"Trust me,"* he said. Trust him I did.

At seventeen, I would have followed Aaron Stone to the very depths of hell and back again if I'd had to. I'm not sure if, at twenty-four, that would be much different.

After forcing me to eat my breakfast, he shoved me into the bedroom and practically pulled my damn dress over my head before getting himself dressed. And I have to admit, that's something I both loathed and enjoyed. Seeing his naked body is always beautiful, but his covering it up? Not so much.

Now we're walking the streets of Paris. His fingers are linked through mine and he's barely said a word as he drags me across quaint cobbled streets I know I should recognize. He shakes his head at all my questions. He curls his lips at all my annoyed prods. He rolls his eyes at all my groans that heels can't take the endless hobbles.

"My feet hurt," I whine. "You could have warned me. I think my feet are actually breaking."

"For fuck's sake, Day." He stops. "Get on my back."

I laugh loudly. "Are you kidding me? I'm wearing a dress!"

"Believe me. I'll make sure no one can see that gorgeous red and black set you thought I didn't notice you sneaking on this morning."

"I don't doubt it." I put my hands on his shoulders. "Do you know how crazy this is?"

"It's only as crazy as you make me, woman. Hurry up before I change my mind."

"Aaron Stone, soon-to-be CEO of Stone Advertising is giving me a piggyback ride through Paris." I snort and bury my face in his shoulder blade. He slides his hand up my thigh and smacks my ass, and I laugh. "Sorry, sorry. It's just kind of funny. How many super powerful businessmen do you see doing this?"

"I wouldn't know. If they don't, I'd imagine they'd have no idea how to treat their women. God forbid she should have sore feet."

I slap his chest. "So shoot me. I forgot how many streets here were covered in stones."

"The only stone you need to worry about is me, sweetheart." He squeezes my thighs. I grin. "I'm harder to deal with than all of these fuckers put together."

"Only because you're demanding and controlling and a pain in my frigging ass."

"Watch it, woman. I'm controlling, remember?"

"Ooh, what are you gonna do? Tie my wrists to a bed and fuck the breath out of me?"

He shifts his body so I fall to one side. He catches me elegantly, flattening my body against his. "Damn fucking right I am." His mouth covers mine with a heat I feel everywhere. "I didn't hear any complaints from you that night."

"Uh-uh." I shake my head and put my finger against his lips. "The next time we fuck, I'm in control."

"Is that right?"

"You have no idea how right it is until you've been truly fucked by me."

"I've been fucked a thousand times."

"Baby, you haven't been fucked by me. Tonight you can put away your controlling demands because I'm the one taking the reins."

He pulls my hips against his, and his erection digs into my hip. "Is that right?"

"You bet your ass it is." I kiss him hard, pushing myself into him. "Now, where are we going?"

His eyes change from dark to bright blue. "You're a temptress, Dayton Black."

"Cock tease is what I'm used to hearing, but I'll take both." I pull him forward. "Where are you taking me?"

"I'm taking you to the place where I realized I was in love with you."

My eyebrows shoot into my hairline. "This isn't the way to the Eiffel Tower."

He smirks and spins us so he's leading the way. I watch him as he walks—his strong strides swallowing up the sidewalk, his gaze focused on his destination, and his jaw firmly set.

"That's where you say, 'No, Bambi. This is the place I realized for the second time I was in love with you.'"

"Dayton Black."

"Aaron Stone."

"Shut up for once in your life. Shut those gorgeous red lips and follow me."

"I've been following you for ages."

"And thank fucking god we're here."

I look to the side. And stop. Everything. I stop breathing and thinking, and my heart stops beating. "*Pont de l'Archevêché,*" I breathe. The narrow bridge is covered with padlocks, every inch of it having one of the metal locks attached to it.

Aaron smirks and spins, facing me. His feet are at the end of the bridge, and he steps back, mouthing something at each step. What the hell is he doing?

"Here," he says and bends down.

I frown at him from the end of the bridge. There's no way he can find it. There is absolutely no fucking way he knows where it is.

"Here," he repeats with more conviction, a padlock in his hands. He turns to face me. "It's here."

"There are thousands on padlocks on this bridge. You honestly think I believe you know the exact place ours is?"

"Twenty-eight steps in, roughly."

"Are you kidding me?"

"Kind of halfway down because you had a freak-out about it not being even."

"I don't believe you."

"Silver and gold. We scratched our initials in with a penknife we found in my suite."

So much emotion rises in me at that memory. The moment I realized forever would never happen with the guy I loved beyond belief.

I swallow the remembered pain. "If it's ours, what's under my initials?"

"A hoof print. Just like Bambi's." He glances at it. "Come see if you don't believe me."

My legs take me toward him. They shake the whole time, and I hide my trembling hands around my waist. I stop beside him and know he's right before I bend down. I know that the padlock he holds in his hand is ours, the one we so lovingly carved our initials into. The one I painstakingly carved a deer's print into so we'd always remember it was ours. So if we ever found it, we would know.

It's unmistakable. A generic lock like so many others, yet so unique.

I stare at it in disbelief and cover my mouth with my hand. "How do you even know where it is?"

"I counted. As we walked away, I counted the steps to the end of the bridge. Just in case." He stands and pulls a second from his pocket.

I reach my hand out but hesitate and curve my fingers back. I swallow all the crazy shit pounding and clenching in my chest and take the padlock from his hand.

Our names are on it. Not our initials. Our names. Perfectly inscribed and underlined by the date we first met.

I curl my fingers around the cold metal. It feels as natural as it did the first time we stood on this bridge with a lock exactly the same. I bend down and hook it around the bridge beneath the first one. Aaron kneels next to me and wraps his arm around my body. His hands cover my shaking ones and lock it into place. My lips part the instant it clicks, and he holds up a small gold key.

"I threw the first time," he says into my ear. "Now it's your turn."

I take it and stand, staring at the River Seine, the way it winds around and through the city until I can't see it bend any longer. I feel his hot breath on my cheek and his hands at my hips and his body at my side.

And I tighten my grip on the tiny key. It digs into my palm but I ignore the sting. I already know I'm going to throw it. And I know what throwing it means. Everyone does. Every damn couple that visits Paris knows what this signifies.

The first time, he threw it, and in my mind, I promised the summer. I promised what I knew I could give. I promised him all I could.

This time, I'm throwing.

This time, I'm the one making the real promise.

This time, I'm promising him that I'll love him forever.

Regardless of what happens when we touch back down in Seattle, when real life intersects with this magical rendezvous, I'm promising him that he'll always have my heart.

I'll never love another the way I love him.

I pull my arm back. With his fingers at my hips, I force my arm forward. He inhales deeply.

The key hits the water with a tiny splash and sinks.

I curl into his hold, offering a forever my heart can guarantee but my body can only hope for.

Moulin Rouge.

The movie every teenage girl watches, wishing she could be Nicole Kidman. The first time I saw it, I know I spent the whole time wishing I were. Wishing I had my own Ewan McGregor acting as Christian.

Except I do. And he's been plying me with wine all night. By the time we leave the building headed by a bright red windmill, the night air certainly gets to me.

I tilt my head to the side and gaze at him all through the journey back to the hotel. Aaron smirks, scratching at his neck, and I can tell by the tightness of his jaw that he's fighting the urge to look at me. Like it's a mammoth, nearly fucking impossible task not to meet my eyes when I'm staring at him as if I want him naked right this very fucking second.

Our journey through the hotel foyer consists of my calculated steps and his hand twitching at my waist. The seconds in the elevator are taken up by the aimless traveling of his fingers up and down my side. They're filled with sparks of need jolting through my body.

Aaron locks the suite door behind us, and I walk to the fridge. The wine bottle is cold beneath my fingers, and I focus on each drop falling into my glass instead of him watching me.

"Dayton." My name leaves him, hot and heavy.

I turn, meeting dark blue eyes filled with a need so intense it engulfs my body in red-hot flames. He approaches me and closes his fingers over mine. Just when I expect him to pull the glass away, he doesn't. He lifts it to my mouth and tilts. His breath is hot against my neck, and his chest smolders against my back as I down the wine before me.

"I've always loved Moulin Rouge." I run my finger around the rim of my empty glass. "Do you think I could do the dances like they do?"

"Oh, Jesus," he mutters.

I spin from his hold and catch my tongue between my teeth as I cast my eyes around the room. They fall on the coffee table in the middle of the room, and my lips curve into a wicked grin.

I throw a glance over my shoulder and move toward it. A deep chuckle fills the room when I climb up onto it. I pause for a second to catch my balance and smirk at him.

"Well, do you think I can?"

"Dayton, get off the table. You'll break your damn neck." He makes a grab for me but misses as I step back.

I waggle my finger in his face. "You don't get to tell me what to do tonight, remember? I'm in charge. Ooh la la!" I wink saucily and spin.

My body contorts and undulates as I recreate a routine from the show from my tabletop stage. I keep my balance and dance like it's what I was made to do—like I should have been a fucking stripper instead of a call girl.

Despite his concern for my safety, Aaron makes no move to get me off the table. I expected his arms to loop around my waist and pull me off or that he'd climb up and sling me over his shoulder. He does neither. He does nothing but stand and watch me with his hands resting in front of his body.

I'm laughing as I dance, but I'm more aware of him that anything I'm doing or feeling. I'm more conscious of the way he's fiddling with the cufflink at his right wrist, the way his lips are curved into a wanting smirk, and the way his eyes shamelessly roam over my body. More than that, more than all three things put together, I'm aware of the gradual darkening of the blue hue of his irises. I'm aware of the building lust and need and raw sexuality that swirl in them, reaching out to me and surrounding me.

And they do. Surround me. Completely and utterly.

My body heats to an unimaginable level, and every part of me begs to be touched by him. Tingles, tugs, wanting trembles… They overtake me again and again, leaving my skin covered in goose bumps and my heart pounding.

Then his eyes meet mine. They finish their visual caress of my body and find mine in a heated collision that makes me stop dead. It takes my breath away—the intensity in his gaze. It makes me brave and shy and wanton all at the same time in a crazy mix of conflicting emotion.

He steps closer and reaches out to me. This time, I let him rest his hands on my waist and lift me from the table. I take a deep breath. He runs his fingers up my arm and across my shoulder, teasing the skin at my neck as they find their way to my jaw.

"Tell me what you want," he whispers, his voice husky.

"You. Just you."

"No." He brings his body flush against mine. "More. Tell me what you want me to do you." His fingers slide around my body to cup my butt, creeping beneath my dress. He brings it around slowly, drawing a path with his thumb from hip to hip, skimming the top of my underwear. "Do you want me to touch you here?"

I part my lips at the touch of his fingertips sliding beneath the material and curl my fingers into his shirt. "Yes."

"How? Like this?" He rubs his thumb across my clit, drawing a sharp breath from me. "Or like this?" Two fingers slip inside me effortlessly, stretching me. He curls them at the tips, hitting my sweet spot, and drags them across it like he knows.

"Oh. That." I release his shirt and sink my fingers into his hair. I'm gripping it so tightly I know I'm pulling it, but he gives me no indication of it. And all I can truly feel are his fingers inside me.

"You sure?" He slides his other hand down my back, undoing my zipper.

I'm left feeling empty when he pulls his fingers from me to slide my dress down my body. The emptiness leaves as his eyes trace me from head to toe, only to be replaced with an all-consuming need that roars through me.

"So fucking beautiful," he murmurs at my neck, dropping kisses across my collarbone.

I drop my head as he travels downward, tracing along the curve of my breast and down my stomach. His hot breath covers my aching pussy, and I know where he's going even before he hooks his fingers in the waistband of my panties and slides them down my legs.

I tremble beneath his touch with nothing to hold on to in order to steady myself, and my knees buckle as he kisses up my thigh.

"Or is this what you want?" He kisses just above my clit. "My mouth… My tongue… Here. Licking your pussy and teasing your clit until you come so hard you see black? Is this what you want?"

His hand cups me, his finger rubbing over me. I groan and reach down to his head.

"Tell me what you want, Dayton."

"Get up," I demand, tugging at his hair. "Up."

He stands slowly, dragging his mouth up my body as he does. His breathing picks up speed as I deftly undo each button on his shirt and ease it over his shoulders. It silently falls to the floor behind him, and I press my mouth to his chest. Over his heart. It pounds beneath my touch, and I settle my hands at his waist as I let my tongue travel across his body.

It's a full adventure from his pecs to his waistband, and I take advantage of every dip and rise of his muscles as my tongue explores him. I unbuckle his belt and undo his pants without taking my lips from his body. He tenses beneath my touch as I pull them down, his boxers included, and free his raging erection.

"Fuck," Aaron mutters at the first touch of my lips at the base of his cock. I wrap my fingers around him and take him into my mouth, my tongue flicking against him.

I work him, my only objective his pleasure, needing to feel his release inside me. My pussy or my mouth. I don't care. I run my tongue along the side of his shaft, reveling in the way he works his fingers into my hair and groans my name, and lick the drop of pre-cum from the end of his cock.

"Dayton," he rasps again when I brush my fingers across his sac. His balls tighten in my grip as I squeeze lightly, and he groans deep in his throat, pulling his hips back and lifting me.

"Kiss me."

His tongue plunges into my mouth and he kisses me feverishly. His hands run across my body desperately, and when they stop at the top of my thighs, I feel his fight not to touch me. Not to take control of this.

I pull away and walk backward. He follows me to the bedroom and drops his eyes when I unclip my bra. I slide it down my arms, freeing my breasts, and my nipples pucker beneath his gaze.

The bed is soft as I lie back on it, and Aaron stands at the end of the bed, just watching me. Waiting. His chest heaving with the force of being controlled.

The familiar feeling rushes through my veins, mixed with desire and heat.

I want to push him.

I want to see how far he'll go until he breaks and takes back control of my body.

With my eyes on his, I trail a finger down my breastbone. His chest heaves and he swallows as I run it beneath the curve of my breasts, teasing but not really touching. His gaze follows my finger as I trace small, lazy circles across my stomach.

Slowly, I take it lower.

His breathing gets even heavier and his cock twitches. He wraps his hand around it and my body reacts immediately. I feel the wetness pooling between my legs, and my lungs constrict at the sight of him standing before me. Powerful. Sexual. Almost primal.

I stop my finger just above the mound that dips to my pussy and wait for him to say something. He tightens his grip on himself, and eyes so dark they're almost black take mine captive.

"Do it," he growls. "But when you come, your hand will be replaced by my mouth."

I don't dispute it or argue as my hand dips lower. My lips part as my finger finds my swollen clit, and it almost feels alien to touch it myself. It's been so long since I had to do this that I almost want to pull away and demand that he skip the waiting and just get his mouth down there right the fuck now.

The tension keeps me going. Aaron strokes himself slowly as I rub circles around my clit, sliding my fingers down and dipping them inside myself.

"Fuck, Dayton. If you had any idea how you look right now…"

The rawness of his voice makes my eyelids flutter shut. "Tell me. Tell me what you see right now, standing in front of me while I touch myself for you."

"You look like perfection. You're sexy in the rawest way, and it drives me fucking crazy. I can see how wet you are, can see it on your fingers each time you slide them back out of your gorgeous cunt. And knowing I did that makes me the smuggest son of a bitch in this city."

I fight the buck of my hips and the pressure from the quickly building orgasm. "And you?" I ask hoarsely.

"Hard, baby. I'm rock solid and it's all because of you. All for you." The bed creaks and dips as he moves forward. His breath crawls over my leg, igniting a new flare inside me, and I cry out softly when he grabs my free hand. He wraps my fingers around his cock. "Feel that?" he questions, rocking his hips and pushing himself through my grip. "That's you. No one else gets me this crazy."

I squeeze him lightly as the first wave of orgasm thrashes through my body, and as quickly as he filled my hand, he leaves it empty. He pulls my hand away and covers me with his mouth, his tongue stretching inside me as I come into his mouth.

It's intense and unrelenting, wave after wave assaulting me.

I need him. I need him to fill me the way he always does.

"I'm going to fuck you now," he says, wrapping his lips around my nipple. "The way *I* want. As hard as *I* want and for as long as *I* want. And it's going to be hard and it's going to be fucking fast."

He gets off me and I open my eyes.

"On your front," he whispers. "Hands and knees."

My lips part as I do it. He moves behind me and slaps my ass lightly.

"Now crawl up the bed."

I crawl.

"Wrap those hands around the top of the headboard."

I wrap my hands around the headboard.

His hand connects with my ass again, sharper this time, and I flinch away from the sting. Never mind that I feel it all the way through my pussy.

He raises himself until the head of his cock is just inside me. I flex my hips to take him deeper, and he leans over me, pulling back.

"I'm trying to control myself, Dayton, but I meant it when I said it would be hard and fast. I won't be nice, not after watching you give yourself an orgasm that should have come from me."

"You told me to"—all the breath leaves my body at his hard entry—"do it."

"I was making a point." He holds himself inside me and turns my face to the side. He takes my mouth harshly, his teeth tugging on my lower lip. "I let you touch yourself simply so I could remind you there's nothing you can do to yourself that I can't do ten times better. I can make you come harder and more intensely than you could ever make yourself." To prove his point, he pulls out and rams back into me. I cry out. "Think about that next time you decide to tease me and take away something that is my right."

"Making me come is your right?"

"You belong to me, Dayton. It's my right to do whatever I wish with you. That includes being the only person who will ever make you come. Starting now."

He picks up a speedy pace, pounding into me harshly and relentlessly from behind. Every thrust inside pushes the breath from my body. I drop my head forward, pushing back against him, taking him deeper until he hits the end of me. He grabs my hips, controlling my movements. Slamming me onto him with each thrust forward.

It's sudden and it's explosive and it's mind-numblingly intense. I shatter. I surrender to the intense rush of blood and adrenaline and spiking pleasure. It consumes me. Owns me. Possesses me to my very core. I tremble. I shake. I fall and spiral into the consuming flood.

This is rough and real. As a second hits before I can center myself again, I know this is what needed to happen. This is the past and the present and the future all colliding in a crazy, fucked-up moment of ownership and pleasure.

I break.

I release my hold on the headboard and drop forward as Aaron shouts his own release in a magical cry of my name. He collapses onto me, our skin slick together, and wraps his arms around my body. His chest is heaving as hard as mine. I can feel his heartbeat pounding through his ribs to my back, and it's perfectly in sync with my own.

My heart is beating so hard it could break through the bones keeping it safe. It's so full of everything—of desire, of passion, of love. All for the man holding on to me like I might run if he doesn't.

And when he eases out of me, kisses me softly, and drags me to the shower, the questions spin in my mind.

How do I walk away?

How do I *stay*?

# Chapter Twenty-Three

"I hated them then, and chances are, I hate them now."

"You barely even tried them. You licked one then screwed your face up all adorable."

"There is nothing adorable about me. And there is nothing tasty about snails."

"Really? Would it kill you to try one after seven years?"

"I don't know, but I'm not willing to take the risk." I fold my arms across my chest. "I'll sit here with my salad while you suck on your snails, thank you."

Aaron smirks. "You do that."

I cringe as he eats one. Complete with a shiver. I wipe snail trails from the mat outside my back door, for the love of God. I'm not about to eat the little bastards. The slime and…ugh. No thanks.

"They're good."

I roll my eyes. "Yes, I'm sure they're the most delicious thing on Earth."

"No. That's you."

My fork freezes mid salad-stab. "I can't believe you just said that out loud."

Indeed, the couple at the table next to us are listening.

"I'm merely correcting you," Aaron replies, unfazed by the

attention on us from whomever they are.

"Could you save your corrections for private?" I shoot an angry glare to my right, and the couple looks away.

"Absolutely not." He leans forward, his eyes sparkling, and lowers his voice. "Do you think I'm ashamed of the fact I would substitute every meal for your coming in my mouth?"

I run my tongue along my bottom lip. "No."

"Then be quiet and finish your lunch."

I stab a piece of lettuce with a force it doesn't deserve. "*Merde*," I mutter.

Aaron smirks. "Most know *bonjour* as their primarily used French word. Of course my woman knows *merde*."

"You taught me it." I chew slowly. "It's an easy word to remember."

I set my fork down beside my plate and ignore his lowered chuckle. My eyes scour the view outside our window until they fall on the familiar shape of the *Louvre*. My heart skips a beat. My favorite place in the world.

"I know what you're looking at."

"Please," I ask without taking my eyes from it. "I promise it'll be the only time I'll make you come with me."

He grins and waves at a waiter for the bill. "I was waiting for you to ask."

Excitement builds, and I smile at him as he pays. Outside the restaurant, I skip along the cobbled street—in my flats—toward the museum.

"You look like the girl I fell in love with all those years ago."

I turn to face him. "Being back here with you, I feel it."

He catches up with me and takes my hand in his. His lips brush across my knuckles, and he pulls me closer to the *Louvre*. "I'm going to hate every second of this, aren't I?"

"It's likely." I lean into him slightly. He loops our arms over my head so they circle my body, pulling me closer to his side. I fit perfectly against him, and I smile as I remember the endless hours we spent exploring the city exactly this way.

If I close my eyes and believe hard enough, it almost feels like no time has passed. Like we could be here for the very first time, just getting to know each other and falling for the first time. I can kid myself that I'm only just finding out how his touch silences the rest of the world and his kiss sends me into a heady spiral of bliss.

I can pretend that I'm only just finding out that looking in his eyes is the best and worst thing a girl can do.

Nothing has changed. Irrespective of my job or the time passed, *nothing* has changed. It feels the same as it always has when we're together.

Being with Aaron is effortless. Just like loving him, waking up to his electric eyes and smirking lips each morning feels so natural that I can't remember it not being so. The time without him far outweighs the time together, but that doesn't make the slightest difference.

And the idea of being without him again makes my stomach clench painfully.

The thought of not waking up to a ready-made pot of coffee, to rumpled sheets on the other side of the bed, to his lips brushing across a part of my body, sinks in deep and claws at every part of me.

I squeeze my eyes shut. No matter how it hurts, how hard it will be to say goodbye, how hard it will be to leave such a pivotal part of my life behind, it has to be done.

Nothing can last forever.

I open my mouth but Aaron speaks before I can. "Wait here."

He releases me and strolls down a tiny street, disappearing into a small building. I stare after him in shock. What the hell?

I wrap my arms around my waist, suddenly feeling a chill from the gentle spring breeze without his arms around me. My foot taps as

I wait. What the hell is he doing?

He reemerges a few moments later, a small bag in his hand. I frown. His face is stretched into a grin, his eyes sparkling with the boyish charm that endeared me to him originally, and he stops in front of me.

"Here."

"A brown paper bag?"

"Just open it."

I unfold the top, the paper rustling as I do, and reach inside. My fingers wrap around a ball chain, and there's a small clink as I pull it out.

"Oh my god."

The Eiffel Tower charm at the end is sandwiched by a star charm and a red glass heart. The bag crumples in my fist as the necklace flattens in my in palm, my jaw slack.

Aaron grins and takes it from me. "I can't believe the store is still here."

"Me either."

He steps behind me and unclasps the necklace. He settles it around my neck and pauses. "Do you remember?"

Do I remember? How could I forget? We were standing in the same place seven years ago when he first gave me a necklace identical to this. It was a crazy, impulsive buy, and he said that he'd bought it firstly because of the Tower.

"The Tower for your love of it and the place we first met," he murmurs, redoing the clasp. His finger trails over my shoulder alongside the chain as he turns me to face him. "The star for what I see whenever I look in your eyes…"

"And the heart so I'll never forget I have yours," I finish for him in a whisper. I reach my hand up and my fingers curl around the charms. "Like I could."

"Just in case." He kisses me sweetly.

I reach into my purse and unzip the back pocket. I grab a chain exactly like the one hanging around my neck and tug.

"You still have it." Aaron takes it from me in awe. "I don't believe it."

I tear my eyes, which are filling with tears, from the necklace and find his. "I promised you I'd never forget."

I wake to an empty bed—something I'm more than used to—and the sound of Aaron talking in an agitated tone in the other room. After rubbing my eyes and pulling on my robe, I pad through silently.

"Yes." He runs his fingers through his hair. "Jesus... I'm not supposed to be working this week. You know that, Dad... Fine... Yes. We'll be there... Okay. Bye."

He drops the phone on the floor and drops back on the sofa. His arm rests over his eyes, and he sighs heavily.

"That doesn't sound like a great way to start your day," I say softly.

"It's not!"

I say nothing at the sharp tone in his voice and flick the coffee machine on. I refuse to do anything to make him feel better if he's going to snap at me like an angry puppy.

"Sorry," he says, wrapping his arms around me from behind. "I shouldn't have spoken to you that way."

"Damn right you shouldn't have." I pour a cup of coffee. "Are you going to tell me what's wrong? If not, I'm going to shower."

He laughs quietly, but I can still feel the tension in his body. Like he'll snap if you push him too far. "Someone I'm not particularly fond of heard we're in Paris this week. They've taken the liberty of organizing a company dinner here at the hotel tonight, and my father just informed me that we're expected to attend. Required to, actually."

"What if we had plans?" I step away and raise an eyebrow.

"We did." He sighs heavily and leans against the counter. "Now we have new ones. Believe me. I'm not happy about it, Day."

"Can't you just explain you're not working this week? That this is a vacation?"

"No."

"Well, who is it?"

"Who?"

I click my tongue. "The person organizing it."

"Oh. No one important. I'm not sure they'll even be there." He turns away and pours a cup of coffee.

"Aaron."

"Leave it, Dayton."

*Ass.* I put my mug down with a little too much force and storm into the bedroom. There isn't a chance in hell I'm going to stay in this room with him in a mood like this.

I change into some workout gear and pack a change of clothes and a bikini in my bag. A session in the gym and the pool followed by the spa should give him enough time to calm the hell down.

"Look, I have a couple of calls to make now. Maybe you should go out for a couple of hours."

I put my hand on the door and look at him. My mild annoyance has morphed into anger, and I'm not afraid to tell him that I'm pissed off. "I was planning to stay out all day. Don't worry."

"Day…"

I yank the door open. "What time do you need me back here?"

"Four," he sighs.

"Perfect. Don't bother calling me unless you've pulled your head from your ass and calmed the fuck down." I slam the door behind me with a childish satisfaction.

I'm not above using teenager-style defiance to let him know that I'm pissed off either.

It's still early, so the gym is empty aside from two older guys on the rowing machines. I snap a band from my wrist and tie my hair back, heading toward the treadmill. If anything is going to work out this annoyance, it's the treadmill.

I ease into it, starting off with a slow walk and gradually building up to a steady run. My feet pound against it with every step, and I turn the incline up a little more.

Why can't he tell me who's organizing the dinner? Or, more to the point, why *won't* he? I know he said he isn't fond of them, but sheesh...

Maybe it's an old friendship turned sour. It happens in business, right? It's a ruthless world. Or maybe it's someone who works at the company he doesn't like very much and is doing it to spite him.

Maybe it's an ex-girlfriend.

I choke on my thought. God, it actually burns to think that— but it's possible. He's bound to have seen someone—maybe more than one someone—in that time. She could work at the company still.

But why can't he just tell me about any of those? What about any of them is so bad that he has to keep it to himself and talk to me like I'm a petulant child when I ask?

Well, there goes burning off my anger.

I give up on the running and leave the gym as quickly as I came. The pool. Water. That's what I need—the weightless feeling of being suspended by its remarkable force. Perhaps it'll take away some of my crap weighing me down.

God knows there's enough of it.

I change quickly and dive into the empty pool. I push tiny hairs away from my eyes and bob in the water.

Just when I'd decided it was worth it to stay. To give up everything I have in Seattle and take a completely different path in my life.

Just when I'd decided to give him what he's asked for, this happens, and now I doubt my ability to make the right decision.

Maybe it's good I couldn't tell him yesterday.

I probably made it impulsively and need more time to make such a huge choice.

But as I dip below the water and jump into my first length of the pool, I *know* it's a good thing I couldn't tell him yesterday. My gut says so.

It also says that the happiness I've finally found again is too good to be true.

And everyone knows that gut instincts are never, ever wrong.

Aaron's waiting for me when I enter the suite with an almost bashful look on his face. I raise my eyebrows and head straight into the bedroom without speaking a word to him. I know he follows—and I don't care.

A long, strapless black dress is laid out on the bed. It's one of mine. I fight the urge to roll my eyes at his presumptuous nature and drop my bag next to my suitcase.

"Are you going to ignore me?"

"Are you going to talk to me like I deserve to be spoken to, or am I still your outlet for your annoyance?"

He folds me into his arms and breathes in deeply, burying his face in my hair. "I'm sorry, sweetheart. I was wrong to take it out on you."

"Fucking right you were." I wrap my arms around his waist and lay my head on his chest. "Don't do it again."

"Ever?"

"*Ever*. Next time I won't be so nice to you, nor will I walk away. Talk to me like crap again, Mr. Stone, and I'm going to tear you a new asshole. Got it?"

He bends his face into mine with a smile playing on his lips. "Got it." He takes my mouth with his.

"Are you going to tell me who has you in a bad mood yet?" I pull away and change. His eyes rove over me as I change from my sports bra to a blue lace one.

"Someone from my past who delights in making my life incredibly hard." He discards his shirt and pulls a new one on. "If there were a way to get out of this tonight, you can bet I'd find it."

"Wow. I can't imagine disliking someone that much." I step into the dress and reach around to pull up the zipper. "Who is it?"

Aaron doesn't say a word as he knocks my hand away and does the zipper for me. He rests his forehead against the back of my shoulder, his fingers still clasped on the pull, and exhales loudly.

"Aaron?"

"The person organizing tonight is my wife."

# Chapter Twenty-four

I jump away from him as if his touch is burning me. And it is. So are his words.

Did he…

Was that…

"Wife?"

There's no mistaking the accusatory tone in my whisper or the way my hands are now clasped against my stomach, shaking frantically. Holy fucking hell.

"Yes."

I feel sick.

I clap my hand over my mouth and turn away from him. Betrayal slices through my body, leaving no part untouched by the overwhelming sting.

"She's my ex-wife, actually. We'd be divorced if she didn't keep stalling on the agreement."

"You're still married. She's still your wife." Oh god.

"We've been separated for two years."

I shake my head. Bile is rising up my throat. I fight to swallow it back down, to kill the sick feeling in my stomach.

"And you never thought to tell me?"

"I didn't know how to. I kept putting it off until it became impossible. I wanted to, Day." He rests his hands on my arms, and I flinch, stepping back.

"Don't you dare touch me." I rub the places his hands were like I can wipe away the pain they've left behind. "Don't you fucking dare stand there in front of me and try and justify this. Shit, Aaron. You're married! Fucking *married!*"

What he said on the boat comes back to me and hits me with the force of a freight train. Everything... About sitting his wife down to work it out... Not going elsewhere... *It was all a great big pile of shit.*

"Didn't she sit still long enough for you to work your shit out, huh? So much for making sure you'd work it out. Fuck!" I fist my hair and spin. "All that was a lie, wasn't it? How much more has been a lie? How many more lines have you said that actually mean fucking nothing?"

"Our marriage was a sham, Dayton. Naomi cares for nothing but money and fame. She was an up-and-coming model struggling to break into the industry. I met her one night at college and could see her potential, so I gave her the in. I set her up with one of our agents, and she was...thankful." He scrubs across his forehead.

"I bet she was."

"We started seeing each other casually, and every time I went to break it off, my father's assistant convinced me it was good for us to be together because of our profiles. Our 'relationship' was no secret, and she was always being hit with the fact that she'd only made it because of me."

"She did!"

"We both knew that. I was a buffer for that. I claimed we met after she signed with our agency and that was that."

"And you woke up one morning and decided to marry her, right? Because it was the 'right' thing to do?" I raise my eyebrows and walk across the room.

"It didn't work out. After eight months, we separated. I've been fighting her for two years. She's not entitled to half of everything I own, but she won't take what I am offering. There's a reason I don't own the company on paper yet."

Of course. There had to be a reason. And it had to be a wife, didn't it? It couldn't be a financial fuck-up or a contractual issue. It had to be a fucking wife.

"I can't even look at you right now. I can't believe you didn't tell me about her. How couldn't you tell me, Aaron? Did it not ever cross your mind while you were watching me sleep or pouring me coffee to tell me? How about when you were kissing me or fucking me? Or when you were writing little fucking notes and hiding them?!"

He meets my eyes and I see the pain in them. Guilt and pain and heartbreak. Good. I hope his heart is being torn apart by razor-sharp claws. Mine certainly is.

"I was so scared to lose you, Day. So scared that if I told you, you'd get up and walk and that would be that."

"So you thought you'd ignore it and she'd go away eventually? That I'd never find out? Even when you were begging me to move in with you—did you really think then that you'd never have to tell me?" I close my eyes and press my fingers into them. I'm not going to cry. Not over this.

"I hoped I could call my lawyer and give her what she wants from our marriage. My money. Then yes, I hoped she'd go away. I had no idea she was in France right now. If I did, I never would have brought us here."

"What a nice surprise that was. No wonder you couldn't tell me this morning." My heart is racing. I don't know if I've even comprehended this yet—that he has a wife. An ex-wife, but a wife. Until the papers are signed, there's no ex about it.

I can't comprehend anything past the sick knot in my stomach, the agony in my chest. The sting of betrayal that just keeps getting sharper.

"I'm so sorry, Dayton. If you had to find out, it never should have been like this. I'm so sorry."

"Believe me, Aaron. You're not half as sorry as I am." I walk into the bathroom and splash cold water over my face. I stare at my reflection in the mirror. My eyes aren't swollen and my cheeks are puffy. My lips aren't chapped. No one would look at me and think I'd just had the shock of my fucking life.

So I can see the tears lurking in the corners of my eyes. They aren't going anywhere.

Aaron walks in just as I pick up my makeup brush. "What are you doing?"

I meet his eyes in the mirror. I know the exact moment it happens. The moment I slink into Mia. "I have a contractual obligation to fill. I'll be there with you tonight, but I'm leaving right after."

He draws in a sharp breath.

"You'll be refunded for the final two weeks that will be unfulfilled. Then you will wipe my agent's number from your phone and not contact her again. I'll be changing mine when I'm back in Seattle."

"Day, please—"

"My other option is leaving right now and letting your wife know she's got between us. I'll leave late tonight and use the company plane. This way you can tell everyone I had a family emergency and had to return home immediately." I pause to brush some lipstick on before turning to him. "We both have reputations to protect, and that's exactly what I'm doing."

He slams the bedroom door shut behind him as I walk into the kitchen and buttons his shirt in the middle of the main room. "Don't look at me with Mia's eyes."

I take a deep breath and pour a glass of wine. My lipstick leaves a red lip print on the rim of the glass, and I slowly turn to him. When I do, his jacket is on and his tie around his neck.

"I'm doing my job, Aaron. You're my client. That's it."

I've been Mia thousands of times in my life. I've buried the real me beneath layers of masquerade and no one has been any wiser. I've hidden every part of me you can imagine, including emotions.

Mia feels what she has to. She smiles at all the right times, laughs at all the right lines, and feigns annoyance at all the right moments.

My life is a charade. I have control but I never really get to pull the strings. I'm always acting under someone else's orders. I'm always fulfilling someone else's wishes. Living someone else's dreams.

I accept that. I have to. If I didn't, I wouldn't have this job. I'd be flipping burgers or smiling politely at snobby women in a high-end boutique somewhere.

I hide. I pretend. I lie.

My life is a lie.

It's full of cheating and things that mean nothing.

I always live for the other side of it. When I'm Dayton, I wish I could be Mia—confident and outgoing and out there. When I'm Mia, I wish I could be Dayton—curled up in my pajamas with a tub of ice cream in front of the television, laughing with my best friend.

Either way, I'm not completely happy.

The last few weeks have changed that. Being with Aaron again reminded me of everything I'd left behind. He reminded me what it is to look into the eyes of someone who cares and smile. What it is to feel red-hot desire rushing through your veins and to feel that desire aimed straight back at you.

He reminded me how to love and be loved.

He also reminded me why I shouldn't believe in love.

And the skinny blond woman walking toward us with her lips curved in an evil smirk is the reason why. Naomi Lane, married name Stone. She's everything I'm not, and the Prada woman's words make sense.

We're polar opposites. She's light and a size zero. I'm dark and a comfy size six.

We couldn't be more different.

"Aaron! How lovely for you to clear your schedule for tonight." She kisses his cheek, an action I notice he doesn't return.

"I believe I had no choice," he responds dryly. "Dayton, this is Naomi. My ex-wife."

Those words punch me in the stomach. Gut wrenching isn't even strong enough to describe it. More like stomach twisting, nausea inducing, heart clawing.

"Naomi, my girlfriend, Dayton."

"Oh, I've heard so much about you!" She fakes a smile and leans forward to air kiss me. It takes everything I have, but I return the gesture. *I'm not Dayton. I'm Mia. I'm strong.*

"Really? I can't say I've heard very much about you at all. A few passing comments, maybe."

She blinks. "Oh. I suppose Aaron's been very busy with taking over the company and you haven't had much time to talk."

"Oh, we've had plenty of time to talk...among other things...but you just never came up." I smile.

Her jaw tightens and she turns light brown eyes on Aaron. "And how is the change going?"

"The contracts are locked in the lawyer's desk, waiting for the day our divorce papers land there." Aaron's fingers twitch at my side. "We can all hope that will be soon."

"Oh, darling. You're being unreasonable in your agreement. Can't we just discuss it?"

"Naomi, you made a point by organizing this tonight. If you found out I'm here, I'm sure you're aware I'm not working this week. I don't wish to discuss anything with you. I'm not paying two lawyers so we can sit and have coffee to iron out your ridiculous terms."

"Aaron, honey." I flatten my hand against his stomach. "Shall we get a drink? I don't think this is the place to be discussing this."

He takes a deep breath and kisses the top of my head. "You're right. Let's go."

We cross the room to the bar, and aware of her eyes still on us, I try not to move away from him like I want to.

"You handled her well," Aaron says softly.

"Nothing like letting the woman your boyfriend is married to think you don't care." I run my tongue along my bottom lip and take a long drink from my wine glass. "She's a bitch, by the way. You picked a real good one there."

I'm fighting inside myself. This was a stupid idea—coming here and pretending my heart isn't shattering inside me with each word. Pretending I can stand in front of her and not give a fuck she's married to the man I love so wholly.

I reach inside my purse and grab my silenced cell. "Excuse me. I have a call."

Understanding flashes in his eyes, and he shoots from his seat just as quickly as I do. I make a show of walking through the room, my finger in my ear, my lips parting in shock. Aaron follows me the whole time I act my charade. I talk trash into the silent phone until I reach the elevator.

I jab the doors shut before he can enter. My chest heaves. I swallow back a lump of emotion and lock myself in the suite, tearing my dress from my body.

I grab the room phone and call down to the concierge, walking through the suite in my underwear, gathering my things.

"Concierge desk."

"This is Miss Black, from the presidential suite. I have a family emergency and have to leave immediately. Can you call for a porter to remove my bags and a car to take me to the Charles de Gaulle airport in ten minutes?"

"Of course, *mademoiselle*. Is *Monsieur* Stone aware of your departure?"

My eyes lock with a pair of tortured blue eyes as he crashes through the door.

"Yes," I say into the phone. "He's aware."

I put it down and throw a dress over my head, still aimlessly throwing my things in my suitcases.

"Don't go," Aaron whispers. "Please. Don't go."

"I don't have a choice." I zip the cases one by one. "If you'd told me before, maybe I could have dealt with it. But to tell me an hour before you expect me to stand face to face to her? No way, Aaron. No way."

"Dayton. Please." He strides forward and cups my face, bringing his forehead to mine. "Please. Just one night. Let me explain everything. Just don't leave me again."

"You knew I was going tonight. I'm just leaving sooner. I can't stay down there with her, and it's ridiculous to expect me to."

The emotion comes crashing through my body. My heart thumps, my chest constricts. Every part of me shakes, and the tears...

God, the tears.

They fill my eyes and spill over before I can do anything. Before I can fight against the drop, they fall down my cheeks.

"Fuck, Dayton," he rasps. His voice is hoarse and raw, holding the pain I feel. He brushes his thumbs across my cheeks. "Don't go, baby. Don't go."

With everything I have, I step back and shake my head. "You lied to me, Aaron. A lie of omission, but a lie all the same. This isn't a tiny thing that can be swept under the rug and forgotten. This is huge and a central part of your life. All the times you asked me to tell you everything about me, you were never willing to return that. You were never going to tell me. You said so yourself. I can't stay. I'm sorry."

I wipe at my cheeks and pull a denim jacket over my dress.

I meet his eyes and look away again. If I stare into them, I'll give in, and I can't do that. I'm too weak to even be Mia. The pain I feel is too much to pretend it doesn't hurt.

A knock sounds at the door and I open it, seeing the porter. Aaron sees him too, and as he gathers my bags, Aaron's gaze sears into me. It burns and it hurts. It breaks my heart all over again.

"Is my car ready?" I ask the short man pushing the cart.

"*Oui, mademoiselle.*" He disappears into the lift, and I place my hand on the doorknob.

"I'm begging you, Dayton. I'm fucking begging you not to go."

"I was ready to give it all up," I admit, my voice small and cracking with tears. "When you gave me my necklace again, I was going to tell you. I was ready to give it all up to be with you. I was going to call Monique, cancel the payment, and leave her. I didn't think I could walk away from you again. I didn't know if I'd survive another broken heart."

"So don't. Stay. *Please.*"

"You were right. True love never dies. It only fades, lingering below the surface until we're ready for it again. Until fate puts us in the right place and the right time and that simmering love can come alive again." I look over my shoulder, the tears falling thick and fast, and bite my bottom lip. "I love you, Aaron, but I have more integrity than to stay with a man who can lie to me so easily. I respect myself too much. I'm sorry. I can't stay."

I run toward the elevator, needing to get away before I give in to the dam ready to break.

"Day! Fuck, Dayton!" he roars in a raw burst of pain.

The doors close and I hear him smacking his hands against it in defeat before I descend to the bottom floor.

The concierge is waiting for me and his eyes widen at the sight of my tear-stained face. "*Mademoiselle,* is everything all right with your family?"

"My grandmother has taken sick. I'm sorry." I catch myself before more tears fall. "I can't…"

He guides me to the car and helps me in. I whisper a thank-you as he closes the door and reach forward to close the partition.

The car pulls away, and I pull out my cell.

"Hello?"

"You knew, didn't you?"

"Dayton."

"Don't use that fucking tone with me, Monique. You knew he was married didn't you?" Nothing. "*Didn't you?*"

"He stipulated I not tell you. Client confidentiality."

"Ha! Client confidentiality? Fuck that! What about the well-being of one of your girls, huh? Did it not cross your mind that it might be in my best interest to know my client, my ex-boyfriend, the man I've loved my whole goddamn life, the very same one whisking me off around the world, might be married?"

"You said you wouldn't fall in love, Dayton."

"I never stopped loving him. You should have told me. I should have known!"

I hear her exhale. A long, regretful sigh. "You're right. I should have told you."

"I'm on my way to the airport. Get my number changed."

"I'm sorry, Dayton."

"Fuck you, Monique. Fuck you."

I hang up and drop my phone into my purse. And I give in.

I let the dam break, let the wall collapse, let the strength dissolve, and I cry. I let the pain run through my body without a second thought. Because I need to feel it. I need to feel it and remember why this never should have happened.

I bring my knees to my chest and stare out the window. Through my blurry eyes and chest-heaving sobs, I make out the Eiffel Tower. I screw my eyes shut and turn away, a fresh hit of pain filling my chest.

It doesn't comfort me at all. Where it was once a reminder of a beautiful time, now it's a mark of heartbreak.

Our journey has ended in the very city where it all began, and once again, I'm leaving Paris with tears streaming down my cheeks.

And without the man I love.

FINAL CALL, book two of the Call series and the conclusion to Aaron and Dayton's story, will release June 2014, exact date TBA.

# Acknowledgements

As always my first acknowledgement goes to my partner, Darryl. This time for dealing with a snotty, teething, screaming baby and a demanding toddler while I wrote like a mad person, then forcing me to relax for an hour. Also for not complaining when I didn't crawl into bed until stupid o-clock because my characters kept me up. And for his encouragement for stepping into the adult erotic romance world. He's a bit of a gem.

My agent, Dan Mandel, for encouraging me to self-publish this and take a new step in my career.

My critique partners, Heidi Tretheway and Katie Ernst, for reading this book and tearing it apart so it could be put back together in a better way. And a huge thank you to Heidi for all her knowledge of Seattle, meaning I could get the setting straight. You guys are the best, and I love you hard.

My betas, Holly and Zoe, for loving Aaron first. Your comments are amazing, and you were my first ego strokers for this novel. I like your strokes. Please do it more often.

Some of the best indies I know. Laurelin Paige, Kyla Linde, Kendall Ryan, S.K. Hartley, Lexi Ryan, Tamsyn Bester, Melody Grace, Lauren Blakely, Rachel Harris, Melanie Harlow. Thank you for all your support during and up to the release of this book. At some point you made me smile, and it's something I needed.

Kendall Ryan, again, for being the first person to read an ARC and for the 4am (for me) conversations that followed. Not much can make me smile at 4am, but somehow you managed it. Thank you for loving Aaron and Dayton as much as you do.

My editor, Mickey Reed. Firstly for squeezing me into your full schedule. You're a star, lady, and I'm so pleased I got the chance to work with you. Now you're stuck with me. Yay you! ;)

Cait Greer, thank you for formatting this book and making it gorgeous. Now technically I'm writing this in the original manuscript and it hasn't been formatted yet, but I've seen your work and I know you'll do this book justice, so extra thanks in advance. ;)

To all the bloggers who have helped spread the word for LATE CALL. There are so, so many of you, and I can't begin to list you. But if you've retweeted, shared, liked, commented on, posted, squeed, anything for anything to do with LATE CALL, know that it's so very appreciated, and you are too. <3

My street team, my Hartbreakers. I love these ladies seriously hard. Your enthusiasm knows no bounds and I'm so lucky to have you by my side promoting my work. You met these guys before it was even announced to the world, and you loved him way back then. You all rock my socks.

# About the Author

By day, *New York Times* and *USA Today* bestselling author Emma Hart dons a cape and calls herself Super Mum to two beautiful little monsters. By night, she drops the cape, pours a glass of whatever she fancies—usually wine—and writes books.

Emma is working on Top Secret projects she will share with her followers and fans at every available opportunity. Naturally, all Top Secret projects involve a dashingly hot guy who likes to forget to wear a shirt, a sprinkling (or several) of hold-onto-your-panties hot scenes, and a whole lotta love.

She likes to be busy - unless busy involves doing the dishes, but that seems to be when all the ideas come to life. She has since invested in a dishwasher, meaning the ideas come at the same time as her son's dirty nappies. She is in the market for a bum-changer due to this.

Emma's works include new adult series THE GAME and MEMORIES series. The CALL series is her first adult erotic romance series, but it's been so fun to write, she doubts it will be the last.

Find Emma online at:

Blog: http://www.emmahart.org

Facebook: www.facebook.com/EmmaHartBooks

Twitter: @EmmaHartAuthor

Goodreads:

http://www.goodreads.com/author/show/6451162.Emma_Hart

Made in the USA
Las Vegas, NV
03 February 2023

66781959R00164